THE LABORS OF DARIUS LINARD

LEAH R CUTTER

KNOTTED ROAD PRESS

Come someplace new…
Are you a traveler? Do you enjoy exploring strange new worlds, new cultures, new people?

Journey into the various lands envisioned by Leah Cutter.

Sign up for my newsletter and I'll start you on your travels with a free copy of my book, *The Island Sampler.*

I will never spam you or use your email for nefarious purposes. You can also unsubscribe at any time.

http://www.LeahCutter.com/newsletter/

The Wild One originally published in Boundary Shock Quarterly: Issue 1, Captain's Log

ALSO BY LEAH R CUTTER

Science Fiction

The Long Run

Project Nemesis

Project Nyx

Project Tisiphone

Project Persephone

War of the Allied Worlds

The Labors of Darius Linard

Huli Intergalactic: Science/Space Fantasy

Origins

The Strawberry Girl

Urban/Contemporary Fantasy Series

The Witch's Progress

Circle of Air

Circle of Fire

Circle of Water

Circle of Earth

Seattle Trolls

The Changeling Troll

The Princess Troll

The Fairy-Bridge Troll

The Troll-Demon War

The Troll-Human War

The Troll-Troll War

The Cassie Stories

Poisoned Pearls

Tainted Waters

Spoiled Harvest

Bloodied Ice

The Shadow Wars Trilogy

The Raven and the Dancing Tiger

The Guardian Hound

War Among the Crocodiles

The Clockwork Fairy Kingdom

The Clockwork Fairy Kingdom

The Maker, the Teacher, and the Monster

The Dwarven Wars

The Chronicles of Franklin

Franklin Versus The Popcorn Thief

Franklin Versus The Soul Thief

Franklin Versus The Child Thief

Epic Fantasy Series

Houses of the Dead

Houses Divided

Houses Fallen

Houses Reborn

Forgotten Gods

A Wind Blown Torment

A Stone Strewn Clash

A Sea Washed Victory

The Tanesh Empire Trilogy

The Glass Magician

The Desert Heart

The Ghost Dog

Mysteries

The Purloined Letter Opener

Dancer in Darkness

Trophy Hunters

The Alvin Goodfellow Case Files

The Rabbit Mysteries

The Shredded Veil Mysteries

Mystery, Crime, and Mayhem

CONTENTS

THE CLAIM JUMPER 1
THE WILD ONE 55
RUNAWAYS 87
HOMECOMING 153
HERO 201

Read More! 259
About the Author 261
About Knotted Road Press 263

THE CLAIM JUMPER

PART ONE

DARIUS SENT OUT THE CALL signal again.

PleaseOhPleaseOhPlease!

He kissed two fingers then reached up and touched the silver medal welded to the center of the ceiling for luck, a habit as automatic as breathing. The side facing out had an image of Jason of the Argonauts, while the side snug against the cabin had the golden fleece.

The cold silence of space replied to Darius' signal.

None of the boundary markers responded.

God*damn* it.

One or two boundary markers not responding could be anything. Space debris, mechanical failure, a short in the electronics, whatever. Hell, an entire line could have been wiped out from the ice shed of a recent comet. His claim was in the outer third of the asteroid belt, after all.

None of the boundary markers responding?

That meant a claim jumper squatting in the single degree

of arc of the *New Athens'* asteroid belt that Darius called home.

Sweat trickled down the back of Darius' light T-shirt. His new pants itched—he'd bought them during his last station call since he'd shot up another two inches and outgrown his previous set. Again. At eighteen was taller than his dad too, just shy of two meters.

Darius rotated the three-dimensional space map splashed across the tiny front window of his spaceship, then he overlaid it with a map of where the boundary markers were supposed to be.

If he was a claim jumper, where would he hide? Inside Darius' claim, or outside of it?

Orion—his little mining ship—could barely map out the asteroids in the claim: its sensors were at least twenty years too old. A ship with any kind of stealth protection (particularly something exotic from, oh, say, the Xi Lien system) would be completely hidden from him. He'd have to stumble on it in real time, see it with his bare eyes.

Would the claim jumper hide behind Big Bertha, the largest asteroid in this section and the only hunk of rock that supported an actual mine shaft? Or would he lay low near the dust field, caused by a collision of two asteroids that had happened when Darius' dad had first claimed the area over forty years ago?

Gods, his dad would know. Darius missed him again with a great fierceness.

Stupid debris. Stupid suit malfunction. Stupid warning signal that had gone off inside *Orion* far too late for Darius to save his dad.

Geez, it hadn't even been a month since his dad had passed. And now, Darius was going lose his father's claim.

Where was that asshole?

Darius had to find him quickly. Any area of the asteroid

belt was considered fair game if the boundary markers went offline for more than twenty-four contiguous hours, as counted by *New Athens'* time. It didn't matter that the claim was registered in the Space Grant offices in the world capital of Heklos, that Darius had re-filed the claim in his own name after his dad had died. He hadn't even had to lie about his age, either, having recently turned eighteen.

Actual boundary markers around the borders of a claim were what the officials cared about.

Were the markers merely offline? Or had they been stolen? Maybe blown up?

Darius would have noticed them being destroyed. *Orion* would have notified him if there'd been a series of explosions nearby.

Wouldn't it? Or was the entire alarm system still messed up?

After his dad's death, Darius had traced every line and circuit he could (without removing all the walls and panels) going from the detectors in the front of the ship to the actual alarms set in the walls of his tiny cabin at the back of *Orion*.

It hadn't taken long to find the short that had made Darius miss the first emergency call that his dad had sent.

Stupid ship was just too old, needed too many repairs that Darius couldn't afford.

Had there been more than one short, though? Had Darius missed other alarms?

He quickly called up the alarm logs, the taste of metal flooding his mouth. He took a deep breath of the too stale air (another repair he couldn't afford) and tried to calm himself.

Luckily, the logs didn't show that *Orion* had issued any alarms. Probably, the boundary markers hadn't been blown up.

That meant there was a good chance they were in their formerly mapped location. They'd just been hijacked.

Darius strapped himself to his seat, Dad's words about not being an idiot pilot and bouncing along echoing in his head, then he quickly plotted the course to the closest marker, twenty minutes away. Or at least where it was supposed to be.

Pinging the marker brought continued silence. Darius grew more tense as the minutes ticked away. He could push *Orion* to faster speeds—but that would use up more fuel. While he had plenty, it wasn't smart to waste it. Not until he really needed to.

Where was that damned pirate? What was Darius going to do? How could he survive out here without his claim? He didn't have the money to be planet-bound, that was for damned sure.

The minute the green light on the console came on, indicating *Orion* had arrived at its destination, Darius unbuckled himself from his seat and left the control room, swimming through the air, pulling himself hand-over-hand to the larger storage bay on the right.

Orion looked like a sloppy capital F, with the control room at the bottom of the letter, two small storage bays in the center, and a larger set of rooms across the top: Darius' quarters, the empty room in the center where his dad had lived, and a smaller kitchen/galley/hydroponics center.

Only three drones remained. Darius had the spare parts from two others that currently weren't working that he could cannibalize and probably make another if he had to.

But it took time to assemble them, time to test them, and even more time to link them up with the rest of the ship's systems. They were much newer than *Orion's* software and just barely compatible.

Plus, it wasn't work that Darius enjoyed. He did it because he had to, because Dad had insisted he learn the new systems coming into the *Greek Union of Planets*, now that the war with the Allied Worlds was over.

If Darius could afford it, he'd be planet-bound, though he'd only touched real earth once in his life (he'd been born on a station). But it would be safe there, and he could just breathe the air. Maybe he could live on a ranch, like what they showed in the holos, with horses and cattle, creatures he'd never actually seen.

But first he'd have to have extensive gene therapy to strengthen his muscles and bones so he could live under gravity. And he'd have to find a job, something he could do on dry land, that would bring in enough credits so he could eat, and put clothes on his back, and…

He was better off in space. At least for now.

Darius quickly ran diagnostics on the little drone. It wasn't much longer than his forearm, triangular in shape, with three thin fins curving down to the bottom. The top tapered off elegantly, with two large blue discs bulging just below the tip, giving it binocular vision as well as wider sensors.

The optics checked out, and he only had to fiddle a little to get the sensors synched up with *Orion*. He pre-programmed the drone to go out to where the marker was supposed to be, circle the area, then return. He could have reconfigured it to react to live commands but he was in a hurry.

Faster to just send it out and let it return on its own.

Dad had put in a special pocket in the side airlock of *Orion*, just for launching the little probes. It was more efficient to open a small latch instead of the full door.

Darius reached for his environmental suit, then hesitated. It would take time to get into his full suit. Time he shouldn't waste.

But what if the door malfunctioned and he ended up breathing space?

Darius compromised and reached for the smaller mouth ventilator instead. It would give him enough air that he'd be able to reach his suit in case there was an emergency.

Fortunately, the probe went out the tiny lock just fine, and everything locked back up tight. Darius took a deep breath of the still too stale air and shrugged his shoulders a couple of times, trying to relax.

The camera on the probe sent back images in real time. Darius watched it bob across the empty space, not much to see.

Wait. Was that the marker up ahead? It was still blinking! It sure looked like it was online.

Suddenly, the picture disappeared. Gray static filled the screen.

Darius raced up to the front control room again, focusing all of *Orion's* sensors forward. He kissed two fingers and touched the Jason medal again, for luck, out of habit.

Nothing. They didn't register anything in front of his ship. Not a marker, not the probe, nothing but space.

What kind of jamming equipment did this claim jumper have? How fancy was this guy's equipment?

And how the hell was Darius going to get his boundary markers back online?

The sour smell of Darius' sweat reminded him once again that he needed to replace the filters on the air scrubbers. They were probably three months out of date. Dad had been planning on replacing them, just before he'd died.

It was dirty, tricky work, folding himself into the tiny space behind the environmental units. And he'd never changed the filters by himself. He really did need to do it soon, though.

After he got his claim back.

Darius worked diligently to modify *Orion's* mining scoop. Almost all of the asteroids in the arc of his claim were too small to support an actual mining shaft. Instead, *Orion* harvested material from the surface of the asteroids by patiently, slowly, scooping up pebbles and rubble then testing and sorting the minerals.

The scoop was three meters wide, made out of an extremely flexible material that folded in on itself if it collided against any boulders that were too big to scoop up. It would straighten itself out again as soon as the obstacle was passed.

Darius needed for the scoop to work in space, not against a solid surface. He also needed to reinforce the scoop itself.

His plan was to fly *Orion* above where the boundary marker still sat and scoop it up. The marker was just over two meters wide and oval in shape, like a squashed ball. It was bigger than any boulder the scoop normally carried up to the ship.

Once Darius had the marker in the ship, he could run diagnostics on it. Maybe figure out why it had gone offline.

If nothing else, maybe it had some kind of log he could record, that he could use it to prove his claim back on *New Athens*.

He wasn't a software genius, though. He was adequately trained, and he'd certainly learned a lot living with his dad on *Orion*. But if the claim jumper's software was really sophisticated, Darius didn't have a chance in hell of blocking it.

The markers were standard issue from the Space Grant office. They had special drones that set the boundaries for everyone's claim, not trusting that the miners would mark their territories accurately.

It was against the law for Darius to pick one up.

However, it was *really* against the law to jam them, send them offline.

Satisfied with his modifications, Darius strapped the scoop back against the belly of *Orion*. He turned to leave, then paused, and turned back. He reached out to touch the scoop, patting the smooth bright metal briefly, hoping to impart luck to it.

This had to work. He needed to get one of the markers.

Darius climbed back up to the control room, checking stats as he went. He had enough fuel, so that wasn't an issue, at least for the moment. He was too far out to receive inner planet radio traffic. Too far out to send any messages, either. None that would arrive in time.

Had the claim jumper planned it that way? Waited until Darius was on the far side of the belt, the outside of his claim, before he started his attack?

Darius strapped himself into his seat and looked out at the rich darkness ahead of him. The familiar hum of *Orion's* engines surrounded him. He kissed two fingers and touched the Jason medal one more time, as usual before he started any venture.

Orion wasn't equipped to handle jump space. It was one of the reasons why Darius lived in low gravity—not enough ship to efficiently generate a true gravity field. And though he had enough fuel to take him all the way into *New Athens*, there really wasn't anywhere else he wanted to go.

If only his dad hadn't died. If only he wasn't so alone up here. If only…

Darius shook himself. Dad had always yelled at him for being too much in his head.

Time for some action.

Even if it was going to be very slow, blind, painfully awkward action.

Darius piloted by the map of the boundary markers overlaid on the map of what was supposed to be real space in front of him. He still couldn't see anything.

Had the claim jumper also blocked *Orion's* sensors?

He couldn't see the lights that the probe had seen. He just had to trust that it was there. He piloted the ship up, then over where the marker was supposed to be.

Here went nothing.

Slowly, Darius lowered the scoop. He had the sensors cranked up to their most sensitive setting so he'd feel if any kind of debris hit the scoop.

Then he haltingly inched forward. *Orion* wasn't set up for such minute maneuvers. It could reverse really well, however.

So Darius went forward a small amount. It was difficult to judge. Then he backed up. Did it again one quarter meter over.

But nothing tinged against the scoop.

Where the hell was that marker?

Darius flew to the far side of where the marker was supposed to be and turned *Orion* around, searching the black sky. But now *New Athens* was directly in front of him, blinding him completely.

Damn it! Where was that marker?

Darius tried again, flying a closer pattern. Just as he got to the edge of the area where the marker was supposed to be, he finally heard a *ting*.

Something had struck the scoop! It was a little bit away from where the marker was supposed to be, but still close enough.

Quickly, Darius brought the scoop back up, into the belly of *Orion*. Then he hurried down to examine the boundary marker.

However, no boundary marker waited for him.

Instead, he'd scooped up his own probe that he'd sent out earlier.

Darius did *not* want to put on his environmental suit and leave *Orion* to go looking for the boundary marker. It wasn't safe out there, in space. The death of his dad had drilled that home but good.

Plus, he was all alone out here. Dad had always said that spacers didn't live alone—they died alone. Darius needed to find a partner. However, no one would want to take a chance on a tiny, singular mining ship like *Orion*.

It was possible Darius and whatever partner he dredged up would hit a patch of some exotic mineral in his single degree of arc and be able to laugh all the way to the next galaxy in their own star cruiser.

No one but his dad had wanted to take that gamble. Darius hadn't been able to find anyone to come and help him.

There were plenty of men available, former soldiers from the war. Darius didn't trust them, even though his side had "won", and the *Greek Union of Planets* maintained their independence within the Allied Worlds.

Unlike the other poor bastards who were now going to lose their cultures and be "merged" with the rest of humanity…

Then again, Darius hadn't looked that hard when he'd been at the space station. Hadn't wanted to advertise his bad luck. Hadn't wanted to open his books up to some stranger on the off chance that they might decide to go in with him.

Maybe that was why he'd attracted a claim jumper. They knew he was all alone out here.

They probably thought he'd just roll over and let them take his single degree of arc of the asteroid belt.

However, Darius wasn't about to give up without a fight.

Kissing his fingers and touching the Jason medal one last time for luck, Darius unstrapped himself from the pilot seat. With slow pulls, he dragged himself to the airlock where his full environmental suit stood. God, he hated that thing. Hated how closed in he felt wearing it. How slow it made him. It was fully armored and protected, though. He'd be much safer in it than in a light suit.

Besides, he'd outgrown his light suit. The legs no longer fit him. His dad had thought he'd finally reached his final height with the last growth spurt, but Darius wasn't sure.

He'd never had any gravity to stop him from growing.

From the airlock, Darius put in the last few programming commands to *Orion*, arming the ship in case someone other than him came aboard.

Not that it would do any good if the asshole who was jamming the markers showed up. *Orion's* software was so ancient that it wouldn't take much to hack it.

Darius lifted the full environment suit down from its hook. Even without gravity it was heavy.

Slowly, Darius slid one leg, then the other into the pants, buckling and zipping them tightly against his skin. Then he loosened them. He needed to be able to move. It was just his paranoia that was making him tighten the suit so much.

After Darius shrugged on the jacket and locked himself fully into the suit he took some time, probably more time than he should have, running the diagnostics on the suit.

It appeared to be in great working condition. Dad had always insisted they have new suits, even if it took a day or more to get them synched up with *Orion*.

The air in the suit had a metallic taste as well, though it was better than the ship's air. Darius swallowed hard against the bile that suddenly rose in his throat. It reminded him of the day his dad had died, of the droplets of blood that had risen in an arc when he'd brought the body back inside the airlock.

He still made himself reach up and open the airlock, depressurizing the tiny compartment.

His breathing was loud in his ears. Though he couldn't actually feel the coldness outside the airlock, he shivered as the door opened.

Darius checked his lifeline, making sure that he was firmly attached to *Orion*. He tugged as hard as he could. It didn't budge.

After another deep breath, Darius took a step outside the airlock into space.

Though *Orion* didn't generate any gravity, Darius still felt lighter outside the ship. Maybe it was because he wasn't enclosed in metal anymore. *New Athens* shone brightly to his left, the single sun off in the distance, behind him.

Most of the asteroids in this degree of arc were darker, not composed of reflective material. It was one of the reasons why Dad had taken this area, even when there had been claims closer into the planet that were available.

"Darker and richer," he'd told Darius more than once with a wink. "Darker and richer will surely bring the gold." Then he'd touch the Jason medal, as if he could touch the golden fleece on the side.

They'd never struck it rich, no matter how many times they'd wished for luck and gold.

Slowly, carefully, Darius pulled himself along the outside of *Orion*, toward the front of the ship and the main control room.

According to the maps, the boundary marker should be directly in front of *Orion's* nose.

And there it was.

God*damn* it. Why couldn't *Orion* see it? Why was it offline? The orange and blue lights on the side of the marker were still blinking as if it were working properly.

Darius pulled himself out in front of *Orion*, holding onto handles just outside the control room window. He paused for a moment, glancing inside the ship. The cabin looked surprisingly ancient, the cushions for the two chairs well molded around their inhabitants bodies. All the controls were scratched and dented. Not a clean surface in the entire cabin. Plus, more than one control had been jerry-rigged, patched together with other parts, the bare wires showing.

It looked nothing like the sleek ships Darius saw in the holos, the new ones coming off the line. Hell, even the ones coming from the Guan Jo system looked newer.

But he couldn't afford to worry about that now. He needed to get that marker. Reclaim his home.

Turning, holding onto one of the handles tightly with his left hand, Darius stretched out as far as he could with his right, reaching for the boundary marker.

As he reached, the marker dipped down, so he missed it.

What the hell? Markers were supposed to be stable.

Darius reached again.

How the hell was the marker moving? It didn't have any kind of thrusters on it.

He swung out with his foot. Stupid thing *was* reacting to him, not just bobbing in space.

No wonder the scoop hadn't been able to grab it.

Wait, was there something hanging off the bottom of the marker?

Darius changed the polarization of his face mask, trying to brighten up the darkness.

Holy shit. What was that?

A black tail hung down from the marker, at least two meters long, ending in a triangular point.

Darius reached out again, watching carefully.

The marker itself couldn't move. But that tail swung away, gracefully matching Darius' reach, tugging the marker to the side.

What was that thing? And who had put it there?

Darius paused for a moment, thinking.

What if every boundary marker for his claim had such a tail attached to it? And each tail was a separate jamming unit? That would explain why he wasn't receiving static when he tried looking for the markers—it wasn't an area effect, but localized.

It would also explain why the probe had died when it got close enough. The jamming effect was all around the marker.

If he got too close, would it short out all the controls in his environmental suit?

Darius *had* to get that marker. Along with its long tail. Even if the claim jumper took his claim, he'd be able to prove that the markers had been tampered with.

But the marker swung out of reach every time Darius tried to grab it.

He was going to have to let go of the ship.

The thought filled Darius with cold dread. Sweat pooled under his arms, across the small of his back. He was going to have to decontaminate his suit when he got back inside *Orion*.

This was how his dad had died. Leaving the ship.

Darius had to get that marker, though.

And that meant jumping.

Turning back toward the ship, Darius touched two fingers to his faceplate, then reached up to touch the top of the control room, where the Jason medal hung on the inside.

Then he turned and *flung* himself into space, pushing off explosively, grabbing for the marker.

It bounced against the center of his chest. Darius quickly wrapped his arms around it.

Ah ha! Got you!

He took a deep breath. He could still breathe. His suit hadn't been jammed.

The speaker inside Darius' helmet suddenly crackled and came to life.

"Hello. Darius? Darius Linard? Are you there?"

Startled, Darius looked over his shoulder at *Orion*.

Who the hell was addressing him on the internal communications line?

But no one sat in the control room of *Orion*. His dad hadn't miraculously come back to life. Or decided to haunt him.

The stars behind *Orion* suddenly winked out. A large diamond shape manifested just beyond his tiny ship.

It was a nebula cruiser. Not capable of jump space, but it did have near-light-speed capabilities.

Darius awkwardly turned himself around.

Had that great big ship been following him the entire time? Cloaked and out of *Orion's* sensors?

"Darius?" came the voice over the suit speaker. It sounded female.

"Yeah?" Darius said cautiously. "What do you want?"

A woman's peeling laugh came over the speaker, cold and ruthless. "Money would be nice. Power. Respect." The voice lowered for a moment, coming out almost as a whisper. "*Justice.*" After a pause, the woman continued. "The list goes on and on."

A light from the dark ship suddenly bathed *Orion's* hull.

"What are you doing?" Darius asked. He could see every scratch and crevice in his little ship, dents he and Dad had always sworn they'd take care of during their next visit to a space station.

"Getting what I want," the amused voice answered him.

Darius felt a slight tug on the rope connecting him to the ship.

The dark ship was pulling *Orion* to it.

They were not only going to steal his claim, but his ship too?

"No!" Darius cried. He pulled himself hand-over-hand along the rope connecting him to his ship, the only home he'd ever known.

Too late.

The dark ship swallowed *Orion* whole, like some great whale eating a minnow.

However, they hadn't cut the line to Darius. He was still attached to *Orion*, and now, to the great dark ship.

"What do you want?" Darius asked again, his sweat now freezing across his back. If they cut his line, he'd be lost. He'd survive in his suit for a day, maybe two, drinking his own piss.

Sooner or later his suit would give out. He'd die like his dad had, alone in space, untethered.

"Let's see. I have your claim. I have your ship. Both have some value, though your ship's greatest value may just be as scrap. What do you have to offer?"

"I know the asteroid belt," Darius said through gritted teeth.

He was starting to hate that laugh.

"My ship knows more about all those hunks of rock than your father learned in over forty years of exploring," the woman boasted. She paused, then added, "Did you know that in the section near the dust cloud there are asteroids filled with heartsoil?"

Crap.

Heartsoil was one of the most expensive minerals

available, not just in the *Greek Union of Planets*, but through most of the local galaxy.

If only Darius, or his dad, had found it.

"So again, what do you have to offer?" his tormentor asked.

"I can work hard," Darius told her. "And I can learn." That was the one skill Dad had always tried to instill in him, to work hard and always learn.

"Good boy! Right answer," the voice purred. "That just might make you compatible. Come on aboard."

Darius paused. A small opening appeared in the hull of the dark ship.

It was his only chance to survive out here. No one would come and rescue him. Hell, no one would even come looking for him.

Live today. Vengeance tomorrow.

Darius would get his claim back. He'd be able to claim the heartsoil as his own. He'd rescue *Orion*, if he could.

And he'd survive.

Because that was something else his dad had taught him to do.

Darius didn't know what to expect as he stepped through the airlock and into the strange ship.

He hadn't expected the airlock to open up onto a staircase several levels above the ground of an active space dock.

Orion wasn't even close to the biggest ship. There were cruisers meant for inner planet travel, lighter flitters for moon and orbital hops, as well as at least two cargo ships that could easily carry *Orion* as well as the rest of their supplies.

Some of the equipment was older than *Orion*, but most

of it was much newer. And from systems outside of the *Greek Union of Planets*. The bigger cruiser had the sleek lines of a ship from the Guan Jo system, while he had no idea where the tiniest of ships came from, sleek and black and odd. Maybe Xi Lien, maybe farther out.

"Hey. HEY!"

Someone was shouting from above where Darius gaped. A young woman in orange coveralls, waving a large wrench, was trying to get his attention.

Since she seemed to be able to breathe the air, Darius reluctantly pulled off his helmet.

The air was fresh—much fresher than *Orion's*. The smell of oil and solder tickled the back of his throat. The noise was unbelievable. Metal screeched on all sides. A spark welder spouted static just below him. And there were people—lots of people. Yelling, talking, cursing.

Darius stopped himself from backing up and going right back to the silence of space.

They had his ship. If he wanted to live, he had to stay here.

At least for now.

But where was the bitch who had stolen it? Why weren't there guards or something?

What were these people going to do with him?

A petite woman strode across the floor of the space dock, waving at him. Her skin was too brown to make her a native of the *Greek Union of Planets*, and her eyes had a fold to them that marked her from the Xi Lien sector. Her black hair was cut spacer short. Even from this distance, Darius could tell her eyes were a hard green. She bore a large scar down her left cheek. A normal woman would have gotten skin therapy to have that fixed. Most of the space stations could do that level of repair.

She seemed to wear it as a badge of honor or something

stupid like that, holding up her face specifically so that he could see it.

Darius started when the helmet in his hand buzzed. He turned it over.

"Would you care to join us down here?" she asked, talking through his helmet speaker.

It sounded as if she were still laughing at him.

Darius nodded, not trusting that he'd be able to say anything without cursing. Or shouting. Or something else that would be stupid and would embarrass him.

He clanked down the stairs slowly, carefully, making sure that this wasn't some kind of elaborate trap. But the metal stairs were solidly attached to the side of the ship. There weren't any holes in the stairs, the railing didn't fold in on itself when he touched it.

Darius was sweating by the time he reached the bottom —the environmental suit was heavy, and while the ship wasn't under full gravity, it was a much higher gravity than what he was used to.

But he refused to remove it, in case the bitch decided to space him after all.

"Darius Linard," she said as she came forward. "Born on the Iaos space station, eighteen point five years ago, as counted by *New Athens*. Raised by Mikilos Linard, on the ship *Orion*."

Darius nodded. That was all true.

Who the hell was this bitch?

"I'm Captain Alana," she said, looking him up and down.

At least she didn't appear to disapprove of his suit. Much.

"You are now a consigned member of *Xinsheng*," she said formally. "In exchange for your life, food, shelter, and certain benefits, I agree to take you on as part of the Pineapple Express Transport company. You'll also be paid a stipend, and if you work hard, will be able to pay off your debt."

"By the time I'm fifty?" Darius asked belligerently. How dare she just steal everything from him? And why the hell would he agree to this deal?

"Maybe," she said, smirking. "If you actually *are* any good at learning and do work hard, you may be able to do it in as little as ten."

Darius blinked, surprised. "Really?" he asked. "I figured you'd make me an indentured slave."

A disgusted look crossed the captain's face. "We are *not* slavers. I only deal with them when I must. You will have a legal contract and a way to buy out your consignment. I do *not* want to hold onto you for life." She looked him up and down again. "Seriously. I don't want to hold onto *you* forever."

Darius refused to rise to the implied insult that he wasn't worth holding onto. He couldn't stop his traitorous tongue, though. "Why deal with me at all?"

"Because you *are* young," the captain said. "And potentially trainable. And we always need pilots. You've been raised in low gravity. Chances are, you're a better pilot than most."

Darius nodded. That was what Dad had always said, that Darius was the better pilot of the two of them because he'd been raised in space and had a better feel for it. "What do you transport?" Darius asked. Was there a legitimate side of her business?

"This and that," she said, waving her hand in the air as if brushing away cobwebs. "Will you sign the contract, Darius Linard? Or do I shoot you now?"

"Do I have any choice?" Darius asked bitterly.

"You can choose to live," the bitch captain said sweetly. "Or you can choose to die. Choose now."

The noise in the space dock hadn't diminished in the

least, but Darius still felt as though the other crew members were watching him.

He glanced up. Guards stood on the catwalk with drawn guns. Probably something that would only shoot flesh and not metal.

His head was uncovered. His suit couldn't protect him.

The captain looked bored, as if she presented this kind of life-or-death deal to people daily.

Maybe she did.

Darius still paused. Did he really want to do this?

It wasn't really much of a choice at all.

Live now. Vengeance later.

"I choose to live," Darius said.

"Good choice. Strip," the captain said.

"What?" Darius asked, shock running through him.

"You took too long," she said coolly. "I won't abide incalcitrant crew members. Strip. Now. Down to your skin. Or else."

The guards had their weapons obviously pointed at Darius now. He couldn't get close to the captain without his brains spilling all over the floor. It wasn't worth it.

If he was going to an assured death, he was going to make damned sure she was coming with him.

With a sigh, Darius put his helmet on the dark gray metal deck beside him and started unstrapping his environment suit.

He took off layer after layer. The jacket. The pants. His T-shirt. His new pants. Even his shorts.

The humiliation *burned.*

The bitch captain didn't even bother to watch. One of the other crew members had come up with a tablet, holding it up for her to read.

Darius stood shivering on the cold deck, his hands covering his privates.

He was going to *get back* at her, he vowed.

Finally, the bitch captain had finished with her oh-so-important work and returned her attention to Darius.

"When I say move, you move. Got that?" she asked, her voice as chill as space pressing in around them.

"Yes, ma'am," Darius said.

"Good boy. Now come," she said, turning and walking away quickly.

Darius paused. Should he pick up his clothes?

No. She said to do what she said, when she said it.

He felt the heat of the guns pricking his bare ass as he followed her quickly, out of the space dock and into the rest of the ship.

The corridor looked the same as all the hallways he'd ever been through on space stations. They seemed to have been designed around a single plan: plain walls with alarms and monitors built in, colored stripes leading the way to unknown areas of the ship, hard metal floors.

Most of the crew who they passed looked away, didn't try to meet Darius' eye. A few did, challenging him.

Fuck them. Fuck them all. He didn't care if they saw him naked or painted red.

He would have his vengeance on *all* of them.

The bitch captain didn't parade Darius through too many corridors. It wasn't long before she stopped in front of a blank door.

"You will stay here until someone comes to fetch you," she announced.

The room beyond had a bed couch and not much else.

It was still larger than the room he'd called his own on *Orion*.

"Can I fetch my things from my ship?" Darius asked.

"No," she said. "It's all scrap."

Darius bit down on the anger that boiled up. *Orion* wasn't merely scrap!

"But my things—"

"Are now all *my* possession," the bitch captain told him firmly.

Darius didn't care so much about his own things, but those of his dad's, that he'd kept…He settled for glaring at her. God, if only he had some kind of fighting training. He'd kill this bitch in a heartbeat.

But she was as muscled as the planet-bound. She'd toss his ass on the ground faster than he could strike.

He'd have to wait until he got her in low gravity, somehow.

"In you go now," the bitch captain said. "Someone will be along shortly," she promised sweetly, her tone cloyingly fake.

"Fine," Darius said. He marched into the room. The door shuttered behind him.

He would not cry. He would not bitch and moan. He would survive.

And he would have his revenge, starting with her, the high bitch queen.

PART TWO

Three months later

DARIUS REACHED DOWN UNDER HIS thick T-shirt and brought his new Jason medal up to his lips, kissing it quickly for luck. This was his third solo "milk run" for the Pineapple Express Transport company in as many months.

He'd barely made it out alive both of the previous times, with whatever shit-hunk of a ship they'd sent with him getting mostly destroyed in the process. The only reason he'd gotten out alive at all was because he was a fucking good pilot.

But seriously, how the hell was he supposed to know that the Guan Jo system responded *without* lasers only if you flubbed the greeting the first time? That responding perfectly every time sent up warning signals?

Though Darius got intel reports on every system he visited on his own, and he spent time memorizing them as he was supposed to, they still left much to be desired.

Complaining to the high bitch captain brought nothing but derision.

He really hated that laugh of hers.

Darius wasn't sure what he was carrying this time. He was pretty sure it wasn't legal. Big rainbow colored boxes were strapped firmly into the storage bay, which had been modified to take up twice as much space as originally designed, leaving him with a cabin barely wide enough for his skinny bed.

However, in order to survive, Darius had had to sign away his life and become an indentured employee of the Pineapple Express Transport company. Oh, they'd pay him, while at the same time charging him for food, bunk space, transportation, and fees to fix the ships he flew.

It was all perfectly legal. There wasn't a court on any world that would revoke his contract, even if he'd signed it under duress.

Besides, he really might be able to buy out his contract in a decade. Or three.

Probably more if he couldn't bring a ship back in one piece.

He didn't even bother to learn the names of the ships he piloted anymore. Most of them were as old, if not older, than *Orion*. He'd learned quickly not to get attached to anything. The bitch captain made sure of that, keeping him on guard and on his toes, switching the crews he worked with, the carrier ships, everything.

Pineapple Express Transport was the vaguely legitimate arm of the bitch captain's empire. Why she hadn't gone into politics, he'd never know. She'd be queen of the universe by now if she'd decided to.

But she also couldn't personally blow shit up on a regular basis if she'd gone straight. There was always that.

Darius checked his fuel levels, put everything he could

into his (very) meager shields, then kicked the ship into gear, skirting the very edge of the system while probing for an opening.

Slipping into the Ecos system hadn't been difficult. The neo-hippies *wanted* people to come and join them in their utopia.

Getting out, however, was a whole different manner.

Particularly after Darius had stopped by three different planets, met dark carriers, collected pharmaceuticals that he'd never even heard of before but were likely banned in the rest of the known worlds.

At least the air scrubbers in this spaceship worked properly, and he wasn't afraid of any kind of contamination from the rainbow colored boxes.

The intel he'd received on the system had claimed that there was an opening in the Ecos system defense grid on the outer perimeter. The strength of the grid fluctuated with the sunspots from their main sun.

Darius had timed his visit with the highest activity of sunspots that season.

But he couldn't find a damn hole in the system. Nothing big enough for him to slip through.

He had enough fuel to pace across this degree of arc of their system a couple more times, but he was getting nervous.

What if one of the dark carriers had been found? Compromised? What if they knew about his visit and were already tracking him? Sometimes trackers were put on containers that could make it through the ship's jamming equipment.

How was he going to get back to the main ship? Then, how did the main carrier and the rest of them make it through the jump point alive?

Had the intel been wrong? That had happened on the first run Darius had gone on solo.

Or were the sensors on this hunk-of-shit ship on the fritz? Again?

Darius had thought he'd learned a lot when he'd been living on *Orion* with his dad.

It was nothing compared to how quickly he'd picked up new systems when it was his skin on the line in an unfamiliar ship.

Unlike *Orion*, this ship had been originally designed for a single crew member. Everything was in arm's reach. Without the force of gravity to hold him down, Darius had grown long and lanky, with a wider reach than most. He could reach everything without even having to stretch much.

Full gravity wouldn't kill him, but it would have been a bitch and a half. He disliked *Xinsheng* for that very reason— far too much gravity for him. He'd wake up with nightmares, dreaming that he couldn't breathe.

Darius ran diagnostics on the sensors up front, then the sides, then the back. The little spaceship was built like an egg with useless wings sticking out from the sides, as if that would help steer the craft when it was operating in deep space. Was he supposed to glide on the solar wind or something equally stupid?

Huh. The readings on the back sensors were different than the front sensors. The back sensors showed a weakening of the defense grid. There. As well as a largish object.

Shit. Was that an asteroid? Or was he being followed? Sweat instantly pooled along his back. The familiar taste of metal flooded his mouth.

Without unstrapping himself from his seat, Darius reached up behind him and flicked the breakers for the back sensors, taking them off line, then on again.

Readings were still different between the front and back. Large object still behind him. It didn't make any sense.

Unless…

Darius spun the ship in place on her gyros, flipping one-hundred-and-eighty degrees, then took the readings again.

The hole was still there. There was a weakening of the grid nearby.

The large object remained there as well. Which meant it was an anomaly, another screw up of the sensor.

So he knew there was something wrong with the back sensors, on the one hand. On the other, it was the sensor that showed him the way out.

Which did he believe?

Fuck it.

Darius spun the ship around so the rear of the ship faced the opening in the defense grid.

He was going to back out. *Orion* had always backed better, so he was quite good at it.

Couldn't see anything directly in front of him, so he threw up a map to show him what was behind him.

It was going to be touch and go, but Darius was at least used to that by now, accustomed to piloting strange ships.

Something winked behind the grid he had on the heads-up display.

Fuck. There *was* another ship out there.

God, he hated space sometimes. And shit for ships. And sensors that were far too easily fooled.

But he couldn't just break his contract—the bitch captain would hunt him down and have his balls for breakfast.

More than one crew member had heard stories about that sort of thing.

She was very good at getting exactly what she wanted.

Darius threw all his power into the engines, leaving almost nothing for the front shields and *slammed* the little ship into reverse.

He squirted through the defense grid like a seed through screen.

Of course, he couldn't hear any alarms he might have set off. No bright lights flashed when he went through.

He'd been spotted, however. And something big was coming after him. At speed.

Time to run.

Darius spun the ship around so he was facing forward, then hit the big red emergency button in the center of the console.

The button turned on the cloaking device/jammer that the bitch captain provided on all of her ships. It was strapped to his little ship along the outside, to the belly of the hull.

Instantly, everything inside the cabin grew hazy, as if had just filled with smoke.

Darius knew it wasn't, though. It had to do with how his ship had just *shifted* sideways, and neither his (human?) eyes or sensors worked as well on this plane.

Was he now invisible from the Ecos system sensors? From whatever the hell that thing was behind him?

Darius shivered as the cabin edges of the control panel and even his seat grew less distinct, while the air turned foul, smelling like burned rubber. What the hell was that thing doing?

He'd only been able to examine one, once, and just for a few minutes. The tail, even inside the artificial atmosphere of the main ship, *Xinsheng*, was freezing to the touch, burning his fingers. It had been made of a black material that ate away the light. He had no idea how it was constructed. Couldn't find an obvious seam. Or even a power source.

Plus, they appeared to be *growing* from the metal they were attached to, the two materials fused together.

They were devil tails.

Mankind had never run into any advanced alien civilizations. The few they'd come across had pretty much curled up and cried "uncle" as soon as the masses of humans arrived.

But if Darius was a betting man, like Dad had been, he would have laid out good gold that those tails were alien. He didn't know any human tech that was that good with organics.

For now, Darius had to find the carrier and get the hell out of this system. Before that damned tail burned his ship out from under him.

Darius didn't go in a straight line. He had no idea how well he was hiding from the sensors in this system. Instead, he bounced around like a rubber ball in a box being shaken by a hyperactive eight-year-old, going up, down, and side to side, as unpredictably as he could.

As far as he could tell, he'd left the big blank object behind him. He still didn't slow down until he was in hailing distance of the carrier.

Just in time to watch all hell break loose.

<hr>

"What do you mean the carrier was attacked?"

Darius winced at the strident tones of the high bitch captain echoing off the metal walls of the space dock. He stayed where he was, though, back behind the others standing and gaping at the carrier, not volunteering anything. It wasn't his place. Sweat still pooled in the middle of his back, stinking of too many hours in an environmental suit and too much fear.

He hadn't realized that one of the benefits of the devil tail was that it built a kind of force-field around a ship. Though it made sense that it would, given that it was a type of cloaking and jamming device.

Even with a huge gaping hole in its side, the carrier had

been able to hold it together long enough to make it to jump space.

"Ma'am," the main carrier pilot hurried forward. "It was an ambush. There was no way we could have anticipated it."

The bitch captain turned her piercing gaze at the rest of the crew.

Darius was glad that he wasn't the only one who shrank back.

Someone other than Darius might have considered her pretty if she'd smiled sometimes. Or didn't laugh so harshly. Or had gotten that ugly scar of hers fixed.

"You," she said, pointing at Darius. "It was your fault, wasn't it?"

"No ma'am!" Darius said, stepping forward, stung. "The attack started before I got to the ship." He didn't add that one of the enemy's ships had probably been tracking him for some time.

The bitch captain's eyes narrowed. "And your ship?" she challenged.

"Mostly in one piece," Darius bragged. It was the first time he'd come back with a working ship.

She sniffed, unimpressed. "I want full reports," she said, pointing to the woman who ran engineering. "And complete logs with analysis," she added, glancing back at the carrier's captain. "And you, I want to see you in my office," she said, snapping her fingers at Darius. She paused, wrinkling her nose at him. "After you clean up and get that stench off you."

"Who, me?" Darius gulped.

He shivered, knowing the others laughed at him. No one pitied him—he was still an outsider, still proving himself, while the rest of the crew had been together for over a year.

But Darius had kept his word, if not to the bitch captain, at least to himself. He would work hard. And he would learn. He would survive until he could enact his vengeance.

May as well go and learn what the high bitch queen wanted now.

<hr>

Darius had been to the high bitch captain's main office twice before.

He hadn't enjoyed the experience either time.

The office was smaller than he'd have thought, not much bigger than a closet. The bitch captain's desk ran from one wall to the other, a wide barrier between her and her guests. It was covered with data crystals, three different readers, scanners, monitors, and other equipment that Darius didn't recognize.

A second long desk ran along the left wall. It held fewer items. At the very far edge, pushed against the wall, were actual books. Darius' dad had had two of those, from the planet *New Athens*.

These looked much older than his dad's books.

Directly behind the captain was a large porthole window. It had probably been expanded from the original design.

Rumor had it that the bitch captain liked looking out on the stars. One of the cooks had even mentioned that he'd seen the captain reading one of her books under starlight.

Darius didn't want to believe it. He didn't want to admit anything that made the high bitch captain human.

This time, when Darius arrived, not only was the captain already there ahead of him, so was another woman.

She was *ancient*. Her face held deep wrinkles, and her hair had fallen out in huge chunks, so only wisps remained. She was pudgy in that way that old spacers got, because they never got out of their pilot chairs. She wheezed as she sat, arms folded over her ample chest.

Ugh. She even smelled old, like those food packets they

sometimes got from *New Athens* that weren't sealed properly, that smelled both musty and sickly sweet, like rotting peach syrup.

Darius squeezed in next to her. What fresh hell had the bitch captain decided to bequeath to him? How many more labors would he be required to perform? Even Hercules only had to do so many.

"Every ship you've run, you've ruined, Darius," the bitch captain said, not looking up from her desk.

Darius gulped and sat up straighter. Fuck. This wasn't a slaver that the bitch captain was going to sell him to, was it?

She threatened that all the time, though she actually hated slavers. She'd told him when he'd first met her that she wasn't a slaver. He'd been surprised at her revulsion when a slaver had actually come on board, though most wouldn't have noticed it—the hard line to her jaw, how all her smiles had been forced, her minute shudders when the slaver had clapped her on the shoulder.

Rumor had it that she'd been a slave, once. Some horrible mine or another. Supposedly, one of the reasons she'd started Pineapple Express Transport was so she'd have a way to employ the people she stole, so she didn't have to sell them into slavery.

Darius didn't believe it. Or at least, he doubted that was the only reason she'd started Pineapple Express Transport. Though he'd never admit to it, even under torture, Captain Alana was actually brilliant. She had plans inside of plans inside of plans, depths that she didn't bother showing to anyone, that only someone watching her very carefully every single minute might see.

"So I'm going to give you one last chance," the bitch captain said, finally lifting her head and staring hard at him, her green eyes like ice crystals. "And I'm going to make it worth your while to not fuck up for a change."

Darius bit his lip. The last ambush really hadn't been his fault. He hoped.

"This is Sara," the bitch captain said.

Darius glanced over at the old woman. He was surprised her eyes were open—he'd thought she'd fallen asleep.

Sara nodded at Darius, then addressed the captain. "Bit wet behind the ears, ain't he, Alana?"

Darius sat up straighter. Fuck. Was this..this *Sara* friends with the bitch captain?

His life could *not* get any worse.

The bitch captain glared at Sara. "Captain Alana," she said wearily, as if she'd had to correct the woman many times before. "That's why I want you to straighten him out. Teach him to fly right."

The old woman snorted. "I ain't got decades, ya know."

Darius nearly rolled his eyes. He wasn't as much of a screw up as they were making him out to be.

Was he? The bitch captain had said he was a good pilot, and he'd proven that. More than once.

"I've got another incentive for you," the bitch captain said, turning toward Darius. "You remember your old ship? *Orion?*"

Darius gulped, torn between anger and sorrow. How dare she talk about his ship? His dad's ship? She'd also assured him that *Orion* was only good for scrap metal.

His ship had long since been deceased.

When the silence drew out longer, Darius realized that the bitch captain was waiting for an answer. "Yes, ma'am," he said slowly. "I do."

She hadn't let him take anything from the ship, not even rescue the Jason medal that his dad had welded to the ceiling of the command room. He'd had to bribe one of the other crew members to buy him a new one when they passed near the next space station.

"I may have been exaggerating when I said that it was mostly scrap metal. Turns out the hull was more sound than I'd originally expected. All the scratches and bumps were only surface deep. And it had some interesting modifications made to the sensors."

Darius tilted his head to the side. What did she mean by that? The sensors on *Orion* were shit. He hadn't been able to find her jamming devices on the boundary markers with the ship's sensors. He'd had to actually leave the ship to eyeball it.

"So we re-commissioned it," the bitch captain said.

Darius couldn't help his gasp. "You what?" he asked, startled. *Orion* wasn't dead?

"Refitted it with better air filters. Better engines. Stronger sensors." The bitch captain paused, then added, "If I agree to let you use *Orion* with your next job, will you bring her back in one piece?"

"Absolutely, sir. Ma'am," Darius promised. He'd do everything in his power to make sure that his ship stayed intact.

"Lord help me," Sara muttered at his side.

"Of course, most of her repairs will be counted against your original debt," the captain continued.

Of course. Bitch. But it didn't matter.

He was going to get his ship back.

And sooner or later, he'd have his revenge.

Darius had never been to the space dock below the main one. He hadn't even realized there were two, stacked one on top of the other.

What other hidey holes existed on *Xinsheng* that he didn't know about? Probably plenty. Lots of doors on the ship that his crew badge wouldn't open, whole areas that he didn't have access to.

The second dock was a lot smaller than the main space dock. And a hell of a lot quieter, too. The machinery all looked the same, old and well-used. But it wasn't big enough to hold one of the jump-capable cruisers.

Three ships littered the dock floor. There was probably room for only one more. Two small little flitters and *Orion*.

Darius spared two seconds to look at the flitters. One was highly modified with sleek, clean lines and what was probably a powerful engine. Was that the bitch captain's private flitter? He'd never seen it before. The same material that made up the devil tails covered the entire rear end of it.

Then *Orion* captured all his attention.

The hull was still pitted and dinged, with long scratches where space debris had run against it.

But the front control room had been fully refitted. New seats, new controls, hell, new *everything*.

Darius could barely control himself from running forward and throwing his arms across the window, giving the ship a hug.

"That piece of shait?" Sara muttered beside him. "We're going to travel in that?"

Darius was in too good of a mood to correct her, to let her know just how wonderful a ship *Orion* was.

He was home.

Darius applied himself like never before, spending twelve to fifteen hours a day, every day, learning the new systems on *Orion*. He couldn't wait to take her out again.

Even if he was working for a smuggling company. It was still *Orion*. Still home.

He didn't know who had saved the Jason medal. But it wasn't merely welded to the ceiling of the cockpit—someone had enclosed in a clear acrylic bubble. He made a habit of kissing the first two fingers of right hand and touching it every time he entered the control room, ritual and habit and home all at the same time.

"That just ain't sanitary," Sara muttered more than once.

Darius ignored her.

However, at least Sara had a clue about what she was doing. She was familiar with the new tracking system, the locks now imbedded into the cargo doors (and more importantly, how to override them if someone came on the ship and locked them in there—knowledge Darius was glad of).

The large red button in the center of the ship's console was something he was already familiar with: It meant that there were devil tails attached to the ship, somewhere.

It wasn't until Darius was crawling underneath the ship that he found them. More than a dozen, long and black, each about a meter long. When *Orion* flew, the tails would blow up against the hull. When they stopped or just hovered, they'd hang down. Were they just for protection? Or did they have other sensors attached to them? They reminded him of the lures that some jellyfish had, dangling innocently until something brushed against them. Then they'd react violently, stinging, paralyzing—even killing—whatever had touched them.

When Darius asked Sara about the devil tails, she just shrugged. "Captain paid a lot of money for those," she said. "As well as the software to use them. Just taking one of 'em won't do you no good."

Darius nodded, thinking.

He was still going to take one, just before he left. Maybe

with one of those he would be able to prove that his claim had been stolen.

He'd have to start searching for where the software for controlling them was located as well.

He still wasn't any kind of computer genius, but he'd been studying. Diligently. Every chance he got.

If he hadn't lost the family claim and the ship he'd called home, his dad might have been proud of him for applying himself.

Finally, the call came in that they were going onto active duty. Darius spent the night before unable to sleep. He ran scenarios through his head. Maybe they'd be close to the *Greek Union of Planets*. He could drop Sara off at a station, make his way to the nearest planet with the devil tails attached to his ship.

Would anyone believe him? Would it be enough to get him out of his contract?

Maybe whatever it was they were transporting would be so valuable that he could buy his way out his contracts with it instead. Have that bitch captain on her knees. Get her to sign back the deed to his claim.

It had been three months. He was no further along on his plans for revenge.

But Dad had always advised patience. So Darius waited, watching, plotting, planning.

His day would come.

Flying *Orion* out of space dock had to be the best feeling *ever*.

In his head, Darius pretended he was leaving *Xinsheng* for good. Leaving the high bitch captain. Leaving slavery and smuggling and indentured service behind. Never coming back.

Sara must have known something was going on with him, because before they got very far into the system she told him, "Now, we don't want to screw up this mission. You hear me?"

Darius nodded. God, if only he could just keep flying! Find another carrier ship to transport him and *Orion* back to the *Greek Union of Planets*…

"I don't know about you, but I'se only got a year left on my contract. Maybe less. Depends on this deal," Sara said sternly.

Darius glanced at her, then back out through the control window. How long had Sara been in service? Had she gone in when she'd been his age?

"This is why Alana had me work with you. She knew I was too close to mess up," Sara said with great satisfaction.

"You two are…close?" Darius finally asked.

Sara wheezed and laughed, rocking back and forth in the other control chair, her arms still wrapped over her ample belly. "Lord, no. She bought out my contract from the slavers. Were going ta work meself to death. Gave me a chance, she did."

Sara had been with the slavers? Doing what?

Darius didn't like the toothy grin Sara was giving him. Gave him the willies. No one had really wanted her to do… that, had they?

"So you do your job. I'll do mine. We get out of there in one piece. With all the other bits intact too." She laughed at some joke Darius was afraid to ask about.

Then Sara farted. The smell of noxious gas filled the cabin.

"Oopps," the old woman said, cackling. "Guess I shouldn't have packed as many beans!"

Darius couldn't pound his head against the dashboard of the control room as much as he might want to. The dashboard might break, long before his head did.

This trip was going to take for-fucking-ever.

Picking up the shipment was as easy as it always was. All a crew ever had to do was to arrive on a world and pick up the cargo.

If a supplier claimed not to have it, or to be short, the crew was instructed to walk away. They never engaged. It wasn't their problem.

Very few suppliers ever tried to cheat the Captain Alana. The ones who did, didn't survive. And their deaths were never pretty.

Or at least that was what the other crew members had told Darius.

Sara backed up those stories with some personal tales of cheating suppliers who had not only their complete livelihoods ruined, but those of their children. Entire generations of families.

"Best not piss off Alana. Or she'll come after you with more than just a knife to cut off yer balls," Sara warned.

Darius still wasn't sure why Sara continued to call the captain merely Alana. Was it her own form of "high bitch captain"? For the captain merely letting Sara work off her debt, instead of buying her free and clear?

They were outside the Ashton system before Darius stopped obsessively checking every monitor, every sensor, staying awake far too late into his sleeping shift just to make sure they weren't being followed.

"Y'alls gonna worry yourself into an early death," Sara told him. "Or I'm gonna space ya. Take your pick."

"It's just—nothing's ever gone this smoothly before," Darius admitted.

Sara shrugged. "Ya lose some. Eventually ya got to win one."

Darius shook his head. Something wasn't right. He wasn't just being paranoid. There was this sense he'd always had about when things were going wrong just out of eyesight.

If he'd paid attention to it earlier, Dad wouldn't have died.

Darius couldn't find a ship following them, however. Nothing could be seen blocking out the stars on any side of them. He played with the sensors, coaxing them beyond their official maximum range.

Nothing but space out there.

"Go sleep," Sara complained. "Yer always here, in my space. I'd like some peace and quiet, if ya know what I mean."

Darius sighed. He did. Only when he was out on a mission did he ever have time alone, like what he'd had on *Orion* after his dad had died.

He'd been lonely, but some part of his soul had also enjoyed it.

"All right, all right, I'm going," Darius muttered as he unstrapped himself from his pilot's seat. "Just don't run us into anything. And wake me if you even suspect something's wrong."

"Sure, sure, kid, you'll be the first one I call," Sara said, rolling her eyes.

Darius stretched, touched the Jason medal welded to the ceiling for luck, as he usually did, before he pulled himself out of the front control room. He rubbed his eyes and blinked in the bright corridor. Okay, he was much more tired than he'd realized.

Maybe he did need to sleep.

Still, Darius couldn't help but stop in the mid-section. To check the doors and the locks on their cargo.

He was surprised when the one on his left opened with the merest touch.

That wasn't right. It should be locked. Even though it was just the two of them. The instructions from the bitch captain were clear. Cargo stayed locked in the hold and was never visited. Period.

Shit.

Of course, one of the things that the bitch captain had *not* bothered to give Darius, or to train him in, was any kind of combat. That was for her soldiers and guards who got special rations as well as slept with extra weight every night.

Darius hadn't thought to check the interior scanners. He added that to his mental checklist of things to scan for next.

Hopefully they didn't have a stowaway.

Cautiously, Darius pushed open the cargo bay door. The lights were already up bright.

The room was too small for someone to hide in. It was maybe three meters in diameter, roundish, with an airlock opposite the cabin door.

If anyone was hiding, they'd have to be living in the walls, and Darius had taken apart too many of the panels throughout the entire ship to believe there was any space large enough for someone to stay there.

He floated over to his right, where the cargo boxes stood stacked from floor to ceiling. Each was made out of a solid white material, maybe twelve centimeters square. Light. Strapped in so they wouldn't bounce around with the ship's lack of gravity.

What the hell was in these? Electronic components? Parts to some fancy machinery? He couldn't imagine what else they might be. The boxes were too pristine for it to be food or regular parts. No, it was something that needed extra cushioning.

Darius found himself reaching for the top box, then pulled his hand back.

No. Things were going too good. He'd gotten the shipment, pulled out of the system, and would rendezvous with the carrier in less than seven hours. No one was tracking them. No one suspected them of carrying…whatever the hell it was that they were carrying.

He was not about to fuck things up by actually going through the shipment.

Something made Darius shiver. A noise, or possibly a wind on a ship that shouldn't have any air movement, not like that.

Sara stood in the doorway.

"Ach, I'm sorry you saw those," she said sadly.

"What do you mean?" Darius asked. "I didn't touch them! Didn't open a single box!"

God*damn* it. Would Sara narc on him to the high bitch captain? Lie about his pawing through the merchandise?

"I know you didn't. You're a good boy," Sara said snidely. "I couldna believe Alana stuck me with you."

Darius stayed silent but slid to his right. It wasn't as if he could get past Sara. She filled the entire cargo bay door. He still didn't know what was in those boxes, though. Felt the need to get away from those.

"Do you not have a clue, boy?" Sara asked, exasperated.

"About what?" Darius asked, confused. What was he supposed to already know about?

"About that cargo," Sara said, sliding further into the room. She closed the cargo bay door after her and locked it.

Darius could get out of cargo bay if someone locked him in. Sara had shown him that, given him that little piece of knowledge that no one else in the bitch captain's crew had thought to teach him.

Then he bit back a groan. Possibly he could get out. If Sara hadn't lied when she'd taught him that trick. Or if she hadn't changed the code on him.

He certainly hadn't bothered telling her that he might have worked out a different way of getting out of the cargo bay if he'd gotten locked in. He didn't know her, didn't trust her that much.

"So here's the deal," Sara said walking directly over to where the boxes were piled, her steps sounding loud in the small space.

Why was she wearing grav boots? Why did she feel the need to be attached to the "floor" of the ship?

Orion didn't have any grav boots as part of its normal equipment. He'd checked every locker, every storage space, even the spaces that weren't completely obvious, that appeared to be mere electrical panel.

Why did Sara have a pair? What was she planning? She could certainly move faster than Darius could in free space, even hauling himself along hand-over-hand along the rungs set across the "ceiling" of the ship.

"This here's some of the most precious cargo anyone can carry," Sara explained. She flipped open the closest box.

Darius stubbornly stayed where he was.

"Oh, come see," Sara said. "It won't bite." She stepped out of arm's reach.

Darius used the rungs in the ceiling to drag himself over to see what was in the open box.

A group of four brilliant blue stones sat snuggled in packing material at the bottom of the box. They were each about the size of half his fist.

"What are they?" Darius asked, cautiously moving back away.

"They're sapphires, boy! Blue sapphires," Sara snapped. "From the mines of Shikura."

Darius had no idea what she was going on about. "I see," he lied.

Sara rolled her eyes at him. "Sure, they look pretty. And some diplomats' wives wear them, show off their wealth. But they're *power*."

"Power?" Darius asked, glancing at the box and back to Sara.

Sara sighed. "They're batteries, boy. Can store enough power to run this here ship."

"What does the bit—I mean, Captain Alana, plan to do with them?" Darius wondered.

"What the hell does that matter?" Sara asked. She took two quick steps toward him.

He pulled himself away, pressing himself flat against the supplies on the other wall of the cargo bay. There really wasn't any room in the small space to get completely away.

If she started swinging at him, it was going to get ugly quickly. She had something to press against with those grav boots holding her in place. He didn't.

"Alana," Sara said, her voice laced with disgust. "Fucking *princess* Alana ain't gonna do nothing. The supply came in short."

"She'll kill the suppliers," Darius said stubbornly. Did he really want to cause the death of someone else by stealing?

"So?" Sara asked. "Us or them, boyo."

Darius shook his head. It wasn't right.

Being indentured to the high bitch captain wasn't right either. However, he didn't want to casually cause the death of someone either. Not like that.

"Here," Sara said, fishing out one of the bright gems. It glowed brighter cradled in her cracked and dry palm. "Alls you got to do is swallow it down."

"What?" Darius asked. He took a calculated risk and pushed himself off the wall, up above her head.

He almost made it to the door before she grabbed him by the ankle, yanked him back. Hard.

Damn it. He'd thought he was too close to the ceiling for her to grab, short troll that she was.

When he looked back, he saw that she now floated above her grav boots. That was how she grabbed him. By releasing herself.

Darius twisted himself in the air to face her, drawing himself together. He'd never become dependent on gravity, not like she had been. All he had to do was bide his time.

"What do you want me to do?" he asked, his arms crossed over his chest, making himself a smaller object.

"Swallow down one or two of the stones," Sara crooned. She held onto his foot with one hand, the gem still glowing brightly in her other. "Why'dja think I brought so many beans? Grease for the internal systems." She cackled loudly.

Darius shook his head. He wanted his revenge on the high bitch captain, not some nameless, faceless supplier. "No."

Sara's eyes narrowed. "I'm gonna have to space you if you don't, ya know?"

"I won't tell," Darius said. "I swear it." And he wouldn't. Particularly if the bitch captain asked. "I just—I don't want to hurt someone else."

"Yer weak, boy," Sara told him. She pushed the gem into her own greedy mouth, swallowing it down quickly.

Darius felt his eyes grow wide. Wow. He wasn't sure he could swallow something so big, so easily. Not like Sara just had.

"How long have you been stealing from the captain?" Darius asked as Sara swallowed down a second gem.

"Heh," Sara said with a wide grin. "Three years, now. Since she bought me out."

"I thought you only had a year on your contract," Darius pointed out.

"Gots to have something to live on afterward," Sara said. "This heres' my retirement program," she added, hefting a third gem.

"So you'll buy yourself out? In a year's time?" Darius asked, feeling a modicum of relief. Maybe someday he *would* be able to work off his debt. If he didn't get his revenge and kill the bitch, first.

"Fuck yeah. But there's no *advantage* to just doing that," Sara scolded him. "Is why I'd been stashing away bits and bobs over the years."

"And she's never figured it out?" Darius asked, curious.

Sara just shrugged. "Seems I have a bunch of bad luck with suppliers," she said.

Darius shook his head. The captain may be a complete and total bitch, and he would still love to fling her out into space without a helmet, helpless and clawing as her lungs imploded, but she wasn't stupid. She was far from stupid.

She had to know that Sara was stealing.

Was this all some huge fucking test? To see how loyal Darius was? If he'd come back to *Xinsheng* now that he had his own ship again?

Fuck. He hated these kinds of mind games. He was always sure to guess wrong. Tricked and fooled like Hercules always had been.

But for now—Darius merely had to get out of the cargo bay. In one piece.

Sara still held tightly onto his left ankle. She also floated, and hadn't bothered to grab onto another handhold.

Seemed maybe she was the one wet behind her ears when there wasn't gravity.

Darius stretched himself out flat then jackknifed together and grabbed Sara's wrist.

"What the—" Sara sputtered.

Darius completed the action, yanking *up*.

Sara floated up and over Darius. She let go of his ankle as she struggled to right herself.

Darius pushed himself off the nearest solid surface and landed directly in front of the door to the cargo bay.

While Sara was still righting herself, Darius entered the general override code for *Orion*, not trusting the code that Sara had taught him. Had the new systems overwritten it? Or would the old code that Dad had put in still work?

Yes! With a quick push, Darius was out the cargo bay door, slamming it shut on Sara. He bashed the emergency override lock, set up in case the airlock in the cargo bay opened unexpectedly or started leaking, sealing off the bay from the rest of the ship.

Darius couldn't hear Sara's curses from the other side. But he'd listened to her long enough to know what she was saying, how she was questioning his father, his mother, his own intelligence, as well as his generally being.

Didn't matter. He had her ass now.

Darius pulled himself forward, back to the front control room. He automatically kissed two fingers and reached up to touch the Jason medal before he slid into his seat.

Once Darius had strapped himself in, he paused. Bringing Sara back to the carrier and to *Xinsheng* was a sure death sentence for her.

But she'd meant the same thing for him. He had no doubt that she would have spaced him if he hadn't gotten away, if he hadn't stolen some sapphires with her.

And who knew if she wouldn't have turned him in anyway? Lied and said that he'd stolen all the gems?

Though Darius could "accidentally" open the airlock in the cargo bay, he wasn't about to space her.

Not because he cared that much about her, but because he'd lose all the cargo as well. And the high bitch captain might take that out of his pay, keep him indentured forever.

No. He'd bring Sara and the cargo in. Let the captain do her worst. *He* wasn't responsible for killing Sara.

It was her fault. And the captain's. Not his.

Or at least that was what he was going to tell him when the nightmares started and her ghost came to visit him, accusing him of her death.

Darius was surprised to see the captain waiting on the space dock when he brought *Orion* into the carrier.

Why was she there? Why wasn't she waiting for them at *Xinsheng*?

Darius hurriedly unstrapped himself from his command seat. He knew the crew would wait until given the go-ahead for unloading the cargo—he'd already called ahead and announced that there was an issue with it and he needed to report first.

He didn't want them opening the cargo bay door and being surprised by Sara.

Captain Alana didn't seem pleased to see Darius. She stood in black coveralls, arms crossed over her chest, glaring at him. Her dark skin seemed darker under the bright lights, shadowed by her scowl. "What happened?" she asked as soon as he got close enough.

"Captain," Darius said with a sharp nod. He paused, taking a breath, before he could continue. "Sara was planning on stealing sapphires from you." Damn it. He hated feeling this heavy again. The crew must have cranked the gravity up since the captain was here.

"I know that," Captain Alana said, dismissively waving her hand. "Why didn't you join her? Steal from me like everyone else?"

Darius blinked, surprised. Then he swallowed. *Fuck.* So it had been some kind of test.

"Because I didn't want you to kill the supplier," he admitted. He winced. He knew it sounded lame.

"Darius Linard. Don't tell me I have a true hero on my hands," the bitch captain said.

God, she was laughing at him again, wasn't she?

He *hated* it when she laughed like that.

She seemed to be expecting a reply.

"I need to pay off my contract," he said, biting off every word. "Not fuck up. Again."

The bitch captain narrowed her eyes and studied him for a moment.

What did she see? Darius made himself stand still under the scrutiny.

Was this another damned test too?

He would not add how he wasn't about to lose *Orion* again. Not when he'd just gotten her back.

His ship meant more to him than she'd ever know. She'd probably never had a home. He didn't ever want to contemplate what her parents must have been like, if they'd raised her to be as hard as this.

Finally, after the sweat had started pooling across his back again, the captain gave a sharp nod. "Good job," she said. "You'll find a bonus in your account after the cargo is… extracted. Those who do right by me get rewarded."

With that, the captain turned away, heading back toward *Orion.*

How had she known what had gone on in the cargo bay?

Were there hidden cameras? Transmitting real time to the carrier ship?

That would make sense. It *was* his first time out on *Orion*, and Sara was a known thief.

Darius nodded to himself, turned and headed toward the crew cabins.

The bitch captain didn't trust him. Yet.

But someday she would. He'd worm his way into her good graces, play the *hero*.

Until it was time enact his revenge, and kill her.

THE WILD ONE

THE WILD ONE

Kiki squatted on her aerie in the middle of the bridge of her space-flier, scowling down on her crew. Though she had a smaller neck ruff than many in the flier clan, it still puffed out around her bald head like a mane of blue-black feathers. She flexed and straightened the three fingers and thumb of her hands, impatiently waiting for *someone* to figure out what in name of the four hells of Tipinia had gone wrong with Lulu, the ship.

Directly in front of Kiki, the great windows looking out into space were still tinted red. Stars glowed ominously through the colored windows, coated with a deadly crimson glow. Foam trickled down the edges of windows, like a washer had exploded and coated everything in soap bubbles. They smelled like fresh kill, which distracted Kiki, making her food stomach growl with hunger though she'd eaten just that morning.

The navigator had coaxed Lulu into staying still, but the ship insisted that he sing lullabies and recite silly, rhyming poetry to keep her there. Communications throughout the rest of the ship were static-y, as if the coms had broken down. The life cabins all functioned within normal parameters, but the temperature in the cargo bays had dropped to just above freezing.

Two ship-breeders knelt beside the window, taking samples, tasting the bubbles, mixing them with chemicals, then tasting again. The ship-herder stood at the back of the bridge, behind Kiki, glowering silently at the entire bridge, disapproving of her, the crew, as well as his charge.

No one understood *why* the edges of the windows had suddenly sprouted bubbles. Were they about to loose pressure? Would the windows suddenly crack and expose them to the cold, hard vacuum of space?

And what did the bubbles mean about Lulu? Was she sick? Was this a new disease none had seen among the space-fliers before?

Kiki's greatest fear was that Lulu had gone insane and that this was just the beginning of her madness. She'd personally known some of the members of the crew of Lulithon, the space-flier who'd grown mentally ill and had committed suicide a few years before by flying into a nearby sun, taking all of her crew with her.

Lulu was young for a space-flier, and relatively immature. According to the ship-herder, after the ship-breeders had released her from the birthing vats, she'd been the runt of her pod (about fifty in all from that brood) for her first year.

But then Lulu had had a growth spurt, not only catching up to her peers but surpassing them, growing to fully mature adult-size in less than a year. Normally, it took three to five years for a space-flier to reach full size.

Kiki had agreed to partner with Lulu though she'd known there would be growing pains, as it were. Kiki was also young for a captain, in her mid-thirties. She'd been decorated more than once during the course of the civil war, however, and felt much older than most of the crew.

Still, this was only the third voyage with Lulu carrying a crew. At least it wasn't a full complement of four times forty, but only two times twenty.

Because of the problems with communications, Kiki couldn't be certain that anyone on any of the nearby planets had heard their emergency calls.

Was it an emergency? Kiki normally wouldn't have called in so quickly. However, she'd learned to be cautious.

War did that, even to warriors. Especially since they'd had to fight their own kind, bringing the rebellious planets back into alignment with the All-World government.

"Captain!"

Kiki turned toward the voice of Tirowli, the scout, who'd just entered the bridge. Though it was unusual to include scouts in a space-flier crew, Kiki had found it had given her an advantage during battle more than once.

Scouts had traditionally been explorers, braving unchartered territory. They were good in emergency situations, as well as conquering new worlds. Scouts had also been trained to deal with humans, should they encounter any. However, human encounters in this part of space would be unlikely. The All-Worlds government had ordered the humans to stay in a single system.

On Kiki's ship, scouts operated a little differently: she had them prowling the curved hallways and side shafts, searching for trouble.

"What is it?" Kiki asked Tirowli. Like most of the crew, the bottom of her command aerie was just above his head. His eyes glared as he stared up at her. The scout was always so serious, his posture stiff and formal. He never bent an elbow to indicate that he was joking.

"You need to come see this," Tirowli reported gravely. "Aft, between the spine hollows."

That was close to the food storage lockers. While the crew wouldn't starve if they turned tail and fled back to the space station they'd started at, it would still be horrible for morale.

Not as though Lulu's antics had been good for it so far.

Kiki glanced toward the front of the bridge. There wasn't anything she could do here, not really, while the rest of the crew worked.

She gracefully leaped down from her aerie, landing beside the scout. Kiki was slightly over five feet tall, and so just an inch or so taller than the scout.

"Kilaleth!" Kiki called, demanding the attention of her second in command. "Send a runner if you discover anything."

"Aye, captain," the dour mate replied.

Kiki nodded at Tirowli to lead the way. Scouts didn't have much of a neck ruff, and his lay flat against his shoulders, indicating that he still felt a measure of calmness. He wore a brown sleeveless tunic that hung down to his knees. The feathers that ran down his arms and legs were a little darker than his tunic. The wide belt around his waist carried many tools she didn't recognize. He'd attached footpads to the bottoms of his feet, to protect the ship from the talons on his toes.

Kiki kept her foot talons trimmed flat as she rarely left civilized areas and preferred to walk unhindered, all eight of her long, elegant talons covered in hard, yellowish scales. Her own sleeveless tunic was dyed bright red, which contrasted nicely with the blue-black feathers that covered her arms and legs. Like Tirowli and the others of the Kinthika race, Kiki's skull was covered with whitish, bare skin. Her large black eyes were set close together, giving her the ability to see minute details at a distance. A sharp yellow beak took up much of her face, hiding a small mouth underneath.

The scout leaped from the top stair all the way to the bottom of the staircase, about ten feet in all. Kiki preferred bouncing from the top stair, to the middle stair, then finally to the bottom.

Tirowli walked briskly, leading the captain along the curved hallways. The skin that covered the walls, ceiling, and floor, looked a healthy pink, no yellow or white patches indicating that Lulu was sick. The hallways were the normal size as well, wide enough for two of the Kintheka to walk abroad. A truly sick space-flier would compress her inner hallways, constricting movement as she struggled to heal.

What was wrong with Kiki's ship?

Though technically, Lulu wasn't really Kiki's ship. Not yet. They'd taken the first steps toward bonding, but it would take many years for them to reach the *pikali*, the sacred bond between a flyer and her captain.

Eons before, on the home world, the Kinthika and the Veeluthians had developed a symbiotic relationship. The Kinthika, or Kin, had originally been hoppers and gliders, able to achieve some level of flight. Though the Kin had lost their wings as they'd evolved hands, they'd never lost their ability to fly, as the Veeluthians, or Veelu, had taken them on their backs, carrying them where they wanted to go in exchange for protection and food.

When Kiki had been a young adult, she'd had her very own sky-flier, a different breed of Veelu who stayed atmosphere bound. She and Raneth had reached the *pikali* quickly.

Then again, Raneth had only ever had to carry Kiki, and never very far.

Lulu had been bred for the stars. She was huge compared to Raneth, and had never set wing to planetary winds. She carried the crew inside an enormous cavity grown specially for them along the length of her belly. While the ship-breeders didn't have the *pikali*, they could still communicate with the ship, encouraging her to grow walls or rooms as needed, or even windows and doors.

Kiki and Tirowli reached the end of the ship quickly. They hadn't passed many crew, as most were at their stations, taking measurements and trying to figure out what had happened to Lulu.

The rear end of the ship always struck Kiki as less developed. Instead of a smooth, round hallway, the area was wide open, about thirty feet square. The ceiling undulated gently, following the curves of Lulu's spine, just above them.

Tirowli led Kiki to the far wall, where a mechanical device had been adhered to the living skin. It looked so ugly and unnatural, a black box, Kin-made, instead of having the curves and colors of nature. It was half a foot wide and a foot tall.

Kiki couldn't help her shiver.

Mechanics.

The first war that had engulfed the entire home world three hundred years before had been fought over mechanics. After that, several smaller civil wars had broken out as mechanical methods were introduced to guilds and centuries-old habits.

Kiki, like the rest of the Kin, both feared and respected anything mechanical. As part of the flier clan, she recognized the necessity of things being made and not grown. She used them regularly, especially during the civil war, as space-fliers had no weapons, though the scales covering their skin gave them a natural defense, even against Kin-made blasters and lasers.

This black box, though…It had a different design to it. Had Tirowli made it? It seemed, well, crude.

Kiki couldn't help but wonder if it was actually human made.

She shivered again.

Five years before, the humans had arrived in the home world system with more machines. Even their ships were mechanical. Kiki couldn't imagine such a waste of materials. Why not just grow what you need?

Tirowli reached out and pressed his three fingers on the side of the machine. It made a whirring sound, then a screen lit up the front of it.

Kiki stepped forward and squinted. While her eyes were incredibly good at long distances, they were less so when looking at things close up.

"What is that?" Kiki asked. A long stream of...*something* was spurting out from behind Lulu. The material sparkled, and had many different colors.

"The camera is located next to Lulu's tail, pointed backwards," Tirowli said. "What you're watching is Lulu excreting."

Kiki blinked, surprised. All fliers were living creatures, whether atmosphere bound, those that made the leap from atmosphere to space, as well as those who were bred in space. They ate and excreted.

But Kiki had never seen...this.

It looked to her like Lulu was releasing glitter out into space. A wide swath of it lay in their wake.

Kiki opened her mouth to ask more questions, such as when had Tirowli done an EVA and placed the camera, who had authorized it, why had he done it, when she shut her mouth again so hard her beak clicked.

She knew what was wrong with the ship.

Lulu wasn't sick. Nor was she going insane.

No, it was much worse than that.

Lulu was bored.

Once the *pikali* had been established, Kiki wouldn't need any organic devices or even mechanical things to communicate with Lulu. They would speak mind to mind.

As the bond grew deeper, they would be able to share other senses as well. Kiki would never forget the time Leethan, her first space-flier, had shared the sensation of the solar winds tickling Leethan's skin. Kiki had giggled like a young chick.

But Leethan had been an older space-flier. His own captain had been killed during the war. About half of the Veelu died after their captains did, usually through suicide, though less than a tenth of the Kin killed themselves when their ships died. So there were always more captain than ships.

Leethan had stopped carrying crews two years before, when the war had ended, the rebellious planets brought back into line with the rest of the Kin, no longer seeking independence.

Kiki tracked the sightings of him and the other crewless Veelu, who flew together in huge pods. They generally stayed in Kin-occupied systems, though occasionally three or more of the space-fliers would connect together and make the leap into jump space and travel to distant systems. They couldn't go on their own—something to do with mass that Kiki never bothered taking the time to learn.

The last report that Kiki had received said that Leethan's skin was no longer a pale gray but had grown more white. He'd also lost what few vestigial feathers he'd carried across the top of his mighty wingspan. He'd die soon, either by flying directly into a sun, or if he died in space, his pod would ceremoniously carry him to one.

After watching a few more minutes of Lulu excreting glitter, Kiki marched back up toward the front of the ship. Instead of hopping back up the stairs to the bridge, she turned left and headed for the small, temporary room that had been grown especially for her to communicate with Lulu.

The room itself wasn't much bigger than a closet. A comforting, golden light emanated from all the walls. Hidden just under the skin were listening and speaking devices that Kiki could use for communicating with Lulu. The devices were an amalgamation of naturally grown and mechanical.

A small, round platform filled the center of the room. It had a foot-high ridge along the edge of it—similar to a ground nest. Kiki stepped into the platform easily, squatting down and settling herself on the padded cushions. She took a deep breath, smelling the scent of the ship that always reminded her of a humid nesting area, someplace warm and safe.

The only decoration in the room hung on the wall directly in front of her: a flat representation of the space-flier, Lulu, from overhead. It was up to date, an accurate portrayal of the image of the space-flier.

It always struck Kiki that Lulu's head, a round protrusion at the top of the figure, was much larger than other space-fliers. Did this make her smarter than average? Or was she going to have another growth spurt soon?

Wings flowed out from either side of the head. Lulu had no neck. She used the wings for gliding and occasionally for gaining momentum, unlike her atmosphere bound cousins. Her movement primarily came from specially grown compartments that Lulu used to explosively push herself in any direction. Ship-breeders boasted that no other ship—

mechanical or organic—could move as fast as a determined space-flier.

A few feathers still clung to the top of Lulu's wings, looking like dark black stripes against the cool gray of her skin. Kiki couldn't see the tiny scales that covered Lulu's body, but she knew they were there. The scales converted light to energy, as well as protected Lulu. The shining scales on Kiki's long talons had similar properties, but to a much lesser extent.

Below the main wing ridge flowed a rippling sail of skin. The earliest space-fliers had merely glided on solar winds.

The body itself was difficult to distinguish from the wings, at least from up above. From the side, the body looked like a round tube, with a second tube below it, that Kiki and the crew inhabited.

Lulu had a smallish tail, particularly compared to the rest of her body, about a tenth as long. It floated behind her like a snake, with a sharp, diamond-shaped tip. While the Veelu claimed that their tail was essential for guiding them while gliding, ship-breeders still talked about creating a tail-less breed, claiming that it wasn't really useful but pure vanity.

Kiki examined the representation of Lulu for a few moments. No part of the ship looked sick or broken.

Still…they had to talk.

Kiki closed her eyes and hummed the notes of her identity song. Each song was unique. There were similarities among the various clans. However, even with mechanical aid, it was close to impossible to exactly replicate an identity song.

A trilling phrase came in response, ending with a rising note, basically asking what Kiki wanted.

Good. Lulu was curious, not resentful or angry.

While there were scholars and diplomats who were fluent in both tongues, the natural vocal apparatus of the Kin had difficulty making all the sounds of the Veelu language, and vice-versa. Kin languages were full of hard constantans, clicks, and short trills. Veelu talked with rounded sounds and smooth words.

Kiki responded to Lulu's inquiry in the creole that had naturally developed between the two races. "I know you're not sick," Kiki started with.

"What do you mean?" Lulu asked in an innocent tone.

"You're not sick," Kiki repeated. "Or wounded. You're bored."

"Gosh, whatever gave you that impression?" Lulu said.

Kiki thought she detected sarcasm in Lulu's tone. While the Kin could use many different tones to indicate their feelings, it was more difficult to indicate humor: instead of using facial features like the Veelu, as their large beaks hid most of their faces, the Kin had to rely on posture, or even the overused bending of an elbow.

"Why are you bored?" Kiki asked, wanting to understand. "What can we do to help entertain you?"

"Stop giving me so many orders!" Lulu said. "You're trying to control every millisecond of my flight. Just tell me where you want to go and let *me* do the flying!"

Kiki managed to control her sigh. Lulu's complaint was common of all youngsters, everywhere. They thought they knew everything, when they actually had so much to learn.

"Have you been paying attention to where it is that we're flying to?" Kiki asked. "Could you get us there using the most expedient route, using the least amount of your energy? Do you already know all the winds and still areas of this sector?"

"No," Lulu said, sounding petulant. "But I could learn if you just gave me the time."

"What we're trying to do is to teach you the sector, teach you the routes by having you fly them. It's much faster this way. That way, you don't have to take years of doing *boring* patrols, just to learn."

Kiki waited while Lulu considered. Kiki knew that Lulu had heard all of this before. However, like most youngsters, she hadn't listened.

This was one of the arguments why females made better captains: they were used to dealing with young chicks. And males, who were frequently just as bad.

"I just...I just want to fly," Lulu said plaintively.

Kiki knew she had to give the Veelu something. "I hear you," she said, a phrase she'd used with her own broods over the years. "I will talk with the navigator and come up with times when you can direct us."

"Promise?" Lulu said.

Kiki paused when she heard the anger that tinged those words. Lulu had been the runt of her pod at the start of her space voyaging. Had others promised her things and then broken those promises?

"I promise," Kiki said, certain that she could keep her word.

***

Kiki stared at Gitakin the navigator in horror. "What do you mean, you're not exactly sure where we are?" They were meeting in a private chamber on the lower deck, just off the back of the bridge, specifically set up for the captain to meet with crew privately. The room itself contained no squatting platforms, just a desk that could be used to hold drinks, food, or occasionally, paperwork.

For the last four days, Gitakin and Lulu had been taking turns flying. Kiki kept an eye on how the two interacted. When she'd become captain with Leethan, she'd inherited most of the original crew, who were used to working together. They were a good team.

Gitakin seemed to do well with Lulu, but Kiki wondered about his tone sometimes. He treated the ship as though she was a little one, just barely hatched.

There had been a brief time on the home world when males had considered themselves superior to females. They'd formed ugly hate groups.

In addition, some of them had even tried to boast that the Kin were the proper "masters" of the Veelu.

That didn't last long, however. The Veelu's religion never condemned suicide: it was seen as the proper solution occasionally. Unlike the Kin, for whom sacrifice was acceptable, but never the taking of one's own life.

The next time those "masters" had tried to gather, all the Veelu they rode drove them straight into the ground, killing everybody in a well-coordinated attack.

While hate groups still sprang up now and again, their message couldn't really get far as they couldn't meet, couldn't travel anywhere.

Gitakin took some time to reply to Kiki's question. "We were sharing the flying, as *you* suggested," he said, putting the blame firmly on her, refusing to accept any responsibility for their current predicament. "It was her turn, and she wanted to show me just how fast she could fly, landing us here, outside of known space."

Kiki cocked her head to one side. Space-flying Veelu traveled much further than the Kin had settled in this sector. "Did you ask Lulu if *she* knew where we were?"

"Of course," Gitakin said. "She said she didn't know."

Kiki nodded. Her second—third?—brood had picked up the ability to lie via technicalities quite early. "Did you ask her to help you figure out where we are?"

"Why would I do that? We're lost," he said. His tone implied heavy condemnation.

"No, I bet she knows exactly where we are. Or at least the correct direction to get us back. You're going to have to work *with* her," Kiki said.

"But—"

"I've looked at your record," Kiki said, overriding him. "You were never popular with any of the crews you worked with. For that matter, you've never lasted more than a couple years on any ship."

Though Gitakin drew himself up to his full height, Kiki still was a few inches taller. "I've always worked with a high degree of excellence," he told her in a frosty tone.

"You are absolutely one of the most learned navigators. That is true. But you can't work in your own shell. You need to engage the others, work as a team."

Kiki could tell the words had no effect on Gitakin. The male believed he could hatch eggs alone.

Before she could continue, an alarm sounded, a harsh wail that had the overtones of young in peril.

"Captain to the bridge," came the voice of the second in command over the comms.

"Coming!" Kiki said, already sprinting down the hallway. She took the stairs up to the bridge in a single hop.

"What is it?" Kiki asked as she leaped up to her aerie.

"There's a ship just at the edge of our sensors. It's broadcasting that it has an emergency," her second in command replied. She sounded worried.

Kiki nodded, a little surprised at the continued loud alarms. Her crew could handle a simple distress call, couldn't they?

"What's the problem?" Kiki asked.

"They're human."

Kiki felt like breaking bricks with her beak: Not because she should, but because she might feel better once she stopped.

"No," Kiki told Lulu, striving to maintain a reasonable tone. "You can*not* just absorb the human's ship and bring it on board." She squatted in the room dedicated for her communications with Lulu. At least the golden light from the walls didn't exacerbate her already pounding head. The normally warm smell of the ship made her food stomach tighten, though, as if she hadn't eaten once this week already.

"Why not?" Lulu asked, sounding petulant. "It would be much faster than building a bridge between the two ships. Particularly trying to maintain an atmosphere in such a bridge."

"Because we don't know what cargo that ship carries," Kiki explained. Again. "It may be harmful. Dangerous."

Lulu made a sound that Kiki couldn't replicate, not with her hard beak. She knew it was a sound of derision, though. "I can isolate it so it can't harm me," Lulu boasted.

"Can you? Even the biological sensors dangling off the bottom of the ship?" Kiki said. "They may be designed to attack anything organic." She wasn't threatening—she'd seen similar "devil's tails" during the war. They'd been set to freeze anything organic that touched them.

"Yes, even those," Lulu said, though she no longer sounded as certain.

"It isn't worth the risk," Kiki said. "I'd rather you stayed safe. Let's just build a bridge between the two ships, so we can dock with it."

Lulu sighed. "That's so much work," she said.

"Are you hungry? Do we need to fly closer to a sun after this?" Kiki asked, knowing the answer already.

"I'm not," Lulu said. "I'm not *depleted* or anything."

"How about this," Kiki said after a moment. "After we dock the ship, we can bring the human over, so you can meet him." A single, isolated human wasn't that much of a threat.

"Really?" Lulu asked. "I get to carry a human for a while?"

"No one else in your birth-pod has done anything like this, I'm sure," Kiki said, hoping the bribe took.

"I'll build a special room for him and everything!" Lulu said, suddenly excited. "I'll let you know how long it will take for me to build the bridge and dock the ship."

Kiki wasn't surprised at Lulu's abrupt departure. The ship was impulsive.

Fortunately, Lulu had time to grow up. It was no longer wartime, they were no longer sending children out to fight.

Lulu would settle down in a few years. She had a good heart. She just needed a steady hand.

Kiki could already see a bump forming at the bottom of Lulu's port wing. It would take another day for it to be complete, with membranes on either side to isolate it from both ships.

With a sigh, Kiki stepped out of the ground nest platform and headed for the door. Now, if only she could get a message out, though none of the nearby planets were inhabited.

As Gitakin had said, they were lost.

Though not really.

Lulu knew exactly in which direction lay home. She assured them that it wouldn't take long to get back to inhabited space.

The original, atmosphere-bound Veelu made sounds that the Kin couldn't hear. It wasn't until the invention of mechanical listening devices that the Kin had even learned that the Veelu frequently talked long-distance with each other.

The Veelu had carried that ability with them to the stars. They had methods of communicating with each other through deep space that the Kin had never been able to replicate through mechanical means.

So Lulu could send an emergency call out, if she wanted to. She assured them that there was no need, however. She could take care of this situation, and the human, herself.

Kiki doubted that Lulu had planned this meeting. It really was just flying into the right place at the right time. The human that they had spoken to had assured them that he'd been flung there when the larger ship, the one that flew his ship and the others through jump space, had been attacked. It was just luck that he'd popped out in this location.

Still. Kiki had a bad feeling about this. It felt as though her neck ruff was permanently standing these days.

But she wouldn't abandon a ship with a distress call. Even in war you picked up survivors.

Didn't matter if they were Kin, Veelu, or even human.

K iki had never met a human face-to-face before. She'd seen vids, and heard about their history. But they had arrived toward the end of the civil war, and she'd been far too involved with the cleanup to pay much attention to the new aliens.

This Darius Linard—and how was she supposed to accurately pronounce his name? It was more like a Veelu name, all smooth and round, without a proper click anywhere—was well over six feet tall. And gangly, like his hands and feet were attached to that long tube of a body with rubber bands. He had dark, thin feathers all over his head, more like thread. The same covered his arms. His eyes were a curious shade of green, set wide between his small nose.

It had actually taken three days for Lulu to build a docking airlock to connect the two ships. A thick membrane grew on either side of the connecting tunnel. Darius had had many questions about what it was, and had evidently been hesitant to just push through it.

He had no idea that by touching it, he'd leave behind valuable information about his body chemistry that Kiki's ship-breeders (and others) would be able to use.

Possibly against him if he turned violent.

Darius pushed cautiously through the membrane, hands first, all bent over. He'd never be able to stand up straight on most of Lulu, just the special compartment that she'd built for him, in the rear.

His ship—he called it another Veelu name, *Orion*—was a mechanical thing. No soul resided under that hunk of metal.

The organic parts of the human ship brought Kiki many questions. How was the input from the organic sensors melded to the unfamiliar systems that ran the ship?

Darius looked at all the Kin standing in the hallway, waiting to greet him. Then he looked directly at Kiki and addressed her in his smooth, alien language.

Kiki blinked, startled that he'd been able to read the group well enough to know that she was the one in charge.

Luckily, Tirowli, standing beside her, was fluent in human.

It made her wonder again about the origin of the viewing machine the scout had attached to the rear of Lulu. And if there were any others stashed away on the ship that she didn't know about.

"Captain Kiki, I presume?" Tirowli said, translating. "I am Darius Linard. Thank you for rescuing me."

"You are welcome," Kiki responded, addressing Darius and not Tirowli. "I understand that your ship runs on *fuel*, correct? And that you no longer have any?"

Darius nodded. At least they had that physical characteristic in common. "And I understand that your ship has no fuel." He paused, peering carefully at the wall of the hallway beside him. "Your ship's organic. Wow."

Kiki glanced at Tirowli. It seemed so out of place for him to say something so…irrelevant. But Tirowli was evidently translating exactly what the human was saying.

There was no way for Kiki to judge, but she'd bet that this Darius was young for a human. (Tar-i-oo? She didn't have the vocal apparatus to repeat that hissing sound at the end of his name. She wasn't certain exactly how Tirowli managed it. Had he been genetically modified at some point? Or—horror of horrors—was the scout *mechanically* enhanced?)

Kiki had many questions, but she impulsively asked the first one that came to mind. "What do you see?" she asked.

The eyesight of the Kin and the Veelu differed slightly but significantly. Learning to see from the other's point of view was considered one of the more important tasks in both races philosophies and religions.

Darius blinked at her, then turned to study the wall.

"I see veins running through the skin," he said, reaching out to trace a line that wasn't visible to Kiki. "There's a pulse to it. Slow."

Kiki nodded, impressed. Yes, the great ship's heart beat very slowly. Auxiliary systems moved the blood through the walls.

"We have a room for you," Kiki said. "The ship—Lulu—built it especially for you."

Darius froze for a moment. "The ship? Lulu? Is she organic? Alive?"

"She's a living creature," Kiki assured him. "Please. Follow us so you can meet her."

The human's smallish eyes grew huge. "Really? Wow."

Kiki was never going to get over the dour scout making that expression.

However, Darius stayed exactly where he was. "Where are you taking me? The ship, I mean."

"We aren't in inhabited space," Kiki said, not wanting to discuss *why*, exactly, they'd flown there. "We are taking you to the next system that is inhabited."

"And then what?" Darius asked.

"We cannot service your ship. Hopefully the nearest space station can," Kiki said, confused. They'd explained all this before.

"If you can fix my ship, which I realize may not be possible, will you let me go?" Darius asked, staring hard at Kiki.

"Of course," Kiki said. "Why wouldn't we?" The Kin and the humans weren't at war.

Darius paused for a moment, considering. "You knew about humans, obviously," he said, indicating Tirowli being able to translate. "However, my government has never told us about you."

"I'm not sure what to say," Kiki replied. "That level of politics is far beyond me or this ship."

Darius nodded. "I will not hold you responsible for what happens to me, then," he said. "Lead the way."

Kiki turned and walked along the corridor toward the back room that Lulu had specifically partitioned off for the human.

The humans didn't know about them? Then where had those sensors on the human's ship come from? The devil's tails hanging from the bottom of it?

More questions that Kiki couldn't answer.

She suddenly couldn't get rid of this human fast enough.

"How long will it take for us to reach inhabited space?" Kiki asked Lulu again, not sure she'd heard correctly.

"Three weeks," Lulu said. "The bridge to Darius' ship won't survive top speed."

"Couldn't you strengthen the bridge?" Kiki said. She blinked, her eyes still unaccustomed to the light that now filled the chamber she used to talk with the ship.

Originally, the light had been soft, a golden hue, reminding Kiki of a delightful summer afternoon.

Now, the light had shifted, growing more white and harsh, like sunlight filtered through clouds on a cold winter's morning.

"Strengthening the tunnel would be a waste of time and materials," Lulu said.

Did Kiki detect an air of superiority in Lulu's reply?

"Plus, creating such a hardened shell would be difficult and costly to re-consume," the ship continued. "Especially for a temporary structure."

"Do we have the supplies for the crew for such an extended journey?" Kiki asked, concerned about the rest of the crew. She didn't want them to have to fly hungry. While all of the Kin could absorb a few nutrients through the scales on their feet, no one was used to living on that meager a supply of calories.

"We do," Lulu said, her smugness continuing. "I checked with the purser this morning."

Kiki blinked, surprised. Of course, Lulu could contact anyone in the crew that she wished. There were lights that Lulu could activate, calling the attention of a crewmember and directing them to a speaking post, where Lulu could talk with them.

"I see," Kiki said. She didn't, actually, understand at all. Why was Lulu insisting on such a slow pace? Kiki knew the ship liked to fly fast.

"Of course, if you'd let me bring the human ship onboard in the first place, we wouldn't be in this predicament, now, would we?" Lulu asked.

Yeap. Smug.

Their speed was in some way a retaliation for Kiki denying Lulu earlier.

"I hear you," Kiki said. Lulu hadn't forgiven the captain her decision about that, even though the ship now had a human to talk with.

For a moment, the air was filled with…something. Kiki had the strongest feeling that Lulu wanted to reply to that, to make yet other strong statement. It was the start of the *pikali*, the ability to communicate directly.

"What is it?" Kiki asked. "You can tell me."

"Maybe later," Lulu said. "If it becomes important."

"You can tell me now, whether it's important or not," Kiki assured the ship.

"We'll see," Lulu said. "Now, if there's nothing else, captain?"

Kiki cocked her head to the side. It still felt as if something was wrong with the ship. But Kiki had no idea what in the world was going on inside Lulu's head.

"Until later," Kiki said, taking her cue and standing up.

On the one wing, it wasn't good policy for a ship to keep secrets from her captain. On the other wing, Lulu had felt the need to be in control. Maybe keeping her secrets would help with that.

While there were a lot of guides for captains and their

ships, one-size did not fit all. Every ship had his or her own personality, as did their captain.

Kiki just hoped that she was doing the right thing for Lulu by giving her such an open expanse of sky to fly in.

***

Kiki was not quite willing to let go of all her bad feelings about the human.

First of all, there was the speed at which Lulu moved. Though Kiki had also checked with the purser to make sure they had enough food and water, it would be close.

The good news was that Lulu was suddenly extremely professional in terms of her duty to the rest of the crew and she stopped all her antics.

The human was keeping the ship from being bored.

The bad news was that every minute of every day that Lulu was *not* occupied with ship duties, she was with the human.

Lulu already had something of a bad attitude. Kiki feared that talking with the human would make it worse.

The human and the ship were learning each other's languages, something Kiki hadn't anticipated. They seemed to enjoy each other's company, which was more than Kiki could say. She made a point of visiting the human at least once a day, midmorning ship's time, though she always had to have Tirwoli in tow, as the human seemed to have a lot more difficulty learning the language of the Kin.

The large cavern that Lulu had built for the human made Kiki uncomfortable. While she was used to open sky above her, ships and cities were more closed in. The tall ceiling made Kiki feel small. Plus, Lulu filtered less oxygen in the human's room, as that worked better for him, making the air seem thin, like it came from a mountain top, as well as stale.

In addition, there wasn't much Kiki and the human could talk about. The human seemed disinclined to talk about where he'd been bound. He didn't really have a home world, as he'd been born in space and spent his entire life on his spaceship.

But the mechanics of the ship were so different than what Kiki was used to flying, they didn't really have common ground there. Their food rituals were completely different—the human needed *cooked* meat, for gods' sake, every day. Totally ruined any delicacy she might have offered him. At least they both shared a belief system, though she thought it odd that he kissed two fingers and touched his religious icon whenever he could.

But Lulu—Kiki couldn't get over how different the ship sounded around the human. Giggly. Swooning.

If Kiki didn't know better, she'd say the ship was falling in love with the human.

Things didn't come to a head until they were two weeks into their journey, when Lulu announced that there would be a delay for a few days or so while she orbited a nearby sun, getting herself up to full power.

All food and water was to be immediately rationed.

The white light of the chamber where Kiki and Lulu communicated had grown much more harsh. That delicate feeling of the *pikali* never returned.

However, instead of talking about the delay, as soon as Kiki got settled, Lulu demanded, "Can't you stop him?"

"Stop who?" Kiki asked. Had the human done something to hurt her ship? She'd space him if he had. Was he the reason why they were delayed? Again?

"Your navigator. He keeps overriding my own damn controls," Lulu said.

Kiki blinked, surprised, both by what Lulu had just said, as well as by her swearing. "Gitakin?" Kiki clarified. "What is he doing?"

"He's always in override mode," Lulu complained. "He won't let me fly at all."

"You did fly us to the edge of known space," Kiki pointed out. "He might be afraid that if he gives you your head, you'll turn around and do that again."

"I know that," Lulu said with a heavy sigh. "I've given my word that I wouldn't, though."

"But you might do something else, just to teach him a lesson, correct?" Kiki said. Her third brood, the ones who'd learned to lie using technicalities, they'd do something like that. Just to get even.

"Who, me?" Lulu asked.

Kiki wasn't fooled by the oh-so-innocent tone in the ship's voice. "There's a reason why he doesn't trust you," Kiki said. "It will take some time for you learn to work together." Though if Kiki had her way, Gitakin wouldn't be part of her crew once she could replace him.

"But he doesn't want to work with me," Lulu said. "He wants to fly, and for me to just *obey*."

Kiki didn't understand the emphasis the ship placed on the word *obey*. It seemed to have some special meaning for her.

"I hear you," Kiki said. "I'll talk with him."

For a moment, that feeling of something not being said filled the small chamber.

"You can trust me," Kiki added after a few moments.

"We'll see," Lulu said. Or at least that was what Kiki thought Lulu said, just as Kiki was closing the door to the chamber.

"Of course, I'm overriding her entire system," Gitakin said. They stood in the small conference room just at the bottom of the stairs from the bridge.

Kiki had watched his interactions with Lulu for the rest of the day after her talk with the ship, feeling her neck ruff flaring anger.

Gitakin still treated Lulu as if she'd just been hatched. He *had* to let go, to allow the ship some control.

Smugness radiated from Gitakin, as if he were the superior here. Kiki felt like slapping him, but she knew that wouldn't knock any sense into the preening male.

"Why are you overriding her system that way?" Kiki asked. "I thought there was to be an even arrangement between you two, with her flying some of the time and you flying some of the time."

"You wouldn't understand," Gitakin said.

"Then explain it to me. Now," Kiki said, raising herself up so she was looking down on him, if only from an inch or so. She was still the captain.

"Lulu doesn't have the maturity to take on a crew yet," Gitakin said. "She may never grow to accept one."

"What do you mean?" Kiki asked, confused. All of the space-fliers, once they reached adult-size, took on a crew.

"She's turning into a wild one," Gitakin said. "Unfit."

Kiki rocked back on her hind toes, shaken. Only once a decade or so a space-flier would be declared as a wild one. The other space-fliers would hound her into the sun, unwilling to accept such a one into their society.

"Lulu is young. She isn't wild. She isn't actively trying to do damage to her crew." Kiki would stand by her ship.

"Really?" Gitakin asked. "She flew us out of known space—"

"She knew where we were the entire time—"

"AND now she's taking her own sweet time heading back. If there are any more delays, the crew will have to go on half rations," Gitakin said triumphantly. "She doesn't care one whit for anyone other than herself."

Did only Kiki add the phrase, *and that damned human* to the end of Gitakin's sentence?

"You have to let her fly on her own sometimes," Kiki said. "That's an order."

As captain, Kiki gave few orders. Her crew, before this one, had been good. No one had to tell them what to do, or how to do it. The only times she'd given a lot of orders had been during battle.

Plus, it was difficult for her to give orders to those from different guilds. Most of her orders while she'd been fighting in the civil war had been to other captains in her squad.

"And if I refuse to follow your order?" Gitakin asked. His neck ruff raised up, as did his arms, as if he was readying himself for a physical attack.

"You know what? Belay that order. You're relieved of your duty. As of now," Kiki said. "The guild's second navigator will take over working with the ship and getting us home." While they were only a skeleton crew, every guild had sent at least two people for each position.

"You can't do that!" Gitakin said, taking a step back, obviously surprised.

"Yes, I can," Kiki said. "You're no longer a part of this crew. I will drop you off at the nearest space station. You can take it up with the guild."

"Oh, you better believe I will," Gitakin said. "Are you going to confine me to my quarters?"

"Yes," Kiki said evenly. "Let's see how Lulu treats you when the feather is in the other hand."

"You'll see," Gitakin sneered. "She's a wild one. Mark my words."

Kiki shook her head after the navigator left, his head held high. She knew no matter how well (or poorly) Lulu treated him, he'd still complain.

There wasn't anything she could do at this point, except to try to repair the damage he'd done on her poor ship.

nfortunately, it turned out that Gitakin's second had been hand-picked and trained by him. He was even worse with the ship.

Kiki was tempted to not have a navigator at all, and just let Lulu fly them back.

But Gitakin's accusation about Lulu being a wild one stopped her.

Kiki needed someone who might be able to override the ship if she did decide to dump them all into space. Hell, she might even put the human in charge. He'd bragged about his ability to fly more than once, as he was space born, like Lulu.

On a whim, Kiki decided to visit the human that evening, after she'd dealt (yet again) with Gitakin's replacement, calling the man to order and reminding him that he didn't have the authority to do all the flying.

The thick membrane covering the door to the human's quarter's surprised her. When had Lulu grown that? Had the human asked for it? There were very few doors or closures in the ship; the ones that existed were mostly for safety. Was it because of the difference in oxygen?

At first, Kiki couldn't push her way through. It seemed as though Lulu granted her access slowly.

The human's high-pitched giggling filled the chamber. It unnerved her.

The human lay on his back on a table. A long rope-like appendage was wrapped around the human's wrist. It slowly unwound as she entered, moving back and against the wall where it disappeared.

Had it really grown back into the wall? Or was it just hiding, partially camouflaged by her own poor vision of things close up?

"Captain," Darius said, sitting up, rubbing his wrist. "What can I do for you?"

He was showing all his teeth like a predator to her. She knew that expression was how humans showed joy. It still brought up all the feathers on her neck ruff.

"What were you just doing?" Kiki asked.

Lulu answered her. "I was trying to learn more about the human nervous system," she said in the creole that the Kin and the Veelu shared.

The human cocked his head to one side. He probably picked up some of the words, but not all of them.

"Ah, very good," Kiki said. She paused, then added, "As long as it isn't taking away from your other duties."

"Have you had any complaints about my duties?" Lulu asked.

"I haven't," Kiki replied. Well, at least not from anyone who mattered. Gitakin's replacement didn't count.

"As this is my free time, I'd like to continue?" Lulu said.

Kiki took the hint. "I'll talk with you tomorrow, then," she said, addressing Darius.

"See you then," he said, the Veelu words flowing out quickly.

It wasn't until Kiki had pushed back through the membrane to the human's chambers that she realized what Lulu was up to.

She'd been sharing the feeling of the solar winds with the human. Only a sensation like that would bring out such joy.

Kiki stopped in the middle of the hallway.

It hadn't happened yet. But soon, she would lose the ship.

Lulu *was* a wild one.

And there was nothing that the ship's captain could do about it.

RUNAWAYS

RUNAWAYS

DARIUS WAS NO CLOSER TO his revenge after a year of working as a pilot for Captain Alana and Pineapple Express Transport. He sometimes still felt like a slave, though strictly speaking, he wasn't: he was closer to paying off his indenture than he would have thought possible. The last job had put quite a dent in the amount he owed the captain when she'd stolen his asteroid claim, his ship *Orion*, and his life. It would still be years before he was free, but that was better than the decades he'd originally thought it would take.

Though Captain Alana was an absolute ass who laughed at Darius more often than not (and gods, he *hated* that laugh), he'd also stopped calling her *high bitch captain* for the most part, except when she deserved it. He'd studied her too closely, watching her every chance he got, for him to be comfortable denigrating her. She was absolutely brilliant.

Since stopping one of the other crew members from stealing from Captain Alana, Darius had found himself moving up in the world, as it were. He still wouldn't consider himself part of the inner circle of the spaceship *Xinsheng*, but he was only a couple of rings from there.

Like tonight. Darius had been seated at one of the small round tables in the cleaned up cargo bay. Not at the absolute back of the room, not at the front, either, with the captain and her closest mates, but somewhere in the middle. He'd stuffed himself on crab puffs, ginger-lemon fish fillets, and pasta in a smoky red sauce that was so yummy he'd wanted to lick the plate clean. He'd even eaten some green beans, which had been surprisingly good, as they'd been grilled with bacon. Now, everyone sat back and talked, drinking tea, coffee, or port, with delicate lavender-sugar cookies that melted on Darius' tongue and disappeared far too quickly.

Though Darius was now well on his way to being twenty years old, he occasionally felt he was still growing because of how hungry he got. However, he was no longer needing to buy new pants every other month since he'd out grown them, and his T-shirts lasted longer as well.

He kept his unruly black hair shorn short, so he never had to worry about it when he put on a helmet. He knew he looked more like his dad now than before, with a proud Greek nose, wide-set dark eyes, a broad mouth, and white skin with a brown tint to it. If he was ever on a planet under the right light spectrum, he'd probably turn a lot darker.

His five dinner companions (assigned by little cards at each plate) all worked in different capacities: engineering (he kept the engines of *Xinsheng* tuned), ship repair (she worked on all the various other spaceships and flitters they carried), cargo (and he didn't stop complaining the entire time about how much work it took to clean out a space like this for a party), communications (or something like that, he wasn't too specific about what exactly he did) and logistics (it took a lot of organizing to keep such a big ship afloat, keep the crew fed, and fuel all the machines).

Darius found he liked being included in more of the crew activities. The excuse for tonight's party was the birthday of the second in command, a towering black man who Darius had met only twice. At least two hundred of the crew were here, maybe ten percent of the total compliment on *Xinsheng*. Darius had seen many of the same people at the various events he'd attended. He was starting to get to know the other members of the crew. He wasn't sure if he could call any of them friends, but he could at least be friendly with them. And it was a good break sometimes from all the hard studying he did to hang out in rec-room five and play a card game, or maybe some pool.

It surprised Darius to learn that some of the members had started out in the same position he'd been in, then had hired on with the captain after they'd finished their contracts.

He swore that would never happen to him. He was still trying to figure out how to get his revenge on Captain Alana. Though maybe not the rest of the crew, anymore.

Nothing had been done to hide the plain, gray-painted wall of the cargo bay, though at the front of the room, above the long buffet table, someone had gone to the effort of creating a long banner with "Happy Birthday Kwasi!" printed on it. Laughter and raucous conversations echoed off the high ceiling.

A small stage had been put up in the front corner of the room. It turned out that eight members of the crew had formed a band in their spare time. They played with an odd combination of three violins, two guitars, two flutes, and with one banjo.

The first time Darius had been invited to one of these events, he'd been surprised to be given a seat at a table instead of being made to serve the others. He'd never met most of the waitstaff, and they seemed to change from event to event.

Had they given Captain Alana some reason to be angry

with them? At least Darius had had skills when he'd been captured by her. Were these the bottom of the ladder in terms of the crew?

He felt guilty sitting there being waited on. He could remember going to a restaurant fancy enough to have actual people waiters once. His dad had dragged him into such a place on a space station when Darius had turned eighteen.

Tonight, Darius stuck to water, despite beer, wine, and mead being readily available. He didn't like how alcohol made him feel.

The conversation turned to speculation about who was attacking their ships. Darius had thought it had been just him and his bad luck, but it turned out a lot of the transport ships had been shot at, even those not smuggling.

"We can't keep up," admitted Yasmin, the ship-repair crew member.

Darius would have liked to get to know her better, but suspected the elegant woman was not only several years his senior, but well out of his league as well.

"Instead of turning around a ship in days, it takes weeks," Yasmin continued. "Not because we have no parts. Too many ships come in damaged. Far too many."

"Hey, believe me, I do my best to avoid being shot at," Darius said in protest when Yasmin glared at him, as if he was personally responsible as a pilot. He reached up and pressed against the amulet he wore under his shirt to ward off any bad luck. On the side facing out was an image of Jason of the Argonauts, and the other side had the golden fleece

"It isn't an organized attack," Li Xi from logistics declared. "I don't see a pattern."

Darius had spent the evening trying not to stare at Li Xi. While most of the crew displayed as male or female, Li Xi had announced as part of their introduction that they preferred neither "he" or "she", but "they" as a pronoun. He wasn't sure how to interpret that. His native Greek had male and female pronouns, as did the English they all spoke, though he'd heard of more modern languages that didn't.

Darius' dad had said more than once that it didn't matter if someone was a boy, girl, or other, as long as they did their job. However, Darius had rarely met anyone like that, mainly because he hadn't met many people, living on *Orion* with just his dad and only occasional trips to space stations.

Li Xi had short black hair, wide black eyes and a broad mouth. While their voice could have been male, their laugh was definitely female.

Yasmin merely raised an stylish eyebrow at Li Xi's proclamation, as if she was questioning the authority of someone who did logistics.

"Who do you think makes sure that you're stocked up on parts?" Li Xi said.

"I agree, I don't think it's organized," Victor from communications said. He also had black hair, and his skin was several degrees darker than Li Xi's. However, his cheeks were flushed from the wine he'd had with dinner. He'd had second servings of everything, and though he was shorter than Darius by at least a foot, they probably weighed the same.

Victor continued. "I don't think we've received any demands or warnings, telling us to stay out of a sector. At least, none that I've heard of at my level." He shrugged.

"Do you think it's because of the devil tails?" Darius asked.

"The what?" "Huh?" "What are you talking about?"

All of Darius' dinner companions looked confused.

"You know, the black tails that hang off the bottom of some of the ships," Darius said.

Yasmin gave Darius a hard stare. "I have no idea what

you're talking about," she said firmly. "I've never seen something like that. And I repair all the ships."

Darius opened his mouth, then closed it again.

Evidently the devil's tails were not something people talked about. He suspected that everyone at the table knew what they were, had some experience with them.

But if no one was willing to say anything, then he shouldn't either.

"Sorry," Darius said. "My mistake. Probably just something I imagined." He pressed two fingers against his Jason amulet again.

Li Xi gave Darius a big smile at that. "Probably," they said.

The band in the corner suddenly started a more lively tune than what they'd been playing all through dinner. The banjo took the lead, the song bouncy and light.

"Come on!" Li Xi said, standing up. "Let's dance!"

Darius shuddered at the thought, but still allowed himself to be persuaded to join all the others streaming to the hastily cleared spot in front of the band.

He should have known that tonight's dinner would include some form of punishment after all.

***

Darius sat at his desk in his cabin on *Xinsheng*, studying the latest system he'd be visiting later that week in *Orion*. It was a binary star system that had a couple of habitable worlds despite how close the stars were to one another. While some people would stay on just a single planet all year round, many migrated from one to the other depending on the season and how close the suns were.

He'd learned not to just study the stars and planets in a system, but the politics of the planets as well. How welcome would he be? Could he escape there? Would they bring in Captain Alana on his say-so? He had signed a contract after all. No court in the Allied Worlds would overturn it, despite how he'd been pressured into it.

It turned out the Mazdujon system was all about justice. But it wasn't the kind of justice that would favor Darius and his plight. He was as likely to be hung for his previous smuggling as helped with his current situation.

Darius turned off the computer and pressed against the back of his chair, stretching. He twisted to the left and right, then stood and started going through a series of stretches. He'd been attending the yoga classes that one of the crew members, Suha, taught. Darius had started going because Captain Alana sometimes stopped in, and it would be another opportunity for him to study his enemy. He kept going because the stretches and exercise made him feel better.

When he finished his stretching, Darius made himself do four sets of twenty pushups, alternating those with various forms of sit ups.

He'd been raised in low-to-no gravity, as *Orion* wasn't a large enough ship to generate her own gravity, nor did she have enough mass to reach jump space. *Xinsheng* didn't have the full gravity of most planets, but it was a lot stronger than what he was used to. His back had hurt the first six months of living on the ship, and he'd had frequent nightmares of being trapped and unable to move. But instead of letting it conquer him, he'd started exercising more, building up his core muscles, so he wasn't always in pain.

When Darius finished his sets, he sat on the floor, breathing heavily, looking around the room. It was "spacer" clean, as his dad would have called it. Nothing was out on the counter or desk. The bed was made, with the pillow tucked under the sheets. His shoes were strapped to the wall beside the door. The walls had been painted a cream color that Darius hadn't bothered changed, though he could have, and were bare of any art or personalization.

When a couple of the other crew had commented on how clean Darius kept his room, he'd given them the easy excuse that *Xinsheng* might lose gravity at some point, though in the year he'd been living there, the ship never had.

It would have been much more difficult to explain that Darius didn't consider this home. Home was *Orion*, his ship. Nothing showed that Darius lived in this room and spent most of his time there. Dad would have wanted Darius to put a Jason medallion next to the door, a good luck charm for him to touch whenever he was about to leave his sanctuary.

Darius had thought about it, but instead, merely kept the one he wore around his neck, touching it when he needed luck.

A chime came from his computer. "Darius Linard, to the captain's office. Immediately."

"Acknowledged," Darius said. He sighed. He'd been expecting the call since dinner last night, when everyone denied the presence of the devil tails.

He folded his feet under him, then stood without needing his hands or to push against anything, a trick he hadn't been able to manage when he'd first arrived. He lifted up his T-shirt and gave it a sniff. Whew. Ugh.

Captain Alana had a more sensitive nose than his. Should he change? Or should he be disrespectful and stay stinky? He was already in trouble, after all.

After another moment's considerations, he whipped his shirt off, threw it in the laundry basket, shut the lid firmly, then grabbed a fresh T.

It wasn't until he was standing outside the captain's office that he realized he'd put his shirt on backwards. Too late to take it off and reverse it.

It would just give her one more thing to laugh at. One more reason why she would underestimate him.

One more thing to fuel his revenge.

Captain Alana's office hadn't changed over the past year. It was still not a lot bigger than a closet. The desk was L-shaped, with the longer side against the wall, the end coming out and separating the captain and her latest victim. A large, roundish porthole broke the monotony of the gray walls, located opposite the door. A winged back chair, covered in dark green upholstery, was pushed up against the far wall. Rumor was that Captain Alana liked to read by starlight, though Darius doubted it was true. She just enjoyed reading, as attested by the number of actual physical books in at least three piles around the foot of the chair.

Darius had watched the books move and change, going from the bottom of a pile to the top, then put away somewhere and the next one on the top picked up.

They appeared to be on every topic: history, navigation, biology, flowers and fauna, and even a few fiction titles, mainly crime.

Darius had never tried to impress Captain Alana with his own meager reading pile, not after seeing one of the newer crew members get shot down. Darius knew he didn't stand a chance. He didn't read as quickly as the captain did, and he didn't remember all the details of what he'd read, not like she did.

Instead of trying to impress the captain, he saved his brain power for learning about the planets he'd be visiting, as well as the computer systems. Despite speaking both Greek and English, other languages didn't come easily to him, in particular, computer languages. It frequently felt as though he was always translating from some alien tongue into something he could read.

Still, he was getting better at deciphering the programs that had been added to *Orion*, in particular, the software that interfaced with the devil's tails, that had been written in yet *another* computer language.

Captain Alana sat behind her desk, flicking through pages on a tablet when Darius arrived. He sat down though she hadn't invited him to, then he waited.

Captain Alana hadn't slept well for a while, Darius would bet. Though her skin was darker than his, dark enough to possibly mark her as someone from the Xi Lien sector, it still didn't hide the black rings under her green eyes. The long scar down her left cheek puckered along the edges, as if it were shrinking. She wore her black hair spacer short, though Darius wondered if the short hair was to make her look even more of a badass. She never wore any jewelry, no earrings, nose rings, finger rings, necklaces or anything else.

She also looked thinner than the last time he'd seen her. Was she losing weight? Or was she gaining more muscles under her loose gray shirt? He'd seen how strong she was when she came to do yoga. It had impressed him—those were muscles that had to be earned, not merely from wearing weights at night.

Finally, Captain Alana looked up, transferring her glare from the tablet to him.

Darius didn't allow himself to flinch under her stare. He didn't glare back, though he wanted to, wanted to express just how much he hated her.

Instead, he took a deep breath and stayed calm. It had taken a lot of effort on his part to learn how to do this. He wasn't even sweating yet.

"I thought you were smart," Captain Alana started off with.

"I'm trying to learn," Darius said. "I study my ass off, memorizing entry points for a system, how to interact with the people there, the customs and politics. I've been trying to learn every system on every ship as well."

Captain Alana narrowed her eyes at him. "And yet you still are asking about things you shouldn't have noticed in the first place."

Darius made himself take another deep breath before he answered her. "As I said, I'm trying to learn. The things that are set before me are much easier to pick up than the social niceties that no one has ever bothered to explain." Darius found himself getting angry. He was at huge a disadvantage compared to the crew members who'd grown up on planets or even space stations. They'd always been with other people, and were used to it.

For the longest time, it had just been Darius and his dad.

Captain Alana peered at him curiously. "You are starting to fit in, though. To mix with the rest of the crew."

Darius nodded slowly. Shit, this wasn't another godsdamned test, was it? Something else that he was surely failing? He always felt that around her, that she was always testing him, and that most of the time he disappointed her.

"It was why I invited you to participate in the larger events," Captain Alana said. "To see if you could let go of a smidgen of your anger, actually open your eyes and see the opportunities in front of you."

Darius kept his lips pressed together hard so he wouldn't reply with something he'd regret later, something about being a slave and having no choice but to learn his master's rules and games.

Of course, that made Captain Alana laugh at him.

Bitch.

"I should have known that you'd be too damned stubborn to let go of your *revenge*," she mocked.

Darius refused to be drawn in, to say anything. He'd never mentioned seeking revenge, she'd just known, and he'd never bothered denying it.

"But you can't speak of the devil tails, as you call them," Captain Alana warned.

Darius blinked, surprised. Why was Captain Alana suddenly being clear?

"Why?" Darius asked. "What are they? Where do they come from? Are they organic? How do they interface with the ship?"

Darius stopped himself from asking the last question, though he felt as though it was the steaming meteor in the room that they were both ignoring—*were they alien?*

Mankind had never met a technologically advanced alien race.

"They're *shifters*," Captain Alana said slowly.

Darius nodded eagerly. He knew that already. What else would the captain tell him?

As if replying, Captain Alana said, "I can't tell you more about them. They're supplied by one of my investors. They're crucial to my enterprise. You do understand that they will self-destruct if they're ever captured or tampered with?"

"I'd heard rumors about that," Darius admitted. There'd been some talk between the other pilots, a brief warning to always run, avoid capture at all costs, because the ships had all been rigged to blow up.

Did the tails, themselves, contain explosives? And what was the mechanism that would set off that chain of events? Was it being in a tractor beam? Or was it someone else messing with the controls?

Of course, he'd never been given any sort of disarming code, so he wouldn't be able to stop the ship from blowing up not only its captors, but him as well.

"Trust me, Darius, that's all you want to know about the

shifters," Captain Alana warned. She paused and narrowed her eyes at him. "I know you won't stop seeking," she said. "But I want your word that you won't spread rumors of what you do learn to the rest of the crew."

Darius fumed for a moment. "That's not fair," he complained.

Shit. There was that laugh of hers again.

"None of the worlds are fair," the high queen bitch captain assured him. "None of us get what we actually deserve. Otherwise, you'd still be in that shithole of a claim, scratching away at the dirt, unaware of the goldmine you actually owned."

That stung. Darius didn't deserve to be poor and without hope, did he?

"No matter how much you personally hate me, you have to admit being part of this crew has been good for you," she continued.

At Darius' stubborn silence, she added, "Think of how much you've learned. How much you know now. How much better *Orion* is, now, with all updated system and parts."

It was the biggest conundrum of his life, his own Gordian sword and knot. He was going to be able to buy *Orion* with his share when he bought out his contract. It would add a few years to his indenture, but it was totally worth it.

He'd still lost his claim, his family's place, all his dad's mementoes. They'd all been stripped from the ship when he'd gotten her back.

Captain Alana probably had never had *family*, not like he had.

And yet, thanks to her, when he finished his indenture, he'd be in much better shape than he'd been in. His ship would be completely updated. He'd have a lot of flying experience with a many different crafts, something that would earn him good money. Hell, he might even be able to buy back his claim from her.

It still rankled that he'd had to lose everything first.

Captain Alana looked at him curiously. "I don't expect you to thank me for where you're going to end up. But I do wish you that for once in your life you to look beyond that proud nose of yours and see what was really going on."

Darius found himself sitting up straighter. Her tone—those words—there was something else going on here.

Damn it! He was so awful at reading between the lines in a social situation. Something else that she wanted him to see. What was it, though?

"So again, I want you to give me your word that you won't spread any knowledge you may gain of the shifters to the rest of the crew," Captain Alana said firmly.

Darius wished he could stand and stretch, to get himself back centered. The captain always did this to him, push him from one end to the other, get him off balance.

However, he was a man of his word. She knew that. He would hold himself to higher standards than anyone else. It was why he refused to steal from her, though he knew other members of the crew regularly did, and that she expected it.

"I won't share any knowledge I may gain about the shifters with the rest of the crew," Darius said slowly. "You have my word."

Captain Alana gave him a smile sharp enough to cut an unwary man to shreds. "My hero," she said, the dripping with sarcasm.

Darius gave her a shrug. "At least I know who I am," he said simply.

Captain Alana frowned at that. It took Darius a moment to realize that he'd implied that the captain didn't know who she was. She had many faces, many masks. Who was underneath all of those facades? Did she know anymore?

"Go take a shower before you inflict yourself on any of the rest of the crew," Captain Alana said, looking back down at her tablet. "And maybe reconsider your style choices."

"Yes, ma'am," Darius said. He knew he couldn't get away without her making some comment on his backwards T-shirt.

On the walk back to his cabin, Darius considered her words. She hadn't forbidden him from learning about the devil's tails—she understood that he'd never give her his word on that.

But that he couldn't share his knowledge…That was probably the only thing that he would have agreed to. And the captain knew him well enough to merely ask for that.

She hadn't actually given him permission to go study the shifters. He knew that if he was stupid about it, she'd stop him.

However, he was aware that if he focused on the shifters, it would set a wedge between him and the rest of the crew, keep him isolated.

Would being separate weaken him? Probably. He couldn't build alliances if he couldn't share his knowledge.

The damned captain had come to a brilliant solution, as always.

Darius wasn't sure what his next step was.

Besides taking a shower.

Darius parked *Orion* on the far edge of the Birlikte system. The run had gone smoothly so far—much better than the last two. He didn't have hours of time to kill before meeting up with the jump ship, however, if he timed it right, he could make it back to the meeting point just before the deadline.

Plus, for the first time in over eight months, Darius was flying alone. Ganghie, the pilot scheduled to go with him, had ended up in the medical unit the morning they were supposed to take off, and Darius had been sent on his own.

If only he could get himself to move.

He stood just inside the airlock on *Orion*. He wore his full spacesuit, the one that was bulky and clumsy but would protect him longer during his EVA. The air from the suit tasted neutral, always a good sign. He'd already double- and triple-checked all the controls, the lines that attached him to the ship, everything.

However, he still felt himself already growing clammy and starting to sweat. Not because the suit was too hot—it kept his body at a regulated temperature both inside as well as outside this ship. But because he remembered all too clearly what had happened on the last time he'd tried an EVA on his own.

That was when Captain Alana had shown up and had taken his claim from him. If he hadn't acted quickly and answered her questions correctly, she would have left him out there to die.

Probably.

No, merely possibly.

Studying her so closely the last year and three months, Darius had figured out that Captain Alana didn't like to waste people. She threatened, and for flagrant insolence or being stupid about stealing, she would kill someone. But if Darius was honest with himself, the person generally had it coming. Captain Alana wouldn't kill someone for a single breach of protocol. They would have had several warnings before she'd act.

Captain Alana understood that people were her most valuable resource. It was why she'd managed to turn most of those who she captured from slaves into employees.

Darius realized that he was one of the few who was stubborn enough that he'd still seek his revenge at the end of his indenture, despite how much she'd given him.

It was just his nature, the nature of the Greek people. No matter how much grudging admiration he had for her. She'd stolen his claim, his family's ship, his life. He'd never be able to forgive her for that.

He took another deep breath. He understood that if she caught him at what he was about to do, it would be considered a mark against him, and that he would only have so many. Because he was so stubborn about his revenge, he figured he had fewer chances to screw up compared to the average crew member.

Captain Alana had also *almost* given him permission to study the shifters. As he couldn't figure out the software that ran them, and he couldn't ask anyone else about it, he decided to go at the problem a different way, and see if he could learn something more about the shifters by actually studying them.

That had turned out to be more difficult than he'd expected. Getting into the repair dock required a crew badge with higher clearance than his.

The only way he figured out would be to arrange some sort of "malfunction" on *Orion*, something that would require an EVA. He couldn't just leave the ship. He had no doubt that all of his actions were being recorded in a log, somewhere, that he couldn't access.

He hit upon the perfect solution—bring down one of the blast screens on the front windows of *Orion*. He could trigger that with a command he'd put into the computer system that maybe someone would find, but possibly not, as he'd buried the code in a completely different place than the regular control section.

In the simulations, when Darius ran diagnostics, the blast

screen would appear as though it was functioning normally. However, it would give him the justification to go do an EVA and check to make sure the blast door was okay and not stuck or damaged in some way.

That would give him time to do some research on the shifters attached to *Orion's* belly, where the great scoop for collecting up minerals and small rocks from the asteroid belt he'd once called home.

Still, Darius hesitated, standing in the airlock. The blast door had come down on cue. He'd tried everything he could from the inside to get it to raise back up. He'd trigger that code when he came back inside.

Doing an EVA by himself was a dangerous proposition.

His dad had always said that spacers didn't live alone, they died alone. Every other trip that Darius had taken over the last three months since coming up with this plan he'd had a copilot. He was finally alone, had some time, and wasn't being shot at.

He wouldn't have another opportunity to study the shifters. Not like this. He had to make himself go outside.

Finally, he reached over and flipped open the protector on the button to open the door, then pressed it, gently. He would have pounded on it, but *Orion* had no gravity, and he didn't want to go floating away.

The door opened. Though Darius couldn't hear anything in the suit, he always thought that outside the ship was quieter. Colder. Absolutely still.

Darius held onto the rungs attached to the outside of *Orion*. He gripped tightly. He wasn't about to let go and be lost. While at least he knew that Captain Alana would send someone to look for him, she wouldn't arrive in time to rescue him. He'd die alone, his suit unable to support him after a while.

All Captain Alana would do would be to retake *Orion*.

His body would float forever, just another piece of space debris.

From the top, *Orion* looked like a sloppy capital F, with the control room at the bottom of the letter, two small storage bays in the center, and a larger set of rooms across the top. Darius had used one of the airlocks in center of the ship.

However, instead of using the rungs to crawl across the ship toward the control room, he crept down the side of *Orion*, toward the bottom. He flexed his hands after a while, willing himself to stop gripping so tightly, but he couldn't do it. Sweat already pooled under his arms and across the small of his back.

No nearby sun lit up the skin of the ship. The only illumination he had was from the lights attached to his helmet: one on either side, close to his ears, as well as a third, larger beam from the top of his skull. All he could hear was the sound of his own breathing. The air still tasted neutral, though his mouth tasted of sour fear. He concentrated on putting one hand in front of the other, slowly sliding his feet along.

He stopped when he realized that the skin of *Orion* had suddenly changed.

The rest of the ship was made from a metal-porcelain mix. It was the best material man had created to date to survive the roughness of space. It wasn't impervious, there were some dents and streaks in *Orion's* skin—which Darius believed just gave her character. The natural color of material was a light gray color. Darius and his dad had never had the money to paint the ship some other color, though they'd talked about making her either a bright yellow or gold, like Jason's fleece.

The skin on the hull of the ship was no longer gray, but an off white. A long seam ran from about mid-way along her long axis to the her end.

Darius held up the spectrograph that he'd "acquired" for this trip. He first checked the material he was familiar with, making sure the unit worked.

It showed that the skin of *Orion* was composed of what he expected.

When he slid the spectrograph to the off-white material, the machine gave him an error. Nothing in its reference library matched.

What the hell? It wasn't just a covering on the old ship. Part of *Orion's* hull had been replaced with something.

Darius had tested the spectrograph in his cabin, learning how to use the machine. Even in his clumsy suit, he could press the library button and change the material setting from "metal" to "organic".

The spectrograph still didn't know exactly what the hull was made out of, but it did recognize that the material was no longer metal and porcelain, but metal and organic.

Darius didn't crow with delight, but at least it had proved his hunch right. When he swung the spectrograph on the tails themselves, they registered as all organic.

Again, the material was completely unknown. He'd expected that.

But these things were *grown*, not manufactured.

And no human world that he'd ever heard of had that capability.

The tails had to be alien. From some planet that Allied Worlds didn't know about.

Had Captain Alana found them during her travels? Were aliens her mysterious investors? Did the Allied Worlds even know about them?

Darius memorized all the readings the spectrograph gave him, both on the hull as well as the tails. Then, though he deplored the waste, he dropped the handheld machine. He didn't want someone to be able to find it, to discover what he'd done.

Still, Darius wasn't ready to leave yet. He attached himself to the rung and hung where he was for a while, shining his lights on first one tail, then the next. He counted at least a dozen, though possibly there were more that he couldn't see. He couldn't crawl across the bottom of the hull either: all the rungs had been removed. And he didn't want to try to swing himself across the bottom of the ship by pulling himself from one tail to the next, like some cartoon hero swinging across a jungle on vines. The tails were cold, freezing to the touch.

Plus, there was always the fear that touching them would set off a counter and cause them to self-destruct.

He hoped that just observing them wouldn't start that sequence.

The tails each moved independently, as if being blown by a solar breeze. They had the same shape, maybe a foot across the top where they were melded onto the ship, then tapered down, coming to a point at the end. The length ranged from one foot to about twelve feet.

Darius wished he could record what he was seeing. Maybe next time he'd bring a hand-held recorder instead of the spectrograph.

He knew better than to lie to himself that there wouldn't be a next time.

He remembered that when he'd tried to pick up one of the markers of his claim, the tail had swung the marker out of his reach, so he couldn't grab it.

As part of his experiment, he reached out and tried to touch the nearest tail.

It swung out of his reach.

They weren't programmed to do that. At least, not with

computer software. The tails that had been attached to his claim markers probably hadn't been networked together.

Had the metal on the bottoms of the claim markers been changed? Probably not. That would have taken too much effort.

Eventually, Darius' suit beeped at him. He'd set a timer for himself of forty-five minutes. That was a reasonable amount of time for him to do an EVA, for him to supposedly get to the front of the ship and tug on the failed blast door.

It was time for him to go.

He realized that for the first time, his fingers weren't cramping. He was still firmly holding onto the ship. But he'd overcome some of his fear of being outside the ship by himself.

He unattached the extra tie he'd used to secure him to the rung, then turned himself around and started pulling himself back up to the airlock.

Though the airlock opened normally, and cycled correctly, Darius found his heart pounding hard until he finally was able to unlatch his helmet.

He couldn't believe it. He'd gone outside the ship, observed the shifters, then made his way back, without a disaster.

Even through his suit, he reached up and pressed against his chest, touching the Jason medal that rested there, thanking the gods for his luck.

That didn't mean that something else wouldn't go wrong. Or that Captain Alana wouldn't space him for finding out too much about the shifters, no matter what permissions she'd given him.

Grinning, Darius shucked his suit, then took himself to the sanitizer. He smelled rank.

But maybe next time he'd get over his fear more quickly.

He might even grow to enjoy the silence of space outside of his ship.

———

As Darius had calculated, leaving the Birlikte system after he'd finished his EVA brought him to the jump point just in time. Luckily, the trip went smoothly. No one shot at him, no pirates showed up out of nowhere and attempted to board him, and no distress signals registered on his systems.

It had been the easiest trip Darius had ever had. He found himself often reaching up to touch his Jason medal, too aware that this luck couldn't last.

Maybe the shit wouldn't hit the fan until he got back to *Xinsheng*, when Captain Alana would march him to the nearest airlock as punishment for his EVA to study the shifters.

The carrier was shaped like a giant V sitting on top of a solid rectangle. The smaller ships were strapped into berths along the inside of the V. The crew of the carrier lived in the rectangle. Though Darius had seen bigger carriers, this one was still quite large, capable of carrying eight *Orion*-sized ships, four on each side.

Orion had been the last to arrive at the jump point: all the other berths were full of ships. Darius had been informed to park his ass at the top of the starboard side of the V. Darius killed the engines and operated on thrusters, perfectly backing *Orion* up until she just kissed the platform.

Darius stayed strapped into the pilot's chair. He knew other pilots trusted the carrier crew to do their jobs right and took off, going to eat or sleep until they arrived back at *Xinsheng*.

Darius couldn't do that. Not that there was really

anything for him to do at this point. But he still flipped the comms to a different channel so he could listen in on the private channels of the carrier and its crew. He also kept the side and rear cameras on so he could watch the operation. He gave himself the excuse that he wasn't a control freak, but that he was trying to learn everything so that if he needed to, maybe he could attach *Orion* to the carrier himself.

He'd figured out early on that it wasn't that complicated a procedure. First, a large tube connected to the tail of *Orion*, sucking her firmly against the side of the carrier. Then, expert EVA workers, who moved more gracefully in no-gravity than Darius could ever hope to, strung cables around the massive storage rooms along the backend of *Orion*.

Though the job itself was simple, Darius knew there was tremendous skill involved. Ships always had different configurations. The crew had to look at the shape and figure out how best to attach it to the carrier, then swim through the emptiness of space efficiently and strap the ship in.

Normally, in addition to the suction tube, four cables were used to attach *Orion* to the carrier. The crew was just finishing with the second one when a loud crackling noise came over the comms.

"What is that?" Brigit, one of the newest crew members, asked.

"Ah, Pierre, did you spoil your suit again?" said another one of the crew, teasing.

"We're under attack!" someone yelled, a voice Darius hadn't heard before. "Return to the ship. Prepare to jump in ninety seconds!"

"What?" Darius said. "But what about my ship?"

Orion wasn't fully attached! If the carrier dropped him midway, he'd never get out of jump space alive! No one would be able to find him there either.

However, the crew outside couldn't hear him. His comms had only ever been set to listen.

A great shudder went through the carrier, shaking Darius and his ship.

What the hell was after them this time?

He watched helplessly as one of the two cables that had strapped *Orion* to the carrier snap.

He knew his luck had been too good to last.

He wasn't about to be destroyed with the carrier, or be lost in jump space. He had to get away. And he had to do it right now.

Orion lurched as the carrier started moving.

Though Darius knew it was completely forbidden to start the engines of his ship while attached to the carrier, he did it anyway. He wanted a fighting chance to get away, and it would take time for them to warm up and get back online.

As the carrier swung around, Darius got a look at the ships attacking them.

Were those Allied World ships? Had Captain Alana finally pissed off the people in power enough that they'd decided to come after her?

The carrier kept swinging around, veering away from the attackers.

Darius clanked his teeth together hard as the next hit jarred the carrier.

Damn it! The carrier had put the attacker just on the other side of where Darius was attached.

The next hit would probably take him out with it.

"Come on!" he muttered, complaining to the slowly warming engines.

Three-fourths of the way there.

Darius was flung to one side, then the other, hard enough to rattle his teeth. Was there more than one attacker? That would make sense. Fortunately, he'd kept himself strapped into the pilot's seat, another lesson that Dad had drilled into his head.

The engines were close to hot. Darius didn't know if the attackers would come after him after he left the carrier. But it was worth the risk. He knew he was a good enough pilot to lose most of those who would chase after him.

He tried to slowly ease *Orion* forward.

The single cable that attached him to the carrier held him in place.

Darius knew he could break away. He paused, then pushed the ship forward again.

Several things happened all at once. Darius was only able to piece together the sequence later.

Another hit, possibly from some sort of missile attack, struck the carrier hard.

At that exact same instant, the carrier leaped away, entering jump space. The stars outside the front windows of the pilot's cabin grew long tails, streaking away.

One instant later, Darius freed *Orion* from the carrier at that same time as well, entering jump space with the carrier, but flinging himself away.

At that moment, the shifters activated themselves. Everything inside *Orion* was suddenly tinged with red.

Had they been about to self-destruct, based on the attack?

The smell of burned plastic filled the cabin. The air grew hazy. Everything inside the cabin *blurred,* as if all the sharp edges of reality had faded away.

Darius pounded on the button to take the shifter back offline. Who knew what they'd do in jump space?

With a shuddering *pop,* the shifters disengaged and Darius re-entered regular space.

The carrier was nowhere to be seen.

Neither were the attackers.

Darius breathed a huge sigh of relief. He kissed two fingers and reached up to the Jason medallion attached to the ceiling above his chair, thanking the gods for his reprieve.

Eagerly, Darius pulled up his space charts from his computer. Now, he just had to figure out where he was. Captain Alana would send another carrier to the second meetup point, as there were always three backup rendezvous points. Maybe that one wouldn't be attacked.

After a few minutes, Darius realized that his luck was still as bad as always.

Yes, he'd gotten away from the attackers in more or less one piece. He wasn't lost forever in jump space.

However, he'd been flung into an uncharted sector of space. The computer didn't recognize any of the stars, couldn't map them to any known chart.

He had no idea where he was.

He was lost, as lost as he could have been doing an EVA of his ship.

And he had no idea how to get back to known space.

***

Darius sent up a distress call, though he didn't have much hope that anyone would find him here. While the scanners on *Orion* were certainly better now than they had been, he still didn't know which way to go. Should he travel toward the brightest star he could find? That didn't necessarily mean inhabited worlds. Or should he just pick a direction at random?

First thing, though, he needed to use the sanitizer and clean himself up. Though he didn't have the sensitive nose that Captain Alana did, he still figured he was pretty rank. That battle had shaken him up.

Now that the adrenaline rush had faded, he also found himself shaking. That had been far too close.

Was it Allied World vessels coming after them? Li Xi had said there wasn't a pattern. Darius had talked with some of the other pilots, and they agreed: it was always different ships that were attacking, not an organized crew.

But maybe it was just local ships attacking, whoever was in the vicinity, and that they were being directed by the Allied Worlds.

Darius unstrapped himself from the captain's chair and pulled himself up to the ceiling. He hung there for a moment, then brought his legs up, stretching his back, before twisting from side to side.

After a few more moments, Darius yawned hugely. He was still shaken, but exhaustion had now engulfed him. He'd read enough field medical texts to realize that he was in shock, or coming out of it.

Should he run the sanitizer? How long could he exist out here without getting supplies? He'd been running close to empty in terms of fuel. However, food was going to be his main concern. He had water, and the recycling system would be able to process his piss adequately, at least for a while.

Gods, this felt like one of Captain Alana's damned tests.

But somehow, he doubted that she'd show up just as he was running out of food and water, merely to laugh at him. The gods couldn't be that cruel.

Or maybe they were.

For now, Darius had a plan. Clean himself up, sleep a little, then run survival calculations to figure just how long he did have.

It didn't feel like much, but it was a plan of sorts.

Darius kept flashing back to the words Captain Alana had said the last time they'd met, about how he'd deserved to be starving and poor, and how there was so much more going on just past his "proud Greek nose" that he couldn't see.

Though he might not have that long to live, relatively speaking, he was still determined to prove her wrong.

Darius nearly jumped out of his skin when a high-pitched tone rang through the cargo bay, echoing off the metal walls and shipping containers.

It was the sensor that indicated another ship was approaching.

He'd been lost for about a week. He'd turned off parts of the ship, and the equations still said he'd starve to death before he'd freeze to death, but it would be close either way. He'd spent some of that time going through the cargo he was carrying. It all looked legitimate to him, though he didn't know what all of it was. Plenty of electronics and some raw metals.

No food. No fuel.

He'd set the emergency call to cycle continuously, then made sure that any reply would come over the ship's speakers, so he could hear it from any room.

A moment after the sensor had pinged that another ship was out there, the comms came on.

"We have your message, ship *Orion* and crew. What is emergency?"

The voice spoke with a heavy accent that Darius didn't recognize.

What the hell? Why hadn't *Orion's* sensors picked up the other ship sooner? Most ships appeared on sensors way before they were in hailing distance.

Darius flung himself out of the cargo area in the center of

the ship, pulling himself along the hall and to his pilot's chair as quickly as he could.

"Hello? Hello?" Darius replied, setting the communication channel to the one that he'd been hailed on.

"Hello," came the chirping voice. It reminded Darius of Li Xi's voice, a tenor that could either be a woman with a low voice or a man with a high one.

"This is ship *Lulu* and her crew, out on training. What is emergency?"

"I've run out of fuel," Darius said, figuring that was the most important problem to focus on. He could also admit to being lost later.

He brought up all the sensors as he spoke, then tried to stifle his gasp.

The ship, *Lulu*, was hailing him from the very edge of his sensors. Most regular ships would be detected before they could speak.

He reminded himself to breathe normally as *Lulu* came into focus.

He'd never seen a ship like that before. It looked to him like a huge manta ray, the kind that had once populated home world's oceans, that man had brought with him to the stars and repopulated alien waters with. It was a cool-gray, much lighter in color than *Orion*.

It took him a moment to understand why, exactly, *Orion's* sensors hadn't detected the massive ship earlier.

The ship was *organic*. He'd bet, looking at it, that there was no metal at all.

Had he just met his saviors? Just met the aliens?

Or would they doom him like their devil tails?

Darius stared at the pictures sent by Tirowli, the scout who spoke the human language over on the other ship. Then Darius stared some more.

Aliens. *They were aliens.* And while the rest of the human races had *no idea* that any aliens existed, the aliens obviously had been in contact with *someone* for quite some time. Decades, probably.

They'd been surprised to find him here. Human ships had been relegated to just one section of the alien occupied space.

However, who was behind such a huge conspiracy? Was it the Allied Worlds? One of the smaller planetary system? Who was keeping it secret?

Darius had no idea, but he was alternately amazed and angry.

The main alien race—the Kintheka, with a click in the middle that Darius couldn't quite master, also known just as the Kin—reminded him of birds. They had a yellow beak that took up most of their face, with large eyes set close together above it. The beak covered over the small mouth they had underneath. They wouldn't communicate via facial expressions, which was going to make talking face to face a real bitch.

Whitish skin covered their bare skulls, giving them a ghoulish appearance. Then there were the feathers. Feathers! According to the file, most of the Kin had blue, brown, and black feathers, with a few albinos, which were uncommon, but not rare.

Darius almost found himself disappointed that there weren't any who were peacock colored.

A ruff of feathers grew out of the base of their neck, like a vulture's. Feathers also covered their arms and legs. They had three fingers and a thumb, and their number system was based on fours and eights instead of fives and tens.

Their legs and feet also reminded Darius of birds. First, their knees bent backwards compared to a human's. Then, their feet had four long splayed toes coming out of a center ankle, covered in hard, yellowish scales, with sharp-looking talons at the end of each toe. As far as Darius could tell, they never wore shoes or covered their feet, though they would wear pads to protect the ship from their sharp talons.

Was there some biological reason why they kept their feet bare? Was it because they were always fighting with their feet? Or simply custom?

Though Darius tried, he found it impossible to recreate a lot of the sounds that the Kin made. They had a beak they could click with, and something in their vocal apparatus that made humming or burr sounds that Darius wasn't sure he'd ever be able to imitate.

He'd bet that Tirowli had had some sort of organic enhancement made to his vocal chords for him to be able to speak to humans so well.

Then there was the other race, the Veeluthians, or Veelu. The file Tirowli sent had a short description of the history of the two races. Eons before, on their home world, the Kin and the Veelu had developed a symbiotic relationship. The Kin had originally been hoppers and gliders, able to achieve some level of flight. Though the Kin had lost their wings as they'd evolved hands, they'd never lost their ability to fly, as the Veelu had taken them on their backs, carrying them where they wanted to go in exchange for protection and food.

If Darius squinted, hard, he might see a little bit of a connection between the young, planet-bound Veelu in the picture and the huge ship *Lulu*.

Both the Veelu and *Lulu* had very little neck, with the wings flowing right out of the base of the skull. While *Lulu* had a broad, flat face, the smaller Veelu had a tiny beak, almost like ridged lips. And both had a long rat's tail.

Or possibly a devil's tail, as some of the Veelu had tails that tapered to sharp points.

The planet-bound Veelu and the ship *Lulu* shared the same ancestors. How did you *grow* something so big? He assumed the ship had no brain or willpower of its own, that it was a stupid system, enslaved to the Kin.

Lulu wasn't quite as big as the carrier had been. But she could easily swallow two or three ships *Orion*-sized whole.

Did she have jump space capability? Or merely travel near light-speed, like *Xinsheng*? *Lulu* might be big enough access jump space, though as Darius understood the physics, it wasn't merely size, but mass. The ship would also have to weigh enough, which had never made sense to him, given the weightlessness of space.

Then again, math wasn't really his thing.

The learning packet that Tirowli had sent of the Veelu speech had been much easier for Darius to learn. They appeared to have similar vocal apparatus, and a tongue that they used for speech instead of a beak.

Soon, he'd learn a lot more about both races. They were building (growing?) a tunnel between the two ships, so *Orion* could dock with them. It was the only way Darius could travel with them. The tunnel would be environmentally sound, so he didn't have to wear his spacesuit while walking the short distance between the two ships.

Darius had had to explain the entire concept of *fuel* to Tirowli. Evidently *Lulu* ran on solar power. He'd also had to explain how he'd run out of food soon, and that he ate more than few times a week, but rather, every day.

Also the fact that he cooked his meat seemed to be met with a level of distaste that had surprised Darius.

Tomorrow, he'd be meeting the aliens face to face.

While it wasn't a first contact for them, it sure was for him.

Hopefully, he wasn't walking to his doom.

———

A thick membrane covered the open door on the far side of the airlock. As far as Darius (and *Orion's* instruments) could tell, it was completely impervious. None of the vacuum of space trickled in around the edges. A similar membrane covered the far side.

It would only take him two steps to walk from his ship to *Lulu.*

He didn't believe it was a trap. Tirowli had assured him that they'd be taking him to the nearest space station, where perhaps they could fix his ship, supply him with fuel.

If they'd meant to kill him, they could have done it days ago.

However, Darius didn't completely trust the Kin. He'd only spoken with the scout, not the captain. He wanted assurances from the captain, herself, about what they were planning on doing with him.

The membrane felt cool against his palms, and smelled like green tea . It was at least half an inch thick. He assumed that it collected his DNA and would give the Kin another opportunity to study him.

What was it composed of such that he could just push through it, yet at the same time, it was tough enough to endure space? It was opaque—he couldn't quite see through it, but it wasn't solid, either.

Darius didn't have a choice, though. And he'd much rather risk himself, going over to the alien ship, than have the aliens come aboard *Orion.* He had a vague hope that he'd be able to get away at some point, though he didn't have a plan.

Right now he had to go meet them. Walk across that emptiness and board their ship.

He pressed his hand against the Jason medal lying against the skin of his chest.

Took a gulp of fresh air.

Then pressed through.

———

The ship itself, *Lulu*, was weird. That was the main thing Darius kept coming back to. The walls were like thick skin, showing veins of blood running beneath them. He'd come to understand that the Kin didn't have good near vision, so they just looked pink to them. He didn't have their far vision capabilities.

Darius had felt Captain Kiki's shock when he'd told her that the humans didn't know about the aliens.

Could he trust her? She assured him that she was taking him to their nearest space station. He believed that. But what would her government do to him, someone who was outside the official channels? Were they aware of the conspiracy? Or was it just on the human side?

All the politics made his head hurt. But at least he was free of Captain Alana. For the time being.

Maybe he could get his revenge on her once he left the Kin systems.

After boarding the ship, the Captain and Tirowli had led Darius to a special chamber that the ship had grown just for him. Kiki was maybe five feet tall, and the ship had been built for her size of people, not Darius's six foot four.

"You'll be able to stay here," Tirowli had announced. Not only was the room was tall enough for Darius to stand upright, the ceiling soared well above his head, maybe as much as eighteen feet. He felt as though he could suddenly breathe, though the air was chewy, and felt thick to him.

Could he get them to tone it down a little, at least in his quarters?

The room itself wasn't very big, maybe twelve by twelve. It was bigger than his cabin back in *Orion*, that was damned sure.

There wasn't much in the room. A long table grown out of something was pushed against the far wall, covered in a whitish skin. At least it didn't look as though it had a pulse.

"Hellloooo," came a voice from a dark patch on the near wall.

"Hello," Darius said, staring at the spot. Both Kiki and Tirowli seemed startled, if Darius was reading their stiff body language correctly. Maybe they were excited, however. Who knew?

"I am Lulu," the voice said, speaking in English.

Darius' breath caught. "The ship?" he asked, incredulous.

The captain had said the ship was alive. He hadn't known if that meant it was sentient or not.

"Yessss," came Lulu's reply.

"Wow," Darius said. He grinned at Kiki and Tirowli before he remembered that they wouldn't be able to interpret the gesture. "I am pleased to meet you."

Tirowli translated, then after Lulu spoke, said, "I am happy meet you. I never meet human!"

"I've never met a Veelu before," Darius said.

"Tell me about your ship," Lulu demanded. Or at least that was how Darius would have interpreted her words.

"The *Orion*? She's my home," Darius said.

"She?" Lulu asked.

Darius made a note of the word. "Yes. She." He repeated the Veelu word. "We call all ships *she*."

"But she no alive!" Lulu complained. "I to talk to her. She no answer."

"True," Darius said, nodding. At least he knew that he

shared that gesture with the Kin. "She isn't as smart as you are," Darius said. While he knew it was important to stay on the good side of Kiki and Tirowli, impressing the ship had to be just as crucial.

Kiki asked, "You have smart ships?"

Darius knew she was asking about artificial intelligence. "No," Darius said simply. There were always rumors, of course, about the military developing ships that could be run completely by automated systems, that had personalities. And there were systems that were smart like that, smart enough to fool a human.

However, mankind remained paranoid about developing a master race of robots or AIs. If such work had been accomplished, it had been quickly bought out and hushed.

After a few more questions about Darius' home world (he claimed not to have one, as he'd been born and raised on *Orion*) and verifying his eating habits (which he could tell disgusted Kiki), Darius could tell the Kin needed to get back to their jobs.

"I'm awfully tired," Darius lied. "Would you mind if I rested for a while? Then we could talk again. Later."

Both Kiki and Tirowli seemed relieved at his announcement. "I will be back later," Kiki declared.

"I look forward to your return," Darius lied.

Something about the Kin just set him on edge. Maybe it was their abrupt movements, the way they jerked their heads back and forth, maybe their sharp claws and beaks made him wary. Or maybe it was because he disliked the relationship they seemed to have with the Veelu.

It reminded him too much of his own situation with Captain Alana. Lulu wasn't quite a slave, but almost.

After the Kin left, Darius sat down on the long table. Was this supposed to be his bed? How could he sleep here? He always had netting over him, in case the gravity went out.

What the hell was he going to do with himself? Maybe he could go explore, though he had the impression that the captain and the scout would prefer it if he stayed in this room.

"Dariusss?" Lulu asked.

"Yes?" Darius said, curious.

"I speak with you?" Lulu asked.

Was she asking for permission? Had she believed that he'd been tired?

"I would like that," Darius said. Then he added, "You teach me your language?"

"Ohhh!" Lulu said. "I know."

A long filament detached itself from the wall beside Darius, deep pink in color, about an inch in diameter.

"Touch," Lulu instructed. "Easy to talk."

What was that thing? How would it make it easier to talk? He could hear and understand Lulu just fine.

"What will it do?" Darius asked, still hesitant.

"Help you see," Lulu said.

Would this thing activate a viewscreen? Or the Veelu equivalent?

"See what?" Darius said.

He heard the frustration in her sigh. "Words hard to understand. This helps understand. Maybe."

Was this some sort of emotional transfer system? Was he about to be assimilated? Did he have any choice?

Still, he trusted Lulu more than any of the Kin he'd met so far.

Cautiously, Darius stroked the line. It felt cool against his fingertips, slippery almost. Though he'd never touched a snake, he imagined this was what snakeskin felt like.

Darius reached up and pressed two fingers against his Jason medal, wishing for luck, before he grasped the line firmly.

A flood of emotions went through him, excitement, fear, anxiousness to please, and beneath all of that, a touch of anger.

Darius couldn't help his gasp. He almost let go of the line, but didn't.

"Wow," Lulu said.

It took Darius a moment to realize that Lulu hadn't been expecting whatever had just happened.

"Feel?" Lulu asked.

Darius nodded. "I feel."

Lulu spoke excitedly to him, long sentences. Darius didn't understand the words, but he caught the gist of it: Kiki should have been able to feel Lulu's emotions like this, however, for some reason, she didn't.

Lulu was lonely. And bored. She really didn't have anyone to talk with.

"I learn," Darius said in the Veelu's language. He didn't know how to say "I promise," not yet. But as soon as he figured out how to say that phrase, he would.

He needed an ally among the aliens. And the ship, despite possibly being a slave, was not a bad place to start.

Every morning, before most of the crew woke up, Darius worked for hours with Lulu, learning the Veelu language. He found it relatively easy, much easier than any computer language. Veelu had the same structure as English, noun-verb-subject. Plus, he was already bi-lingual. He'd learned Greek as a child, as well as English, and had no problems switching between the two.

He missed being able to speak Greek, as he had with his dad. No one on the crew of Captain Alana's ship knew how. When Darius had realized that he was starting to lose the language, he'd instructed the computer aboard *Orion* to start speaking to him in Greek.

In exchange for teaching him the Veelu language, Darius taught Lulu English, as well as a smattering of Greek.

After his lessons with Lulu, Darius spent the rest of the day either exploring the ship (Lulu let him into all the areas, even the ones he wasn't necessarily supposed to go into) as well as studying the local star systems. He tried to learn more of the Kin language, but it didn't come as naturally. Not only could he not make some of the sounds, it was a tonal language.

He didn't understand why the Veelu language wasn't tonal—they'd all started out as birds, right? Maybe it was because both the planet-bound and the space flying Veelu could communicate at great distances, further than the Kin could, and such tones didn't work well across miles.

Kiki made a point of coming to see Darius every afternoon, with Tirowli in tow. There really wasn't much for them to talk about, however. Though they both were captains of their own ship, *Orion* was a completely different flying experience. Plus, Kiki didn't fly the ship, that was the asshole navigator's—Gitakin's—job.

Lulu really didn't like Gitakin. Darius didn't blame her one bit. Gitakin seemed to want to treat Lulu like a child.

And while Lulu was young, and sometimes seemed immature, she was still the godsdamned ship. Gitakin needed to show her more respect.

"Talk with Kiki about it," Darius recommended, more than once. He sat against the wall in his room. They communicated verbally, though frequently Lulu would extend a filament for Darius to touch, so that he could feel how she did. When he couldn't understand the meaning of a word, sometimes sharing how the word felt helped.

They spoke in English and Greek in the evenings, after

Lulu was done for the day, as more of the Kin were awake and it would be difficult for anyone to listen in. Mornings they spoke in Veelu, so they both had the opportunity to practice.

Lulu had dimmed the lights in Darius's cabin, making it feel more intimate to him. She'd also added a golden hue to the light that remained, giving the room a warm glow.

While Darius had been able to give Lulu the chemical signature of air he preferred to breathe, she hadn't really understood what he'd asked for. She measured organics using different component pieces. After some trial and error, she'd managed to get the combination of air molecules right, and Darius finally felt as though he could breathe here. She'd also tinted the air with a faint perfume, a sweet floral scent, instead of the fresh meat scent that the Kin found comforting.

The gravity on Lulu was much lighter than on *Xinsheng*, evidently the same as the Kin's home world. It was why the Kin could hop up and down the stairs, why they built aeries so far above the ground on the bridge and in the large conference rooms where the crew sometimes gathered. Darius still preferred the no gravity of *Orion* but he'd adapted to Lulu quickly.

It was weird being someplace that had no chairs, but did have a fair number of nests, either built up high or on the ground. The Kin never sat—their knees wouldn't allow for that—they did squat when they rested or slept.

The first time that Darius had folded his legs underneath him to sit in lotus pose had drawn a good number of clicks, the Kin equivalent of a gasp.

"I don't want to talk with Kiki about the navigator! She'll just take Gitakin's side," Lulu said.

Darius could hear the pout in her voice. "If he's as much of an asshole as you say he is, she might not," Darius told her. "Besides, aren't you supposed to be paired with the captain?"

"She doesn't *feel*, not like you do," Lulu said.

Lulu had complained a couple of times about Kiki. Darius could tell she felt conflicted, though. She knew her first allegiance should be to the captain and the Kin, not an alien like him.

"Why doesn't the captain feel like I do?" Darius asked. It didn't make sense to him. Lulu and Kiki were supposed to be bond together through a process called *pikali*. They'd be able to sense each other without words, feel each other's feelings, respond to any situation as though they were one being.

It would give them a huge advantage in a battle. But a huge disadvantage as well. Take out the captain, and the ship would be lost. Lulu had told him about the Veelu frequently committing suicide when their captains died.

"Kiki had another ship, before me," Lulu said. "She keeps comparing me to him. She doesn't like me, not like how she liked him."

"She doesn't know you yet," Darius said. "Give her a chance."

"I have!" Lulu said.

"Give her one more chance," Darius said.

On the one hand, it felt wrong for him to stand in the way between a captain and her ship.

On the other, given how this captain was treating her ship, maybe it was up to Darius to step in.

Be the hero that Lulu thought he was, that Captain Alana always teased him about being.

Lulu was the only one who knew Darius's real plight. He'd shared with her how he'd been captured by Captain Alana, how he had to work off his indenture. Lulu understood the concept of slavery, though it hadn't ever really been practiced by the Veelu or the Kin—every time the Kin had tried to treat the Veelu like slaves, they'd learned the hard way how difficult it was to control an airborne species.

Particularly if you then tried to fly on slaves who weren't afraid to fall out of the sky and kill themselves, with their "masters" on their backs.

"I will talk with Kiki about Gitakin tomorrow," Lulu vowed. She paused.

Darius didn't need to be touching the filament that Lulu often extended to exchange their feelings to sense how expectant Lulu waited.

"And I will help you if she doesn't," Darius said eventually.

Really, what more could be asked of any hero?

Darius was pleased that Kiki acted quickly, replacing Gitakin with another navigator.

The problem? His replacement was worse. He kept hitting the emergency overrides on Lulu's flying, trying to control every movement she made.

The ship breeders had placed mechanical controls on some of Lulu's systems. She could override them if she had to, but only at great pain and cost to herself.

However, Lulu was almost to that point.

She wailed quietly with despair that night while talking with Darius. The lights were low and golden, the room warmer than usual. In order to keep the equilibrium on the air in Darius's cabin, Lulu had grown a membrane over the doorway—the filters she'd set up just weren't as efficient.

Instead of being floral scented, the air had a chemical undertone to it, acrid and dangerous. Darius felt as though the hairs on his arms and the back of his neck should be standing up. If Lulu had a physical body, she'd be pacing right now.

Darius sat against the wall on a spot that Lulu had made more comfortable for him, contouring the edges of the ship to his back. Lulu spoke from just over his left shoulder. It was as though if he turned his head, he would see her.

"I can't stand him!" Lulu complained. "I don't know how to get rid of him!"

The Veelu weren't encouraged to commit suicide, but it wasn't frowned on by their society. The Kin had different morals and values, something that Darius kept getting tripped up on.

The Veelu felt so much more "human" to him.

"Does Kiki know how awful the new navigator is?" Darius asked, still trying to play the peacemaker.

"She was the one who put him in charge," Lulu said darkly. "She must know."

"I'm so sorry," Darius said.

He really was. It just wasn't fair that Lulu had so many restrictions. She was a sentient ship, born to space. She really should just be given her head. Let her blow off some steam, then she'd be much more accommodating.

Couldn't they see that?

"Is there anything I can do to help?" Darius asked.

The silence between built, growing more expectant.

"Yessss," Lulu said. "There is. I want to join in the *pikali* with you. Then you can help me escape the Kin."

"Are you sure?" Darius said, sitting up straighter. "That's a big step." His heart beat hard and sweat started trickling down his side.

If he escaped with Lulu, back to human space, he'd have the chance to enact his revenge on Captain Alana.

And to tell all the human worlds that there were aliens.

"I'm sure," Lulu said. "They will label me a wild one, like

they have others. There were many declared wild during the civil war that ended only a few years ago—young Veelu who wouldn't join the fight against their brothers and sisters."

Darius nodded. He'd read about the civil war among the Kin. Some of the worlds had declared themselves independent and turned away from the central government. They'd lost. It reminded him of the recent human wars with the Allied Worlds—many of the independent systems had lost their individual status and had been subsumed by the larger conglomerate.

"Will all of the Veelu turn against you?" Darius asked. That would be hard, for your people to no longer welcome you.

"Most will," Lulu admitted. "But there will also be a few who would help me. Older Veelu. Crewless. Some of the veterans from the war who never felt right about it."

"You'd be safe in human space," Darius assured her. Even if there was a huge conspiracy to hide the aliens, even if the Allied Worlds government knew about them and didn't tell anyone, the Union of Greek Planets would listen. They were his people. Stubborn, yes. However, they were one of the few groups who maintained their identity after being absorbed by the Allied Worlds.

"I know," Lulu said. "You'd protect me."

Her obvious hero worship made Darius a little uncomfortable. But she was also right. He would do everything in his power to keep her safe.

"But—we'd have to leave the crew behind. Leave them safe someplace. Unharmed."

A light tinkle of laughter filled the room. "You are so gallant! Always thinking of others before thinking of yourself and your freedom."

"No, I'm not," Darius said automatically. He knew what it meant to ally himself with Lulu, how this could save him.

They'd talked about the physics of jump space, and she was certain that she could put on the extra weight necessary to achieve it if they couldn't talk two of the older Veelu to jump with them.

"So will you join with me? In the *pikali?*" Lulu asked.

"I will." Darius pushed himself up to standing, ignoring how his heart jumped, how his hands shook. "What do you want me to do?" He trusted Lulu more than the Kin, though he also understood her to be immature.

That just meant spending extra time with her, teaching her, coaxing her. It didn't mean she wasn't capable.

"Lay down on the table," Lulu instructed.

Darius walked over and laid down. The surface instantly conformed to his body, nestling up against him, perfectly supporting him. It also warmed, making him feel even more comfortable.

A filament detached itself from the wall and slowly raised itself toward him.

Darius took a deep breath. There was no going back from this. He'd be allowing an alien to access his deepest feelings, as he understood the *pikali.* They'd be able to communicate, feel what the other felt, possibly without the filaments, though they might always need to be in physical contact, as he was human and not Kin.

After kissing two fingers and pressing them against the Jason medal on his chest, Darius reached out and grabbed the line.

This time, instead of being distinctly cool, it felt hot against his palm. Light filled the entire room, a white glare that made him close his eyes.

He'd expected an onslaught of emotions, but they seemed to come slowly, dripping down the line to him. Anger, Lulu's constant underlying emotion, spreading over him. He understood she'd been picked on by the space-fliers she'd been raised with. She'd been the runt of her litter until her last year, when she'd suddenly grown larger than all of them.

He felt himself flying with her, a memory of being chased by the meanest, biggest members of her pod while the ship herder was busy. They forced her to fly too closely to an asteroid. Unable to avoid it, she nicked one of her wings on it. The pain and humiliation of being scolded by the ship herder for injuring herself washed over Darius. Along with the shame of how the others had laughed at her.

Darius found himself reliving some of his painful memories, of being made to strip naked in front of Captain Alana because he'd responded too slowly to her demands, of losing his dad to faulty wiring, of how stupid the captain made him feel every time she laughed at him.

Happy memories also surfaced for both of them, Darius and his dad, Lulu basking in the heat of the sun. How strong Lulu felt as she'd grown bigger than the bullies, how smug Darius had felt after successfully studying the devil's tails.

Darius found himself giggling at the feel of the solar winds caressed his skin. He couldn't help it. Some level of his consciousness was aware at how awesome this all was—he *was* the ship, Lulu, and she was him, the human.

Suddenly, the rush of emotions cut off. Darius woke up in the chamber.

The filament unwrapped itself from around his wrist. He rubbed it as he sat up, seeing Kiki standing there.

This wasn't her normal visiting time. Was there something wrong? Had she figured out what he and Lulu were doing?

"Captain," Darius said, address her in the Kin's language. He knew he didn't have all the sounds, but he still tried his best. "What can I do for you?"

He couldn't help his grin. He still felt too good with all he'd shared with Lulu. Maybe he should feel scared, as he was helping Lulu turn away from the captain. But he just felt too damned happy.

"What were you just doing?" Kiki asked. Or at least that was what Darius thought she said. He still didn't know their language well enough.

"I was studying the human nervous system," Lulu replied in the creole that had developed between the Kin and the Veelu. Darius had picked up enough of both languages to be able to follow it, though no one had officially been teaching it to him.

The captain talked with Lulu a bit more before leaving. Darius could tell that the captain felt uneasy.

"Does she know?" Darius asked as he laid back down.

"She suspects," Lulu said. As the filament wrapped around Darius's wrist again, he realized that Lulu might never be able to lie to him ever again.

And he wouldn't be able to lie to her.

There wasn't anything he could do about that now. Instead, he eagerly wanted to share some more. To learn all there was about Lulu, to feel again what it meant to be such a mighty ship.

Tomorrow would be time enough for work, after their night of wonder.

Time to plan their escape.

And if they didn't make it, well, Darius wasn't sure how strongly he'd object to diving into a sun with Lulu rather than going back to Captain Alana.

<hr>

Darius woke late the next morning. Lulu had let him sleep. He felt sluggish, as if his blood had grown three times thicker overnight, swelling his veins, making his joints ache. Yet at the same time, he felt wired and tense, as if he'd already drunk three shots of caffeine.

He was glad that Lulu couldn't necessarily feel everything he felt, all the time. He didn't feel regret, not exactly.

It was more like he now understood just exactly what he'd committed to. It was as though he'd finally slept with a woman, only to wake up the next morning fully married, already expecting kids.

He wasn't likely to ever get married, now. He had a partner for life.

He remembered how his dad had loved Darius's mother. But she'd died when Darius had been two. He didn't remember her. Dad had never even looked at another woman, at least not as far as Darius knew. Maybe if they'd struck it rich, his dad would have found someone else to love.

Kind of hard to meet people when you were living on a spaceship out in part of the asteroid belt, away from *New Athens*, rarely even setting foot in a space station.

Darius tried to catalogue the changes he felt inside himself as he drank the protein shake that the Kin had finally come up as the best way to feed him, at least breakfast.

The walls—all he had to do was to stare at them to feel the pulse running through them. It was much slower than a heartbeat, but just as strong and steady.

He knew that Lulu's attention was elsewhere. She wasn't present in his room. He'd always feel her approach now, when she was there. Probably, all he'd have to do would be to call her name, and she'd shift her attention to him.

Would they be able to share more feelings, more thoughts, without deliberate effort? He still didn't know.

Darius found himself drawn to one of the walls of his chamber, the one with the darkened spot that hid vocal apparatus for Lulu to speak with him.

With one finger, he reached out and pressed against the wall, drawing an arc.

The wall darkened over the path of his fingertip, the arc fully represented.

Fascinated, Darius let his hand just draw. He didn't have something in mind, just a shape. A form.

It didn't surprise him when he found himself drawing a small head with wings flowing out where there would be a neck. The image of Lulu appeared. Like a grand manta ray, soaring up out of the floor, toward the ceiling.

Darius had the feeling that the image would change as Lulu did. For example, if she injured a wing, the representation would show exactly where the damage was, how extensive it was.

Though he didn't draw them, the few vestigial feathers that clung to the cross ridge of the top of her winds filled themselves in. As did the small tunnel, that connected Lulu to *Orion*.

Darius felt guilty looking at his ship. *Orion* had been home for so very long, his entire life. Even though he spent most of his time living on *Xinsheng*, he still considered *Orion* his true home.

Or at least, until last night.

What was he going to do about her? He couldn't just sell her. Maybe Lulu could bring *Orion* aboard? But when would he fly *Orion* again?

That gave him another idea, however.

Above the image of Lulu, Darius placed his cupped hand against the wall, willing the flesh of the wall to bubble up against his palm. Then he thought strongly of the Jason of the Argonauts medal that lived on the ceiling of *Orion*, the image he always wished on, that brought him luck.

When Darius removed his hand, he uncovered a vague representation of the medal. It wasn't exact. The face wasn't clear, and instead of being bright white and gold, it was pink. But Jason knew that in time, Lulu would perfect it for him.

She would do anything for him.

Would he do anything for her?

A true hero would.

It took some persuading, but Darius finally got Lulu to agree to his plan.

One of the awesome things about having a sentient, living ship like Lulu was that she could grow any part of herself. Make her wings bigger, smaller, thicker, stronger, whatever was called for. She also grew internal chambers as the ship growers directed, built storage rooms, doors, and so on.

However, they quickly learned that Lulu needed help pinpointing where she needed to make an adjustment. In addition, Lulu needed guidance about what she needed to do.

Darius related it to being able to control his own heartbeat. If he ran, his heart would beat faster. But he needed the external stimulus in order for his heart to work that hard. And it wasn't that Lulu lacked imagination. However, she was young, inexperienced. A lot of her early growth and development had occurred in the ship grower's vats. She'd live another eighty years or so, but she was literally only a few years old.

Or was her lack of control deliberate? Had the ship breeders made it so that Lulu could only improve herself at their direct command?

Later that night, after most of the ship's crew had gone to sleep, Lulu directed Darius to a hole that she created just for him in the ceiling of his chamber. It didn't take much for

Darius to pull himself up and into one of Lulu's internal sections.

The air up here was humid. All around him, he heard the rushing of Lulu's blood. It felt intimate, being completely enclosed by Lulu, in a way that the start of the *pikali* hadn't been.

Darius stood in a special vein that Lulu had constructed beside her spine. It was basically a service tunnel, that the ship breeders had used to have access to her internal systems. The walls weren't completely clear: A glowing whitish film covered them, allowing Darius to see not just where he was, but illuminating everything around him.

He looked around with wonder.

The vertebrae of Lulu's spinal cord, or the Veelu equivalent of such things, were hollow, as were most of her bones. The Kin were similar, though they had more solid bones.

Each of Lulu's vertebrae were taller than Darius, if he'd been able to straighten up completely, and probably twelve feet long. Black veins and bright pink arteries, thick tubes bigger than his outstretched hand, ran through the cluster of spine bones. Thick white tendons lined the ceiling and floor, connecting to healthy red muscle. What looked like black wires grew randomly from the spinal cord to the muscles— maybe part of her nervous system? Darius wasn't certain.

"Wow," Darius said. He reached out and deliberately touched the wall of the service tunnel, trying to communicate his awe at being granted such an intimate view.

He felt Lulu's pleasure, as well as her shyness of showing so much of herself to him.

However, she needed to grow some new material, something that no one else would realize she had, not until it was too late.

The crew parts of the ship were basically a second stomach hanging off the bottom of Lulu's torso. The section that Darius lived in had been created just off Lulu's spine, toward the tail of the ship.

Darius walked up the service tunnel, dragging the tips of his fingertips against the wall so Lulu could feel him, pinpoint his movements, make a map of her internal pieces. The floor grew thicker as he walked from the tail section and headed up toward Lulu's stomach section. He wondered at the many veins and arteries, how the blood flowed, how her heart beat. He gained an understanding of her internal form, and could now picture what she looked like without her skin, how the muscles flowed into one another, how her bones connected.

Lulu followed along, comparing his location to where she felt the crew quarters. It gave her a better understanding of her own body construction as well, and would help her later make adjustments as necessary.

The tunnel narrowed as it reached the center of her chest, then ended abruptly in a T, with more tunnels branching out, heading towards Lulu's wings.

Here, Darius saw the evidence of the ship breeder's meddling. Thick yellow tubes ran up from the floor on either side and ran down the center of tunnels going to the sides.

These were the overrides that the navigators used to control Lulu's flight. While they were natural and organic, they were still alien to Lulu. He couldn't control the revulsion he felt, though part of him wondered if all of that feeling came from him, or if he was also feeling what Lulu did.

The space beyond where the first tunnel ended was dark. Darius understood that the ship breeders had no access to Lulu's brain. Possibly that was beyond their skill, to make adjustments there physically.

Chemically, he was certain that he'd see their splotchy fingerprints everywhere.

With a shaking hand, Darius reached out and touched what Lulu referred to as her brakes. He touched the wall of the service tunnel with his other hand, trying to communicate exactly where he was.

A sense of gratitude washed over him.

Lulu now had an exact idea of where she was being controlled from.

It would take a lot less effort, and possibly less pain, for her to neutralize the controls of the Kin.

———

Kiki came into Darius' cabin to personally announce to him that they were close to space station, and would be arriving the next day.

"Thank you for letting me know," Darius replied, familiar now with the creole that existed between the Kin and the Veelu. The *pikali* had speeded up his familiarity with the two languages dramatically.

"They understand your situation," Kiki continued. "They are not sure if they can help you find *fuel*. But they will try."

"Thank you," Darius said again. He paused, then added, "But you do realize that *fuel* isn't enough? My ship isn't large enough to achieve jump space."

Kiki nodded. "The Veelu can carry you through jump space, once you can fly on your own."

"Have you already called the Veelu to help?" Darius asked, curious how involved Kiki had been.

Kiki paused.

Since joining with Lulu, Darius had a much better time reading the Kin's body language.

Kiki was uncomfortable with his question.

Finally, though, she replied. "I didn't call them. But some Veelu have gathered."

"Did Lulu call them?" he said.

"Don't you know?" Kiki challenged. Her neck ruff raised. Though she was shorter than Darius by a good foot, she suddenly seemed bigger and more dangerous.

Darius held himself very still. He wasn't armored, had no weapon. In a hand-to-hand combat with one of the Kin, he'd lose. Badly. While growing up, the Kin were taught how to fight and defend themselves. Plus, Kiki was a warrior. She'd fought many star battles during the recent civil war. She wouldn't shy away from violence.

"I don't know if Lulu called them or not," Darius said. He was only kind of lying. Lulu had said she'd send out a call when they got closer, but she'd never actually told him that she had.

Kiki stared at him with her large eyes, as if she could discern the truth that way. Her neck ruff started to wilt. "I would fight you for her, if I thought it would do any good. It is not my choice that matters, though."

With her usual abrupt movement, Kiki turned away and started walking away.

"Take good care of her," Kiki said as she reached the far door.

Darius couldn't help but reply. "I will," he promised.

Kiki shuddered once, as if he'd struck her between her shoulders. She didn't turn around to stare at him, though, instead, pushed her way through the membrane grown over the door.

At least she didn't ask why the membrane was now so thick.

On the one hand, Darius wished he could have gotten to know Kiki better. He recognized that she wasn't the villain here. It was as much a combination of bad luck and chance.

Still, he didn't regret that he'd joined with Lulu.

It was the only way they'd both be able to escape.

"I t's time," Lulu announced quietly.

Darius kissed two fingers and pressed them against the Jason medal he always wore. Then he quickly moved to the section of the wall in his cabin that Lulu had previously prepared for him. He sat down and grabbed the filaments on either side of him, strapped them across his chest in an X, and plunged the ends of them back into the wall.

He wasn't completely immobile, but he wouldn't be hurt by what was about to happen next.

Being in such close proximity to Lulu also gave him a better view of what she was doing. Their *pikali* was still new and young, like both of them. It would grow stronger as they aged. Or at least that was how it happened between the Kin and the Veelu.

Abruptly, Lulu gave a great shake, rotating along her central axis, like a wet dog getting to shore.

Darius grabbed onto the filaments holding him to the wall, glad he was strapped in.

When Lulu stopped shaking, he gasped. He could *feel* the crew cabin, that second stomach, coming loose from Lulu's body. It was as if a fan blowing a freezing wind had just started up, aimed at his chest. Darius shivered.

Reaching his awareness along Lulu's sides, he found the rope-like ligaments that still connected the crew sections to Lulu's chest. He wished he had a sharp knife and could just cut them. They'd talked about him flying *Orion* during this part of their plan, but in the end, had decided that they were stronger together than apart.

Lulu shook herself again. Darius had the impression of the crew compartment rocking hard.

The lines between them stayed connected.

Darius gave Lulu the impression of bouncing up and down. Lulu abruptly rose vertically then stopped.

Some of the ligaments tore. A brief stinging sensation went through Darius at the point of former contact, along his left side, just below his ribs.

Darius smoothed a hand over the location, willing it to heal while Lulu bounced a few more times. The last abrupt jerk made Darius's head snap forward then back.

Maybe they'd have to get a neck brace for him if they were going to be doing this sort of thing often…

The last of the lines snapped.

The container for the crew floated free of the great ship.

Lulu and Darius had talked through the probable scenarios. There would be a few injuries among the crew, but nothing severe as the cabin lost gravity and was shaken around.

It was why they deliberately didn't release the compartment until they were close enough to the space station that the crew could be easily rescued. The air would quickly grow stale as Lulu couldn't grow additional apparatus to circulate it. It was well insulated, so it would stay warm for quite some time. None of their lights or communication equipment would work, but Lulu had already sent a distress call.

Lulu's crow of triumph echoed through Darius's cabin. The cold feeling along his torso lessened as Lulu thickened the skin there, blocking out the vacuum of space.

Darius stayed strapped to the wall, however much he wanted to get up and dance around his cabin, celebrate with his best girl.

He felt the menace before Lulu did. Something big and fast approached them over her left wing.

"They're coming."

As Lulu had predicted, some of the other Veelu would turn against her. She would be declared a wild one, unfit for living among them. The other Veelu would hunt her, harry her, never leave her in peace, until she flew herself into a sun.

Darius caught a glimpse of the large Veelu coming to attack. His skin was whiter than Lulu's cool gray. Darius would bet that he was old, much older. As Lulu turned to face him, Darius saw that he, also, no longer had a crew compartment.

He was an old, retired space flier. Probably a war veteran, based on the scars that ran across the top left ridge of his wings.

Lulu had no offensive weapons, no clawed feet, finger talons, or even a sharp beak. She carried no weapons either. The ones that had been used in the war had all been created by the Kin, *mechanical* things mixed with organics. No one had ever even suggested growing a Veelu with internal weapons.

She had great defenses, as her skin was actually composed of small, living scales that naturally deflected most energy blasts.

Lulu had agreed to try the one thing that Darius had suggested. It may or may not work. Perhaps the Kin had tried it already and it had failed. Or perhaps it would damage the Kin much more than a human.

But in addition to growing the extra skin along her belly to protect herself after dislodging the crew cabin, Darius had suggested that she grow the apparatus she used to communicate with the other Veelu, and make it stronger as well.

He still wasn't sure of all the physics of how the Veelu

communicated with one another. Was it psionic? Since it happened simultaneously over unthinkable distances? He suspected it was.

By making her "speaking" organs stronger, Lulu could achieve quite a mind blast, now.

Lulu *screamed* at the older Veelu set on attacking her, the one who'd been prepared to fly directly into her and body check her.

Darius laughed in triumph when the older Veelu visibly flinched, then hesitated.

"I bet his head is ringing with that blast!" Darius said out loud, encouraging Lulu.

He heard her girlish giggle.

It cut off abruptly.

"There are more," she warned. "Coming up fast."

"You can outrun them," Darius told her, bolstering up her courage, despite the fact that they were now outnumbered six to one.

They had to win, or else they'd never escape.

<hr>

Darius realized that he *had* picked up a thing or two from working with Captain Alana all that time. Before they'd arrived at the space station, Lulu had arranged not one, but two other meeting points with Veelu who she felt certain would be sympathetic to her cause, who would join with her and send her into jump space, help her escape.

And while Lulu had been born in space like Darius, she'd always been the runt of her litter.

She had no idea how to use her much larger size to intimidate the others. All she knew was running away.

"Turn!" Darius yelled, feeling Lulu rotating slowly to face the fastest of her pursuers.

He was also used to *Orion*, which was a much smaller ship, and much more maneuverable.

After this battle, Darius and Lulu were going to do a lot of space flying together, learning the exact limits of her abilities, how they could meld their styles together.

In the meanwhile, they just had to escape the three determined Veelu who still pursued them, having already out-flown the others.

The problem was that the other ships didn't attack one at a time. They came at the poor young Veelu as a pack, harrying her on all sides.

The good news was that Lulu was much faster than any of the older Veelu coming after them. She was younger, at full capacity.

However, they'd agreed that they couldn't keep running. Lulu needed to turn and face her attackers, see if she could at least knock one or more of them from her path.

The three following split up, intent on attacking her from the sides as well as from the front simultaneously.

"You need to throw them off balance," Darius declared. He was used to being able to fly in any direction, turning quickly or pinging around like a ball being shaken by a hyper-active two year old. "How about this?"

He imagined Lulu turning on her wings, as if doing a cartwheel.

The other ships would never perform such a maneuver. They were used to crews who wouldn't be able to handle being shaken up that way.

Darius felt Lulu's grim satisfaction as she gracefully began to roll.

The other ships paused, unused to such maneuvers.

What they didn't understand was how close the roll would bring her to them.

The old female approaching Lulu's left wing was suddenly in range. Lulu let out her blasting howl again, rattling the older ship's head.

Then Lulu swung around, somersaulting, coming face to face with the older of the two males. Lulu shrieked again, then, while he was dazed, bashed his head with her wing.

The female attacked, but her wing missed Lulu's belly. Lulu reared up, abruptly rising, then falling, hard. The head of the female landed square against Lulu's chest.

While the female was dazed, Lulu screamed again, practically in the other Veelu's ear.

Abruptly, the female ship dropped down, out of the plane of flight. Only then did Darius realize that the male they'd attacked had done the same.

Then they both turned, slowly, showing their bellies.

Lulu had assured Darius that they weren't just resting: this was how a Veelu indicated that they were giving up.

That left one last pursuer: Leethan.

Lulu felt great antipathy toward the graying ship. He had been Kiki's first ship. He was a grizzled war veteran, who still had much affection for his old captain.

Darius wondered if he was partially deaf, given how Lulu's sonic cries didn't shake him up as much as it did the others.

"Can you grab him with your tail?" Darius asked as they faced off with the huge ship.

"No," Lulu said.

Darius got the impression that while she might enjoy having a prehensile tail, she couldn't control it like a monkey could. None of the Veelu could.

They feinted at each other, trying to strike one another

with their wings. While Leethan had a greater reach, Lulu was still faster.

"Can you smack him in the chest?" Darius asked. He gave her the images of bashing her chest against his.

It wasn't typically how the Veelu fought one another.

Darius hoped the element of surprise would work in their favor.

Lulu arched her back, then rammed herself forward, moving faster than the old ship.

Darius lurched under the impact, glad again for the straps that tied him to the wall.

The older ship seemed shaken at that.

Lulu rose up abruptly, jumping faster than the old ship. He tried to match her, but Darius had given her full control of all her flying capabilities.

Leethan may still have "brakes" that the Kin had set. Or he could just be old.

Lulu didn't have to gain much height on the older Veelu. Just enough so that she could swing forward and come down abruptly on his head, as she had with the last female.

Finally, Darius thought he saw the old veteran shaken.

For the first time, Darius heard Leethan trying to communicate with Lulu. "Why are you doing this?" he asked.

Maybe he had asked before, and Lulu hadn't thought to include Darius in on the conversation.

"Tell him the truth," Darius warned before Lulu could reply.

"Kiki loved you more," Lulu said.

The words hurt, Darius could tell. He soothed the ship as best he could, pushing love and warmth toward her.

"I don't understand," Leethan said. He was still trying to close on Lulu, but she wouldn't let him, easily skitting back and away.

"What don't you understand? Why you stayed in her heart?" Darius said the words for Lulu.

"How can you travel alone?" Leethan asked. He sounded forlorn. Though he'd been the one who'd insisted on no more crews, he was obviously still lonely.

Lulu hadn't mentioned Darius to anyone. None of the other ships had been able to spend enough time studying her to recognize the alien mechanical ship hanging off her side.

"I'm not alone," Lulu said.

The warmth that Darius felt coming from Lulu, the love meant for him and him alone, made him blush.

"A human?" Leethan said, scandalized.

"A true partner," Darius counted.

That gave the older ship pause.

"You will leave Kin space, never to return?" Leethan challenged abruptly.

"I will," Lulu promised.

Darius didn't want to make such a promise, though he understood that he must.

He was stealing one of their ships.

Did that make him as much of a pirate as Captain Alana? And not a hero? Possibly to some.

"We won't be back," Darius finally said.

"Then go, child," Leethan said as he floated down, beneath their plane. "And bring peace with you."

Darius wasn't sure exactly what the old ship had meant about that.

But they had his blessing to leave. He'd no longer fight them. Possibly, none of the others would either.

It meant they could make their getaway. Meet up with a couple of sympathetic Veelu who would join together with Lulu, give her enough mass to enter jump space.

Lulu and Darius would arrive in human space close to Darius's old home world, *New Athens*.

What would happen then, Darius didn't know. He wouldn't go back to his old claim, that was for certain.

He and Lulu would have to find some other way to support themselves, though they would have a lot fewer needs than most ships, as Lulu ran on solar power.

Maybe they'd fly private trips for the rich and famous. Maybe they'd end up a plain carrier.

And somehow, Darius would get his revenge on Captain Alana.

Lulu had promised him that.

HOMECOMING

HOMECOMING

Darius gave a great *whoop* as he and the great space flier Lulu hopped out of jump space and back into regular space. Then he stretched his jaw wide a couple of times, trying to pop his ears.

People reacted differently to jump space. Though Darius had never been submerged in a pool or lake, having been born and raised in space, he believed that for him, the experience of jump space was similar to being underwater: all his movements slowed and became languid, sounds grew muffled, and pressure built up in his sinuses.

"Are we there yet?" Darius teased as he unstrapped himself. While Darius might have been more comfortable sitting in a chair, he knew it made Lulu feel better when he sat on the floor and had his back pressed up against one of her walls so they were in close contact. The straps he used were grown by Lulu specifically for the purpose of keeping him safe in case the ship had difficulties.

Darius lived in the compartment that Lulu had originally built for him when he'd first encountered the Veelu ship and her crew of Kinethka. Since Darius and Lulu had escaped the

Kin the month before, Lulu hadn't added space to Darius's quarters: they were still roughly twelve by twelve, with eighteen foot ceilings. A long table that served as Darius's bed lay against the wall.

Lulu had grown Darius a short, square table, as well as a cube he could sit on, where he took his meals. Communication filaments hung from the ceiling every couple of feet or so, so Darius could easily reach up and directly communicate with Lulu. The rest of the time, they spoke out loud, either in Veelu, English, or Greek.

While Darius had tried personalizing his quarters, getting Lulu to tint the pink skin walls with its barely discernible veins in different colors, they'd finally agreed that her natural coloring suited them both the best.

The bond between Lulu and Darius had grown stronger during the past six weeks since they'd first started the *pikali*—the sharing of senses between a Veelu flier and his or her captain.

When Darius was pressed against one of Lulu's walls, he could detect her heartbeat if he listened closely, feel the slow pulse pressing against his skin. Even when they weren't in close contact, he frequently sensed her mood now. They still needed one of the communication filaments when they wanted to share a sensation, such as the tickling feeling of the solar winds, or to directly communicate an emotion, some shade of extra meaning.

Maybe some year they'd be able to share such things without the filaments. Lulu had told him that the Kin and the Veelu could do such things. As Darius was human, neither of them knew exactly where the limits of their partnership lay.

As Darius stood and stretched out his back, Lulu painted a map on the wall across from him, rendered from the stars just outside of the ship. They'd worked together to learn each other's iconography so she could display maps that they both could understand.

Then Lulu superimposed one of the star maps Darius had shared with her, from his original, fully mechanical ship, *Orion*.

Darius gave a low, long whistle. "Home sweet home," he said after comparing the two maps. Out of habit, he kissed two fingers and pressed them against the Jason of the Argonauts medal that Lulu had grown for him on the wall, just above where he regularly strapped himself in.

"Or, as Dad used to say, sector sweet sector." Darius missed the ability to display the maps in three dimensions, as he was used to seeing them, as well as being able to spin them around, but Lulu hadn't figure out how to do that yet.

Darius wasn't about to suggest that they integrate something *mechanical* into Lulu's systems. Both the Veelu and the Kin had an aversion to anything that wasn't naturally grown.

It had taken Darius and Lulu of them a couple of trial jumps with the other Veelu to figure out exactly how to get Darius and the renegade Lulu back into human space, in particular, the systems that held the *Greek Union of Planets*.

The planet *New Athens* hung in the middle of this sector. Though from this far outside the system, Darius couldn't see it, but he could still place it, and imagined it as a brilliant blue ball around which the rest of the nearby galaxies orbited.

"I wish I could have met him. Your dad," Lulu said softly.

"I do, too," Darius said. He hadn't realized how melancholy he felt until Lulu mentioned it. He was getting used to her knowing his feelings before he did.

One of the greatest regrets of Darius's life was that his dad had died while doing an EVA of *Orion*. The old ship's warning systems had shorted out when they'd been most needed, when his dad had had an emergency.

Darius tried not to dwell on what his dad would have thought of his relationship with Lulu. Not only was she was an alien, she was a huge, manta-ray shaped, sentient spaceship. Since the *pikali*, they were tied together more closely than husband and wife. While Darius might be able to continue without Lulu, he knew the ship would kill herself if anything happened to him, rather than go on living alone.

Darius knew he couldn't hide his sadness. Hopefully, Lulu would think that the emotion came from him still missing his dad, and not their current relationship.

"We should go to *New Athens*, first," Darius told Lulu. He pressed his finger against Lulu's warm pink wall, approximately in the location where they needed to go.

This turned out to be one of the advantages of the maps painted against Lulu's skin. It was easy for them to communicate to each other where they were going.

Lulu blew up the image, magnifying it so that Darius could better pinpoint the planet. He'd spent his entire life mining a single degree of arc of the asteroid belt in the *New Athens* system. It wasn't difficult for Darius to orient himself and find the world he was looking for.

"There," he said, tapping the wall again after double-checking his bearings. "There's an orbiting space station that you'll be able to dock at."

The Veelu had been bred for space flight. She would never be planet bound. Darius wasn't sure how she would take the separation if it ended up that he had to go down to the planet itself, to the Space Grant offices on Heklos, the capital.

His asteroid mining claim had been registered there,

though it had been almost two years now since Captain Alana had stolen his claim, his ship, and his life.

While his indenture-ship to Captain Alana might still be legally binding, he doubted that the officials on *New Athens* would care very much about that.

Because Darius had something much more important than a breach of contract to show the human governments.

Aliens existed. Aliens with sentient space fliers. Aliens with advanced technology, some of which was still attached to *Orion*'s hull.

Aliens who had regular contact with some sector of humanity.

Aliens who had been hidden from the rest of the worlds.

D arius hailed the space station Euthalia using the codes from *Orion*. He spoke in Greek, declaring himself as Darius Linard and announcing that the approaching vessels were *Lulu* and *Orion*.

He figured that the fact that he was able to send his communication from *much* further out than a normal ship would be to their benefit. They needed to get someone's attention during their slow approach so that the space station didn't freak out.

"No, no one will shoot at you," Darius assured Lulu again. He tried to send feelings of warmth and security, but he wasn't sure if he was successful—he was too excited about finally being back in his home system.

It would have taken too much effort reconfiguring and re-growing Darius's quarters for him to have windows to watch their approach. Those had been in the crew cabin that Lulu had ejected during their escape. Instead, Lulu projected what she saw on the wall in front of him.

Darius still wasn't used to seeing how the Veelu saw. The focus always seemed off to him. Then again, Lulu could see much further than a human, unaided. Like the Kin, the Veelu didn't have good near vision. In addition, what Lulu saw had a 3-D quality to it that made Darius dizzy if he wasn't careful.

The station Euthalia came steadily closer. It didn't take much effort to see the blooming flower it had been named after. The top of the station had multiple landing ports arranged around the center hub like a daisy with two rows of petals shooting out from the yellow disc, overlapped and staggered. Four "stems" grew down from the top, each with singular "leaves" jutting out here and there, built for corporate and private ships to dock.

"I'll run if someone does shoot," Lulu warned, as she had before.

"Which is why I'm strapped to a wall," Darius countered, trying to give his ship the support she needed.

Lulu's skin had natural defenses and was tough enough to shrug off most laser attacks, at least from the weapons of the Kin.

Darius wasn't about to give the humans a chance to experiment on her and build a weapon that would get through.

Finally, a voice came crackling through Lulu's sound system. "Ships *Orion* and *Lulu*, this is Melitta on the space station Euthalia. What the hell are you flying, Darius Linard?"

Darius grinned. "This is the all organic ship *Lulu*, one of the Veelu," Darius replied. "*Orion* is attached to her."

"The what?" Melitta came back. "You're just on the edge of our sensors now. Organic, you say?"

"Yes," Darius said. He hoped that Lulu could feel his delight.

Showing all the worlds how badly they'd been lied to made him grin. This was important news that should be shared.

"Hold where you are," Melitta warned after a few moments. "I need to contact my boss."

Lulu decreased her acceleration and came to a halt more slowly than a mechanical ship. She could have stopped sooner, but Darius had wanted to hide her abilities. The humans needed to underestimate them if everything did go sideways.

He really had learned how to be sneaky while working as a pilot for Captain Alana.

Just as they'd agreed not to mention that Lulu was sentient, at least not right away. Better for the humans to think that Darius piloted the ship, not that she drove herself.

"Can they shoot us from here?" Lulu asked.

"First of all, no one's going to shoot at you," Darius said. "Second, the space station only has the ability to shoot oncoming debris out of the way. It isn't a military installation with tons of guns."

"How do they defend themselves?" Lulu said.

Darius was puzzled by the question. The Veelu had no natural guns or offensive weaponry. During the civil war, the Kin had integrated mechanical and organic weapons onto the space fliers, removing them once the war was over.

Why would Lulu care about the defense of a space station?

"The assumption is that if someone attacked Euthalia, they wouldn't want to destroy the station, but to take it over," Darius said. "All the petals around the center disc will automatically disconnect during an attack. No one would be able to land or leave. Not without blowing a huge hole in the station. And there are systems to block access, isolate each arc of the station from the others."

"And the stems off the bottom?" Lulu said.

"Can easily be isolated as well," Darius said. "Why this interest?"

Before Lulu could reply, Melitta came back online. "Representatives from the Allied Worlds are enroute to the station. They ask that you hold your current location until they can continue communications."

"How long will that take?" Darius asked, anticipating Lulu's question.

"Twelve hours, *New Athens* time," Melitta said. "Do you need supplies?"

"We can hold for a while," Darius said. Though he had food—Lulu was originally outfitted to carry a crew of forty for a month's time, and he still had some rations left aboard *Orion*—he couldn't eat all of what the Kin digested, and he was getting sick of the lack of variety.

Besides, he wasn't really sure how he'd pay for any supplies. He didn't have money in any of the accounts that he had access to. When he'd been on *Orion*, he'd been barely getting by.

The money he did have was in accounts held by Captain Alana's purser, and was supposed to be used to pay off his indenture.

"Let us know if you need anything," Melitta said. "Good luck. Gods' blessings walking on foreign fields."

Darius blinked, surprised at Melitta's response. He unstrapped himself from Lulu's wall, thinking.

The blessing she'd said was generally given when sending off soldiers for war.

Was the saying just tradition with the station? Or was it a warning?

Darius slept well while he waited. It was a habit he'd developed early on, then refined when he'd become a pilot for Captain Alana. You couldn't always time docking with a station or meeting a connection with your own personal sleep schedule. In addition, the clock you ran on may or may not have aligned with the clock of the system you just few into.

Darius had learned to just lay down and sleep at the drop of a ship, no matter whether he was fully rested or not.

He awoke with the gentle alarm that Lulu had set for him. The first time she'd set an alarm for him he'd nearly jumped out of skin at the cacophony of noise.

Since both the Kin and the Veelu had originated as birds, they found the sound of morning birdsong sound restful. Or enlivening. Or something.

As Darius had been raised on a ship and not on a planet, he'd never experienced live birdsong before. He had Lulu play it again for him later, after he'd woken up and was at least vaguely coherent. He'd judged it as pretty in the end, in part knowing that was what Lulu wanted to hear.

But he needed mechanical sounds, bells and chimes, to wake him up.

"Have they hailed us yet?" Darius asked as he blearily left his cabin and made his way down to the galley where he cooked his food, something that both the Kin and the Veelu had found unusual, as they required fresh, un-charred meat for their meals.

"No," Lulu said. "I've been listening to what station chatter I can. Mainly it's ships coming and going. The station is warning people away from this sector."

Darius grinned. "Yup. Quarantining us until they figure out what the hell to do with us."

The galley had been originally configured for the Kin,

who were a least a foot shorter than Darius's six foot plus height. Lulu had stretched first stretched the ceiling up so that Darius didn't have to spend all his time hunched over.

Lulu kept the original configuration of the galley, basically just a corridor about six feet long, just off the main hallway, with shelves rising from floor to ceiling on both sides of the four foot wide space.

The upper shelves on the right side of the galley held whitish containers for the various types of food that the Kin ate: raw meat for their food stomach; smaller containers of grains, nuts, and pebbles that their second stomach needed for digestion; as well as foot-long canes of different grasses that tasted sweet to Darius, that the Kin used as dessert.

The upper shelves on the left side of the galley held dishes, glasses, and eating utensils that Darius really didn't need. Some of the items had a similar enough chemical composition that Lulu could reabsorb them. She didn't really need to eat, not like he did—she was completely solar powered, as far as he could tell.

Lulu had made the shelves on the right side at bellybutton level jut out, then added two burners that worked through a focused chemical reaction. She had been equal parts fascinated and repulsed by the idea of flame inside her.

Darius pulled a thick, red hose from where it had been tucked against the wall and squeezed the end so water flowed out into his cup. He set that on one of the burners while he went rummaging for food in the containers.

Lulu had explained how she brought foot out of storage for Darius. She'd even shared the entire process with him through the filaments. However, it was still too strange for him to fully understand the entire chemical processes: first, she initiated a process to dissolve the storage container, used a second to portion off just some of the meat, then yet another to "melt" the floor of the storage room above the galley so the food landed in the appropriate container.

What had she gotten for him that morning? Seemed to be a meat stew. The Kin ate a lot of meat, along with vegetables that, for the most part, he couldn't digest.

However, the Kin knew nothing of bread or baking. He'd eaten some of his last crackers while sharing the experience with Lulu, who marveled at the taste and crunch, but who had no way of replicating it.

Darius poured the stew into a pan and set it on the second burner. The cup of water was hot enough for him to make tea. At least that was something that the races had shared, despite their distaste for heating their food. Concoctions of herbs appeared to be universal between them.

Their tastes varied widely, but Darius had finally found some that was good enough, reminding him of the few times he'd been on a planet, smelling freshly mowed grass, though the tea had a sweeter, heavier taste.

Breakfast heated and tea made, Darius walked back to his quarters. He sat down on his cube, warming his hands once again with his tea before setting it down and starting his breakfast.

Lulu had learned his moods, and knew better than to interrupt during this quiet time. Darius was the one to break the silence that morning.

"I know we've talked before about what we're going to do for money," Darius said. He couldn't help but think about it every time he ate. "Have you given any more thought to what you'd like to do?"

"Transport," Lulu said firmly. "I know we could make more being a tourist destination or selling rides inside an alien ship. But I don't want a bunch of strangers going up and down my halls, their grubby fingers rubbing up against my walls."

Darius nodded. He'd suspected that was what Lulu would eventually decide. While he had a say in her decision, he was also very clear that it was *her* decision. She would be taking on the passengers, allowing them to board her. And while she'd been bred for that initially, he suspected that she preferred having the attention of a single crew member instead.

He suspected they'd be safer as a tourist attraction. Much more difficult to make disappear if everyone knew about you.

Still, they'd get by. He had smuggling contacts now, and a much better idea of how to look for jobs, thanks to his time with Captain Alana.

Darius and Lulu spent some time talking about the various types of cargo that Lulu would be able to carry. If they decided to pursue the exotic chemical market, Lulu felt certain that she could grow the necessary specialized, non-reactive compartments.

If they decided to stick with more mundane transport, there was always a need for moving large amounts of mechanical hardware either in system or between systems. While Lulu by herself wasn't large enough to reach jump space, she could still reach near light-speed speeds in system.

They'd also talked about what they'd need to do for her to gain the mass and muscles necessary for jump space.

Darius had a better feeling for why a ship needed to have a certain amount of *weight* in order to achieve jump space (which had never made sense to him, because ships were weightless in space, right?)

But jump space was *below* regular space, at least how the Veelu saw it. They had to drop down out of regular space, not hop up to jump space. And that evidently required some type of weight.

Darius had been amazed at Lulu's experience of diving into jump space when she'd shared that with him. She couldn't communicate all of it—Darius was a human. Lulu didn't know if the Kin would have a better sense of it. She suspected they would.

However, Darius still made a good flying companion for Lulu, as he'd been born on a ship and flown for most of his life. He understood moving in three dimension as the planet-bound Kin didn't.

As Darius was finishing his second cup of tea, Lulu interrupted his contemplation.

"They're hailing us again."

"**D**ude!" came the friendly voice over Lulu's speakers. "My name's Norm. I'm one of the local representatives of the Allied Worlds. How you doing?"

Norm spoke with an easy, clear English. Darius didn't think that Lulu would have any trouble following it, though the pair of them tried to share all three languages equally—Veelu, English, and Greek.

"I'm doing well," Darius said. He was a bit puzzled at Norm's friendly, overly casual tone. He'd been expecting a fussy bureaucrat—not a guy who sounded almost the same age as Darius, who had spent a lot of time in the lower levels of the space station where most pleasures were available for a price.

Darius could almost see the other guy—he'd have a dark complexion, like most of the Greeks in the union, with dark, maybe hazel eyes, a generous nose, and a broad mouth. His hair would be long but curly. He'd wear a T-shirt with some saying on it and jeans, maybe barefoot.

Though Darius would have preferred to be standing and pacing while talking to the Allied World representative, he stayed seated and pressed up against one of Lulu's walls. He had a communication filament wrapped around his wrist so that Lulu could at least follow his emotional journey.

While it was possible for Lulu to put a visual sensor in Darius's cabin, it didn't make any sense. Lulu couldn't read Darius's facial expressions. While the Veelu had more of a "face" than the Kin, as their beak was smaller, as a space flier, the Veelu hadn't been bred to read posture and expression.

The "speaker" Lulu had grown was merely a dark spot on the wall just above Darius's head.

They were still hiding her existence, their "ace in the hole" if everything went wrong.

"How are you doing?" Darius asked Norm after the silence dragged on, trying to be polite.

"Doing good, man, doing good. Bit of a surprise when you just showed up, though," Norm said.

Darius grinned but still asked, "Why do you say that?" He wasn't sure what Norm and the rest of the station knew about him.

"Your claim went dark, what, eighteen months ago? It was rapidly picked up by Tulip Enterprises."

Darius nodded. He knew that Captain Alana had several businesses that covered for each other, hiding her illegal activities by moving them rapidly from one shell to the next.

"Nobody heard from you after that. Your status is 'presumed dead, body missing'," Norm continued.

"Not so dead yet," Darius said. Of course, whoever took over his claim would profess complete ignorance as to his location as well as disposition.

"What happened?" Norm asked, casually.

"It's a long story," Darius warned.

"I got time," Norm said.

Darius grinned. He could just imagine how Norm would be annoying whose ever office he'd borrowed, now leaning back in his chair with his still potentially bare feet up on the borrowed desk.

"I'll take it from the very beginning, then. First, a claim jumper stole my claim," Darius said. He was still angry about that.

"Dude!" Norm exclaimed. "Are you saying that Tulip Enterprises illegally moved into your territory?"

"Yes," Darius said. Satisfaction swept over him. Finally! He was going to get revenge on Captain Alana!

"But, how could they do that?" Norm asked. He sounded completely perplexed. "Your claim markers went completely dark for over seventy-two hours. At least that's what it shows in the records."

Darius sighed. "I know my claim markers went black." He'd been in a panic at the time. The officials only gave twenty-four hours for a claim to be dead before it would start showing up as "pending sale" on some boards.

"And it wasn't like, you know, just one or two went off line. The entire set just went dark. Like you'd dead-switched them or something."

Some of the older asteroid miners had their claims tied just to their name. They "dead-switched" their claims, so that when the miner was found dead, the claim automatically became inactive. This was so that an "heir" wouldn't get too eager for the older miner to pass away. Once a claim went inactive, anyone could scoop it up.

"I know, I know. I know that all my claim markers went dark at the same time," Darius said, sighing. Maybe he wasn't going to get to his revenge right away. "Captain Alana of the Pineapple Express Transport Company jimmied my markers."

"How could she do that?" Norm asked. The total confusion was back in his voice.

"She attached alien artifacts—devil's tails—onto each

claim marker. They blocked the entire network when she turned them on," Darius explained.

Norm gave a long, low whistle. "Sounds like a lot of work," he said. "Attaching, what did you say? Devil's tails? To every single marker? Just to steal it? Why didn't she make you an offer? Buy it off you?"

"That isn't how she does things," Darius said darkly. While Captain Alana had his reluctant admiration, he also suspected that she didn't negotiate when she didn't have to —she just took when she thought she could get away with it.

"But that isn't important," Darius continued before Norm could go on. "I have proof of the alien artifacts, the devil's tails."

"Really?" Norm asked, sounding very surprised.

"She attached them to my ship. *Orion*," Darius said.

"Yeah, dude, that's where we're having a problem. I hope you can help me out, here," Norm confided.

"Sure," Darius said, starting to feel confused himself.

"Seems as though *Orion* is a registered ship of the Pineapple Express Transport company," Norm said.

"And?" Darius asked, a hole starting to form in the pit of his stomach.

"And Captain Alana is claiming you stole *Orion* from her," Norm said.

"She stole it from me first!" Darius exclaimed. How could he get the "dude" on the other end of the line to understand the importance of what he was bringing to the Allied Worlds?

"She does have a contract," Norm admitted. "Shows that you agreed to work for her and pay off your debt to her. And that in exchange for all the repairs and upgrades she's made on *Orion*, you're working for her."

"But the only way she got me to sign that contract in the

first place was by stealing my claim!" Darius said. "My ship! My life! I have proof!"

"Those are serious accusations, man," Norm said. "Heavy. What do you have for proof? Did you record her as she took your claim? Do you have one of the claim markers with that, what did you call it, *devil's tail* still attached?"

Darius went silent. He didn't, actually have any proof that Captain Alana had stolen his claim. All he had were the devil's tails, as well as the ship he sat in.

"I have devil's tails attached to the hull of *Orion*," Darius said, trying to get the man to see. "They're of alien manufacture. *Alien*."

"So you have no proof?" Norm asked.

"I'm flying an alien ship!" Darius said, upset. "Why aren't you paying more attention to that?"

"Dude, sure, that ship's as fly as anything I've ever seen," Norm said. "But alien? Naw."

Darius sat, frozen in shock. "What do you mean?"

"It *can't* be alien. There aren't any aliens," Norm said. "Otherwise, we would have met with them. Ages ago."

"But we did meet with them. We have been," Darius said. "Look, I have the 'culture' file that they sent me. The aliens are in regular contact with humans."

"Like who?" Norm asked.

"Hell if I know," Darius said. He didn't know how to convince Norm that what he said was true. The representative from the Allied Worlds kept getting tied up in details that weren't important.

"But I can send you a copy of the file," Darius added. "Show you pictures of them."

"Do you have any aliens with you?" Norm asked. "One of these mysterious beings?"

Darius sat in silence for a moment. They hadn't wanted to reveal Lulu's existence. Not yet.

But he may not have any choice.

"Tell them," Lulu said quietly.

"Are you sure?" Darius asked. He knew that Lulu was still worried that the humans would shoot her if they knew she was a living ship.

"He doesn't seem inclined to believe you, otherwise," Lulu said dryly. "Are all humans this stubborn?"

"Yeah," Darius said, smiling for what felt like the first time in a while. "Particularly the Greeks."

He heard Norm talking in the background, asking if Darius was still there.

Warmth and affection flowed through the communication filament wrapped around Darius's wrist.

"It will be okay," Darius whispered.

He wasn't sure how he could promise that, but there was nothing else he could say.

"What do you mean that the organic balloon attached to *Orion* is actually a ship itself? Called *Lulu*?" Norm asked.

Darius sighed. This was starting to remind him of the arguments he'd had with his dad, two stubborn Greek men unwilling to bend, both certain they were right. He was finally pacing, though not in too large of a circle, as he still had the communication filament wrapped around his wrist.

"It's not a balloon!" Darius said. "She can fly on her own."

"Wow," Norm asked. "You must have some really amazing computer systems if you can do that."

"You could come over and see for yourself," Darius suggested. He did *not* want to bring the station officials onboard Lulu.

They might not have any choice.

Why wouldn't Norm just believe the evidence of his sensors?

"Tell you what," Norm said. "Why don't you bring *Orion* over here? Let us examine those 'devil tails' of yours. This ship, Lulu, right? She'll be okay on her own."

"Don't go," Lulu said immediately.

Darius knew that Lulu was speaking to just him—that Norm couldn't hear her. Norm hadn't asked to be introduced to her, claiming that she was just a smart computer system.

"We've talked about this," Darius said. "You know that I'm going to have to leave sometime."

It wasn't that he wanted to leave the ship. More than *Orion*, Lulu was home.

But sometimes even *Orion* hadn't been enough. As much as Darius liked being alone, he missed being with other people sometimes.

He'd never have a wife. Lulu took up too much space in his heart for that. He would like a crew sometimes, other people to talk with.

"I don't trust these people. I don't trust this Norm," Lulu said.

"Yeah, Norm, I'm still there," Darius said. *Just arguing with the wife.*

"You keep cutting out on me," Norm complained.

"I'm talking with Lulu," Darius said.

"Man, you must be lonely if you're talking to a ship's computer like she's a person," Norm said. "You really need some station time."

Darius sighed. While he might privately agree with Norm, it was for different reasons.

"Let's introduce you to Lulu," Darius replied.

He waited for a moment. No disagreement.

"Norm, I would like to introduce you to the Veeluthian

space flier, Lulu," Darius said. After another moment's silence, he added, "Say hello, Lulu."

"Hello," Lulu said. Then she added a phrase in the Veelu language, basically, "It's nice to meet you."

Norm paused on the other end, then gave a low whistle. "You came up with your own language and everything? Gotta hand it to you. That's one complete fantasy package."

Darius rolled his eyes. "If you're not going to treat her well, you're not going to get another chance to talk with her."

"What would I have to do to be able to prove my existence?" Lulu asked. Norm had never properly answered that question before.

There was a pause on the other end of the line.

"Tell you what," Norm finally said. "Darius, why don't you bring your fancy flier *Orion* into the station. We'll take a look at those devil's tails. If they prove to be organic, and of alien nature, then we'll talk more about how to get the right classification for Lulu. All right?"

"We're going to discuss it, and I'll get back to you," Darius replied.

He didn't want to go into the station alone. He knew Lulu didn't want him to go either.

But it was starting to appear as if they didn't have any choice.

<hr>

"You've got to give me a month," Darius said. "Please, Lulu. Give me some hope that if I get captured or something stupid that I'll at least have something to live for outside of prison."

"Why would they put you into prison?" Lulu asked.

"Because I broke my contract with Captain Alana," Darius tried to explain. Again.

They weren't using the communication filament at this point. There were too many emotions flowing back and forth, and it just ended up confusing both of them.

Instead, Darius paced in his quarters and talked with Lulu while Norm and the space station waited.

Lulu had already started the chemical process to dissolve the airlock that she'd built between herself and *Orion*. She'd strengthened the bridge between the two ships after they'd escaped the Kin. However, she'd never brought *Orion* all the way into her main cargo bay.

Darius knew that it was as much jealousy as that she didn't want to be carrying something so *mechanical*.

"It sounds like you had a horrible contract with Captain Alana," Lulu said.

"I did. However, it is *legal*. There isn't a court in all the worlds who would throw it out." Darius had asked around, discretely, and had never found a system that would have been happy to take on the captain's lawyers.

No matter that he'd been coerced into signing the contract at the time. He had no proof of that either.

"Will they acknowledge the existence of aliens once they see the devil's tails?" Lulu asked.

"They may. They may not," Darius admitted. "But once I'm on the station, I should be able to make some contacts. Get a job lined up."

"Won't this Captain Alana come after you?" Lulu asked.

"She will," Darius said grimly. "But not right away. I'm small fry. She has other fish in her kettle to skewer first. Once she gets around to me, we'll already have a good business going. I'll be able to buy out my debt."

"And if we don't?" Lulu asked.

Darius smiled and wished she could read his face. He reached up and snagged one of the communication filaments, pushing warmth and affection toward his ship.

It had surprised him, but it appeared that Lulu was turning into the more practical one of the pair of them.

"If we don't," Darius said slowly, "Then I sell *Orion*. She has been updated. She would fetch a pretty *drachma*."

"Are you sure?" Lulu asked.

"We'll still need to get something that can take me from wherever you're parked to a station, to meet with clients," Darius said.

"I could grow a flitter," Lulu offered.

"Really?" Darius said, surprised. "How?"

"I don't have the right chemicals on hand," Lulu admitted. "But it is possible. We would just have to find them."

"Let's think about it," Darius said. "And maybe that will be our solution, later. Right now, I need to get on *Orion* and to the space station. I will be back as soon as I can be. Hold tight. But you must give me at least a month before you disappear."

He didn't want to talk about her killing herself, though he was aware that she probably would.

"I won't disappear, Darius," Lulu said, disapprovingly. "I will commit *liapku*."

Darius had never heard that Veelu word before. "What is that?" he asked.

"It is the opposite of the *pikali*," Lulu explained. "When the partners separate."

"Oh," Darius said. "Is it permanent?"

"Only if I take the last step and fling myself into the sun," Lulu said. "Some Veelu do. Some do not. I won't know until I reach that time."

"Thank you for waiting for me," Darius said.

"You said one month, right?" Lulu asked.

A chill went through the line they shared. Something

about the ship's words, how she was feeling. It was as if Darius was already alone and they were already separated.

"At least one month," Darius insisted.

"You better get started then," Lulu said. "Because your time starts now."

Darius pulled himself into the old captain's chair of *Orion*. Out of habit, he kissed two fingers and reached up to touch the Jason medal embedded in the ceiling for luck.

Maybe he'd have to find a new medal while he was on the station. He already had a Jason medallion that he wore around his neck. Maybe he could get a second one that had a manta-ray on it. Something he could wear that would remind him of his partner.

The air in the ship smelled wrong. It had the right mix of oxygen and other chemicals. But it no longer had the right scent. Instead, it smelled stale. Darius had forgotten that Lulu had a warm, slightly floral scent to her. It wasn't a human scent.

He already missed it.

Though Darius loved the captain's chair on *Orion*, it didn't fit his back as well as the wall he leaned against when he was in his quarters in Lulu. They both molded directly to his shape, so they had the same support. Still, it wasn't as comfortable for some reason.

Darius started doing his pre-flight check, making sure that nothing in the old ship had broken while he'd been staying with Lulu. This was the first time that he'd bring the engines all the way up and fly her in more than six weeks.

"Am I clear yet?" Darius asked as he watched the engines warm up.

"You're clear," Lulu replied after a few more moments. "Just be careful out there."

"You too," Darius said.

He wasn't sure if that final moment of disconnect with Lulu was just his imagination or not—when the *pikali* that had held them together finally stretched too far, the distance too great, and it broke.

They were suddenly completely separate beings again.

Darius thought about it as he flew. The difference he felt now as compared to just a few moments before. When before there had always been a comforting background hum surrounding him, now there was true silence. Sure, *Orion* beeped and made her own noises, but Darius finally *felt* alone.

It was both frightening as well as a relief.

But which feeling was more prominent?

Darius easily nosed *Orion* down onto the landing pad for the Euthalia space station. He couldn't help but grin. He hadn't lost his touch as a pilot. If anything, his time with Lulu had given him more of a feel for flying.

And he'd already been a pretty damned good pilot to start with.

The "petal" of the station that Darius had landed on wasn't one of the parts of the station that he'd been to before. Then again, he'd never come in to meet with a representative of the Allied Worlds.

When it had just been his dad and him, or even just him, they'd been assigned to one of the upper petals used for merchants and cargo. Generally, those pads had seen better days. The landing pad usually appeared scorched, the rigs used for hauling cargo had been assembled out of mismatched parts and broke down regularly, and the airlocks had all been patched and dingy, making both Darius and his dad worry that they could blow at any time. Particularly given how they hissed as they cycled.

This time, Darius landed on a pristine section of metal. Instead of derelict rigs for cargo hulking on the edges of the landing petal, sleek needle fighters were arrayed in a row, lined up on *Orion*, ready to do damage. The airlock that Darius ventured into looked as if it was brand new, with shiny white walls and unscratched operational signs in both Greek and English.

Darius wore his lightweight work suit going into the station, not the heavy environmental suit that would completely protect him. The work suit was newer, courtesy of Captain Alana, and fit him nicely.

He wasn't planning on taking it off once he got into the station. He knew lots of miners did that. They never trusted any system and lived in their suits.

Three people waited for Darius on the other side of the airlock. He could see them in the small porthole as they all waited while the air and pressure in the lock cycled.

The man in the center looked like a stereotypical bureaucrat, the type Darius had seen in vids. He was short, round, and balding. He had the pale skin of an anglo, with washed out, blue eyes. The rumpled suit he wore looked cheap. And who wore a tie on a space station? He'd sure look silly if the gravity suddenly gave out.

Behind him stood two taller guards. Station personnel? No, that wasn't right. Something about their uniforms…

It took Darius until the end of the airlock cycle, the door unlocking with a loud *thunk*, before he realized that the other two were military guards from the Allied Worlds.

Did they think he was some kind of threat? That was

laughable. Darius had spent all his time in space. He didn't have the muscles or strong bones of someone who'd grown up in gravity. He might have a longer reach, but he had no strength.

"Darius Linard?" the bureaucrat asked.

"Yes," Darius said, nodding. He took his helmet off and tucked it under one arm.

The other man looked up at Darius expectantly.

"Are you…You're not Norm," Darius said, confused.

The bureaucrat gave Darius a huge smile. "Dude!" he said, nodding his head as if he'd smoked too much high quality relaxant.

Then he dropped the act. He straightened up, grew stiff and formal. "I am Norman Weller, Allied World representative, here to place you in protective custody."

***

Darius sat on an uncomfortable metal chair. The room was cold. They'd made him take off his work suit, so he shivered in his sleeveless shirt and lightweight pants. He kept just his bares toes on the floor, and regretted every time he put his whole foot down, the cold hard concrete never warming.

At least he was still on the space station. They hadn't taken him down to the planet. So the gravity wasn't weighing on him as much as his conscious.

A thin unbreakable wire connected the cuff Darius wore on his left hand to the metal table. Despite the searing bright lights overhead and the antiseptic smell of the air, the room felt dark and dingy. Maybe it was the matching gray of the walls, floor, and ceiling, or maybe it was the dark brown of the chairs and table.

Across from Darius sat an empty chair that looked as

uncomfortable as the one he sat in. Beyond that, a door. It rested flush against the wall, fitting so well Darius could barely see the seam. Though the wall behind him appeared to be solid, Darius suspected it was actually a window and that people were constantly watching him.

Plus the cameras. They were tiny, just spots on the ceiling, but Darius knew where to look, thanks to Captain Alana's training.

The Allied Worlds had held him in this room for about ninety minutes, letting him get colder and colder.

It was one of the changes inside himself that Darius had noticed, that he assumed had come as part of the *pikali*. He had a sense of time that he'd never had before. He didn't know if this awareness was a permanent change or if it was part of the countdown that Lulu had started when he'd stepped out of his quarters.

He'd know up to the minute how much time had passed, exactly when his month's time was up.

What was Darius going to do? How was he going to get out of here? He'd misjudged Norm badly. Then again, Norm had deliberately misled Darius.

It reminded Darius of an old joke, how if you were communicating long distance, no one would know it was your dog flying the spaceship.

Was Norm a spy for the Allied Worlds? It kind of made sense. No one would look at Norm and think, "Ah. Here's a criminal mastermind!"

Darius had tried to warn Norm of the dangers of the devil's tails, how they'd been programmed to self-destruct. He'd just mocked Darius, "So you want us to study them, but now you're saying they may destroy us? Dude. What kind of con are you running?"

The door finally opened. Norm came walking in.

Or maybe Darius should think of him as Norman, seeing

him in person. "Norm" was merely a character that bureaucrat/spy Norman Weller played.

Norman held two steaming cups of something that he placed on the table, shoving one toward Darius as he sat down in the other chair.

Darius quickly cupped his hands around the warmth. He didn't care what was in it. All he cared about was the heat.

"Why am I here?" Darius asked he felt normal circulation return to his fingers and heat to his fingertips.

Norman continued to sit and silently sip his drink, studying Darius.

"You said you were putting me into protective custody. Why? Who are you protecting me from? Why are you holding me?" The questions kept spilling out of Darius. "Why were you pretending to be 'Norm'? Who are you? Why won't you believe me?"

Norm nodded to himself, as if coming to some sort of decision.

"You present a difficult case, Darius," Norman admitted slowly. "As well as an opportunity."

Great. Now someone else was planning on using him, like Captain Alana had.

Darius couldn't wait until he had enough evidence that Norman was actually a bigger asshole than the captain.

"Did you examine my ship?" Darius asked. "The *Orion?*" he felt the need to clarify, because he knew that no one was getting close to Lulu, not without his say-so. And even then, he'd have to do a lot of persuading before his girl would let just anyone near her.

The ships of the Allied Worlds could hound her through the system. She had no defensive weapons. No place to hide. No friendly Veelu to help her achieve jump space.

Norman grimaced. "My experts have started their examination. I do need to thank you for bringing your ship in, by the way. We've never been able to study the devil's tails before."

"You knew about them already?" Darius asked, surprised. "Why didn't you say that in the first place?"

Norman sighed. "I'm going to try to explain our position to you. I'd really prefer to not have to kill you, though that may end up being my only choice. You're young. Maybe you can learn."

Darius nodded grimly. It sounded awfully familiar, like what Captain Alana had once said to him. Plus, once Darius had realized that "Norm" was actually Norman, he knew that was probably his only choice.

But why? Darius didn't understand at all.

"We did know about the devil's tails," Norman said. "Smugglers and other miscreants use them to escape the Allied World's guards. However, as you warned, they have to be approached carefully, or they'll self-destruct."

Darius wasn't sure if he felt better or worse that his warnings had been heeded. He didn't want someone to die unnecessarily, however, maybe it was better that the Allied Worlds didn't understand them.

"So you already know about the aliens," Darius said. Bitterness flooded his mouth. He brought the cup up and took a small sip of what smelled like chicken broth. The salt and the liquid tasted marvelous. It made him realize just how much he'd missed human food.

Norman shrugged. "If you insist on going around and telling people that you've met aliens, they're going to lock you up. Declare that you're having delusions, right? It's why you're in protective custody. To save you from you from yourself. You've got quite an imagination there."

Despite the warm cup between his hands, Darius felt cold spike through him.

Was this why the aliens weren't known? Because anyone

who tried to report on them were declared insane and disappeared?

Darius had been taught by his dad to always speak boldly. To tell the truth.

Captain Alana had taught Darius subtlety.

Darius searched for the right words, speaking slowly. "What if I wanted to talk to you about maybe a *shared* delusion?"

Norman shook his head. "I don't have any delusions, buddy."

"Then maybe I could ask about the delusions you've heard other people talk about?" Darius pressed on.

Norman considered for a moment. "Go on," he eventually said.

"So, suppose there's this delusion that some people have about aliens existing. These bird-like races," Darius said.

"I may have heard something about that," Norman said slowly, not giving anything away.

"And maybe some people think they've had contact with these aliens. And have received some sort of tech from them, building it into their ships. Of course, it isn't real," Darius said before Norman could object. "It's something that some human race came up with. Maybe the Xu Lien have better organics than we realized."

Norman smiled at Darius. "Exactly! Now you're getting it!"

"So the aliens are just a figment of some people's overly active imaginations," Darius concluded. "But why?"

"Who knows why some people go crazy?" Norman said, spreading his hands wide. "None of them persist in their delusions, though. Not when faced with the truth."

The words, though spoken lightly, had ominous undertones to them.

"And what is the truth? Exactly?" Darius asked. He didn't want to hear it. He knew that already.

But he had to know.

Norman sighed, sounding like a put-on teenager. "The Allied Worlds have worked long and hard to bring all of humanity together."

"But don't you think that if aliens existed, they might bring all of humanity together further? Like, if they were perceived of as a threat to humanity?"

Norman gave Darius a sad smile. "That might be the truth. And maybe people have thought about that before. But only if the aliens would play along. Only if they were a war-mongering tribe set on conquest."

Darius thought for a moment about what he knew of the Kin and the Veelu. On the one hand, they were warriors and would fight if necessary. However, they weren't conquerors. In fact, based on his conversations with Lulu, they were right now just figuring out how to recover from the civil war they'd just had, mend the cracks in their own society and heal their wounds. They weren't expanding at this time.

In addition, the Kin and the Veelu were much more likely to seek a peaceful co-existence with any outsiders they ran across. Their two races lived in harmony with each other. Their first assumption would be that they could do the same with any aliens.

"So, because these supposed aliens won't cooperate and try to kill us all, they have to stay hidden? But why?" Darius asked. He just didn't understand. The races could learn so much from each other!

"The Allied Worlds takes pride in being a melting pot," Norman said.

Darius nodded. He'd heard the propaganda before, how the Greek people could still maintain their own identity while being part of the bigger whole.

Some of the races and planets hadn't been as lucky, though, when they'd lost the war. Their ideologies weren't compatible with the Allied Worlds, and they were being forcibly subsumed. Religions were banned, as were native languages.

"How can you melt down an alien?" Norman asked.

The entire world shifted under Darius's cold bare feet. It felt as though the space station had taken a direct, physical hit.

However, nothing had happened outside of Darius. The shock running through him was just that strong.

"The Allied Worlds can't allow the existence of aliens," Darius said slowly. "Or you'd have too many rebels, seeking to break off and live their own lives, away from the core worlds."

"Dude! You got it!" Norman said, using the "Norm" voice.

Then the bureaucrat returned. "However, that doesn't answer what I'm going to do with you."

<hr />

Darius sat alone in a locked cell. It didn't look like a cell from the old vids, with bars and such.

It more resembled a padded room, where the criminally insane were kept.

Darius wasn't sure that was an improvement.

The walls weren't padded. They were white, and made of a hard impervious plastic. Darius would bet it would take nothing short of a laser to carve his name in them.

The square room was about the right size for a cell, three paces long and two paces wide. A padded table was shoved up against the far wall. He supposed it was a bed, given that a raised area—probably meant to be a pillow—was built into the far end of it. No sheets, of course.

The toilet and sink were hidden behind steel panels at the foot of the bed. They would jut out of the wall if he waved his hand in front of the sensor. Maybe buttons were too much of a risk?

Opposite the toilet was the only way in or out of the cell. Like the interrogation room, the door was flush with the wall, and the seam blended in, making it difficult for Darius to find.

He could easily imagine going crazy in here, that after a while the room would shrink down to become his whole universe.

The ceiling was at least twelve feet high. Even leaping from the bed, Darius wouldn't have been to reach it. Bright lights, covered in wire mesh, shown down on him.

Would his jailers turn the lights off later, during what was considered night on the station? Or was he expected to sleep with it so bright?

Darius had seen a vid where they tortured prisoners in such a room by always keeping the lights on, then by blasting loud music at random times, depriving the prisoners of sleep.

Was this his final resting place? He'd been away from Lulu for most of a day, now. The thought depressed him. At least if they decided to space him, his last vision would be of the stars.

He missed the stars. One of the first things he'd ask Lulu to do when he returned would be to build him some windows so he could see the stars with his own eyes again.

And he missed Lulu, the smells and sounds of her all around him. He missed talking in Greek to her, teaching her about humans, learning about the Veelu.

Though he wouldn't lie to himself—part of him was relieved to be alone.

He still missed her.

When he got back (and he kept telling himself it was a *when* not an *if*) they would have to work out some arrangement where he got to spend time with her as well as some time apart.

Did the Kin need that as well? Or was this because Darius was human?

And what was he going to tell Norman the next time he saw him? Norman hadn't spelled out Darius's choice, though he knew it was coming.

If Darius wanted to live, he'd have to disavow all knowledge of the aliens. Never speak of them.

And maybe Darius could lie to them. Give the Allied Worlds what they wanted. Live to fight another day, as he had with Captain Alana.

But that meant giving up Lulu. And he couldn't do that.

Darius was fairly certain that the Allied Worlds didn't know about the *pikali*, that he was connected to the Veelu ship. If they had known, they would have just killed him. They would know they couldn't really offer him a choice.

What would they do to Lulu? Would they try to board her? If they already knew about the aliens, they would know not to try. She wouldn't let them.

The worst case scenario flashed before Darius's eyes.

Him, disavowing all aliens, stating for the record that he'd never seen them, that it was a delusion to think they existed.

They'd play that for Lulu. Make her think he'd left her. Cut off her hope. Then they'd start to hound her.

She'd kill herself rather than stay in a system where she'd be regularly hunted.

There was no lying to the Allied Worlds.

Which meant, basically, death.

Darius tried to reach out with his senses, straining them across the emptiness of space, trying to find Lulu.

But there was nothing on the other end except cold silence.

While Darius tried to come to terms with dying, a million wild fantasy escapes played across his imagination: bribing a guard to let him go, overcoming a guard with a strength that had been hidden to him before, finding a gun floating in the toilet (hey, it happened in vids), taking his meal tray and beating a guard to death before escaping, being led to his death and the station takes a meteor hit, being spaced out an airlock and Lulu flying to the rescue…

No matter what, however, Darius didn't see any real way out of his impending death.

And while he really wished he could see the stars one last time, what he truly wanted in his heart-of-hearts was to apologize to Lulu for ending her life so soon.

Darius slept badly. The guards did turn down the lights at one point, so the room was dim, not dark. But there were no sheets or blankets, and Darius was still cold. Plus, he was used to something always being on top of him when he slept. When he was on *Orion*, he'd always used a light net to keep him in his bunk because of the lack of gravity. On Lulu, he'd found he still needed something, so Lulu had devised a couple of lightweight filaments that she strapped him in with, keeping him snugly bound to his bed.

Without something to hold him down, Darius found he kept having nightmares about floating away, the walls dissolving and he found himself dying in the blackness of space.

One particularly bad nightmare had Lulu watching him. She could have saved him, but since he'd disavowed her existence, she didn't.

When the lights did brighten, Darius was already awake. Groggy, he sat on his bed and waited for the door to open. Maybe they would just shove breakfast in on a tray, through an opening he hadn't found. Or maybe they wouldn't feed the damned.

He'd really like at least one last meal before he died. Chicken, baked with a crispy garlic skin, and served with tzatziki. Mashed potatoes, the kind that his dad had made, with rosemary and butter. Maybe even green beans, as his dad had always tried to get Darius interested in vegetables, and green beans weren't too bad. Then ice cream for desert.

Darius hadn't been expecting Norman to come walking in.

He wore a similar suit to what he'd had on the day before, though this was more blue than brown, and didn't look as rumpled yet. The tie today was a dark blue. The shirt looked identical, as did the rest of Norm.

"Get up," Norman said.

Two guards stood just behind Norman. They wore helmets with visors down over their eyes. Neither of them had their guns drawn, but Darius knew if he made the wrong move, they'd draw and probably fire between one breath and the next.

"What's up, Norm?" Darius drawled as he slowly pushed himself off the bed up onto his feet.

He couldn't believe how much he wished for socks. Again.

Norman gave him a shark's smile. "It appears that you aren't going to be my problem for much longer."

Darius didn't like the sounds of that at all. "Why's that?"

"It appears that Captain Alana of the Pineapple Express

Transportation company has some powerful lawyers and knows some of people in high places," Norman explained. "You're still under contract with her."

Darius opened his mouth and closed it again.

"She also claims that she has no record of the devil's tails on *Orion*. Sent us the last maintenance records they have on the ship. Seems as though you got those attached on your own," Norman said, his eyes peering at Darius.

Darius hung his head to hide his surprise. Of course, Captain Alana would disavow any knowledge of those things.

He could argue that she'd hung them on his ship. But what would be the point? He didn't have any proof.

"She's also promised to *take care* of you like she would any traitor who tried to escape her employment," Norman added smugly.

Darius gulped.

He'd been contemplating his death for the last twelve hours.

Seemed that while it might have been postponed, it was now guaranteed.

Darius was surprised when the guards brought his lightweight work suit into his cell and told him to put it on.

When he thought about it, it wasn't that surprising at all.

Captain Alana had supplied the work suit for Darius. Charging his account for it, of course, yet more debt he had to work off.

She'd want her property back. *All* her property.

Though he doubted that she could force the Allied Worlds into releasing *Orion*. He'd lost his ship forever, now. She'd probably add the bill of that to his contract.

That is, if he could have lived long enough to pay off his debt.

The guards waiting impatiently for Darius to don his work suit. They didn't give him his helmet, though they had it with them. When he was ready, they marched him out of his cell. One walked in front of Darius, one behind him.

What, were they afraid he had some sort of raucous jail break planned?

Darius couldn't help but feel relieved as they left that portion of the space station and moved into one of the general hallways.

He still might die within the hour. But at least he wasn't dying in a locked cell.

Captain Alana didn't keep any sort of jail on her ship. Someone egregiously broke the rules, they got spaced. Simple as that.

Would Captain Alana at least listen to Darius before she spaced him? He did have something to bargain with, this time.

Lulu.

Though Captain Alana wouldn't understand that she couldn't just take Lulu. She'd have to work with Darius and his ship. Maybe it would be worth keeping him alive for a while?

No. She'd already promised to *deal* with him.

Better not to hope.

They hadn't gone far when the guards stopped at a closed door, with another guard standing outside it. They nodded to one another, then the guard let them into the room.

It wasn't a large room—maybe ten feet long and four feet wide. A table with chairs took up most of the space.

Darius pulled up short when he saw who was already in the room. The guard behind him shoved him, though not unkindly.

Darius had *not* expected Captain Alana to come and fetch him herself. He expected a flunky, or one of her guards.

He *really* didn't expect to see Captain Alana sitting at a conference table and laughing with Norman. They appeared to be sharing a bottle of something alcoholic, something fierce and fiery, given the smell of the room.

She looked the same as he remembered her, with darker skin than his, and a huge scar running along the left side of her face. She might have been pretty without it. She barely came up to his chest, but seemed taller here. Maybe someone brought her a high chair or something.

Of course, Captain Alana was laughing when he walked into the room. She usually was laughing at him.

Standing in the corner of the room behind her were two of her guards. Whenever she left the ship, she always had guards with her. Those these two seemed awfully well armed.

Such was the life of a pirate.

"So you would not *believe* the tale this young man has been telling us!" Norman said.

Captain Alana snorted. "I bet. He's been going on and *on* about that claim of his."

"Exactly," Norman said.

Darius blinked. That wasn't Norman's regular voice. He was playing a part. Then again, so was Captain Alana. Her eyes didn't reflect her smile. She watched Norman carefully, like one might watch a newly patched air hose, something you didn't trust to not suddenly break and kill you.

"So I take it my permits and fees are all good, now?" Captain Alana asked.

"Yes, and the Allied Worlds thanks you for all the fees you've been paying," Norman said.

Darius understood that *fee* was the bureaucrat's word for *bribe*. Just like *tax* and *license*.

"It's my pleasure to be working for such a smooth

running organization," Captain Alana said. "You can't imagine some of the chaos that I've been running into recently."

"Tell me about it," Norman said with a sigh. "It's hard enough to bring the rogue system in. Then there are the special cases, the deals that were made during the war, that we're still honoring. Like the Greeks," he said, rolling his eyes.

"Tell me about it," Captain Alana said. For the first time, her eyes bore into Darius's. "Stubborn. Pig-headed. Deliberately obstinate."

Darius glared back at the bitch captain. He didn't try to say anything, but he gave his hatred of her free reign.

Norman chuckled. "Still, I'm sure they have their uses."

"I'm sure they do," Captain Alana said. "Be sure to let me know if you find any."

Darius bit his lips together rather than blurt out anything he might regret later.

He knew his hours (minutes?) were numbered. Still, he was going to go out a how a hero should, stoically, and with grace.

"Come," was all that Captain Alana said to Darius before she swept from the room.

Darius fell into line behind the captain, her two guards coming up close behind him.

What, were they afraid he was going to escape or something? Run away? To where? He didn't know a soul here. Couldn't get off the station. And if he was going to die, it wasn't going to be while trying to escape, shot down in a featureless hallway.

No, he'd bide his time, and at least see the stars again before he died.

Captain Alana led them quickly through the station, then out further, to the furthest ring out. Darius breathed easier.

At least he'd get a glance at the stars as they boarded the transport flitter to take them from the station to *Xin Sheng*, Captain Alana's main starship.

"Here," one of the guards said, shoving Darius's helmet into his hands after they'd all stepped into the airlock.

"Thanks," Darius said. He latched the helmet on securely.

"Can you hear me?" Captain Alana suddenly sounded loud in his ear.

"I can," Darius said.

"Can I get you to promise me you'll wait until after we reach the ship before you die heroically?" she asked.

Darius really was rather impressed by the amount of sarcasm she managed to get in such a simple sentence.

"I'll wait," he said.

He'd been waiting now for quite some time. Waiting to get his revenge. Now, waiting to die.

"Good," Captain Alana said. She nodded to the guards, and the airlock shut tight.

Darius wasn't sure what Captain Alana had in mind. What sort of torture she'd subject him to.

But maybe, just maybe, she'd listen to him before she killed him.

Darius couldn't help but shudder as *Xin Sheng* swallowed the flitter, like a whale swallowing a smaller fish whole. When he'd been flying for Captain Alana, the experience hadn't been as disturbing. He was the one guiding his ship. This felt too much like being sucked into a black hole.

He'd spent the entire trip—all sixty-seven minutes of it—staring out into space, looking at the stars.

He didn't bother trying to get Captain Alana to fly closer to where Lulu had been. There was no guarantee the Veelu hadn't already left the area. He didn't know where she was.

Besides, that would probably go directly against the direction of the station. They'd deliberately kept Lulu out of sight of the station, off the radar of most of the ship flying in and out. And they'd cleared the entire arc of space around them.

No one would have seen that alien ship out there. And if someone did see it, they'd be lied to about it. Some experimental craft, or some rich kid's plaything.

No one but the station would have scanned it, would realize that Lulu was fully organic. But again, even if they did, the station and the Allied Worlds would have a wonderful excuse ready.

What would happen between the Kin and the humans? Since the Allied Worlds couldn't allow the existence of aliens? Would they attack the Kin sometime? Try to destroy them? An inconvenient truth that must be eliminated?

Neither the Kin or the Veelu deserved such a fate.

But Darius didn't expect anything less than annihilation lay in their future at the hands of his own people.

Captain Alana pointed at Darius after the flitter landed on the main ship's bay of *Xin Sheng*. "My office. Now," she said. "And strip off that work suit before you come."

Darius gulped, then nodded. Of course. She wouldn't want the equipment wasted. Someone else would get good use out of the suit. It was practically brand new.

Shivering, bare foot again, Darius followed the guards to Captain Alana's office. It was still the same small space with the one porthole for looking out at the stars. More books sat piled up near the chair at the back of the small space. The desk looked messier than usual, with tablets, notebooks, and other smaller devices scattered across the surface.

"Sit," Captain Alana ordered, pointing to the chair across from her.

Darius slumped down. The door closed behind him. He didn't think Captain Alana would have one of the guards shoot him here. The blood would be too messy to clean up.

What did she have to say to him before she killed him? Had she just brought him here to gloat?

One of the tablets nearest Captain Alana's right hand blinked to life. "Ready, captain."

"Make sure you get a good shot," she warned.

"Roger that."

Captain Alana watched the screen for a moment, then turned it and shoved it across the desk at Darius.

He watched with horror as the guards wrestled with a dark-headed man wearing a lightweight work suit. The guards shoved the man into an airlock, then cycled it.

The man wasn't wearing a helmet.

The instant change in pressure shot the man out of the airlock, rocketing him away from the ship.

The camera watching the figure didn't get too close, but Darius felt his own throat closing in sympathy, the air growing thicker.

The figure stopped moving quickly.

"Darius Linard, you are now officially dead," Captain Alana said as she turned the tablet back around and then flicked it off.

"What?" Darius asked, confused.

"That work suit? Was yours. The ID tags are registered to you. This recording will be sent back to Norman on the space station."

"Shit," Darius said. They were going to show that recording to Lulu. He just knew it.

"Excuse me?" Captain Alana said. "I've just wasted a good work suit to make you appear dead."

"I'm aware of that," Darius said. "And thank you. But you know why they wanted you to kill me, right? I came here with a Veelu ship. The bastards are going to show her that recording. She's going to think I'm dead."

Captain Alana smirked at him. "You have been busy, haven't you? Okay, I want to hear everything. From the top."

Darius blinked at her, surprised. "You—you aren't going to kill me for real?"

Captain Alana rolled her eyes at him. "Not yet, no. I want to know everything you learned about the Kin and the Veelu. You always said you could learn. Impress me with your knowledge."

"Why?" Darius asked. "I mean, I realize you already knew about them. But why are they working with you? Or you with them? Why aren't you falling into line with the Allied Worlds?"

Captain Alana blew out a huge sigh. "I know, you don't get it. No one is supposed to see the entire picture. Yet, some people, who aren't as obstinate and as pig-headed as some Greeks I know, manage to figure it out anyway."

"Okay," Darius said. He remembered the last time he'd argued with Captain Alana. She'd accused him of not being able to see beyond his proud Greek nose.

"Tell me about my business," Captain Alana challenged Darius.

"You're a smuggler," he said.

She raised one eyebrow at him.

"Okay, that isn't your entire operation. You have a lot of legitimate contracts with the Allied Worlds as well."

"And where do we smuggle from?" Captain Alana asked pointedly.

"From other Allied Worlds," Darius said, bewildered.

"Who are we smuggling for?" Captain Alana said.

"I don't know!" Darius said. "I only do pickups. Not deliveries."

Captain Alana sighed again. "And you've never talked with the other pilots about their deliveries."

Darius shook his head no. "I mean, not besides the fact that the places we're smuggling to don't seem to shoot at us as much."

"And why would that be?" Captain Alana asked.

Darius shrugged. "Because they don't have the guns? The equipment? Because they're poorer? Because…oh crap."

The picture suddenly formed in his brain.

Captain Alana smuggled goods out of the Allied Worlds, and into the poorer places, the places that had lost the war.

She was actually still fighting *against* the Allied Worlds.

"Crap," Darius said again.

Captain Alana gave him a smug smile.

"So tell me what happened to you. Don't leave anything out," she said smugly.

"Then can we go rescue my ship?" Darius asked.

Captain Alana got a calculating look in her eye. "It might cost you."

"She's the only alien ship in human space," Darius said.

"That might not be completely true," Captain Alana said.

"She's the only alien ship that you'll be allowed to step a single foot on," Darius replied.

Captain Alana nodded. "That's true. So tell me what you know and we'll go rescue your princess. Deal?"

Darius swallowed against a suddenly dry throat.

He was making a deal with the devil. He knew it.

But it was the only deal he could make.

"Deal."

HERO

LULU

ulu knew the exact moment when Darius left what she'd heard other ships call her *sphere of influence*.

The *pikali* wasn't broken. They were still connected. Lulu still felt Darius's presence thrumming inside her, as much a part of her as the blood that flowed slowly through her veins.

However, she no longer had access to his feelings. They couldn't communicate with just a touch. She couldn't share the ticklish feeling of the solar winds, or how bathing in the bright sunlight of a nearby star fed her, or even the joy of flight.

Lulu had been bred by the Ship Breeders as a space flying Veeluthian. She would never know what it was like to be planet bound. While Darius was merely Human, he'd spent most of his life in space, and was as natural a flier as Lulu.

It was one of the things that drew them closer, that made their connection possible.

No Veelu had ever paired with a Human before. Normally, her kind committed to the *pikali* bond with one of the Kin, a race who'd come from the same home world. Both races had started out, eons ago in their shared past, as birds. As they'd evolved, only the Veelu had retained their ability to fly. But it made the Kin proper companions, as flying was baked into their genes.

And now, Lulu was here, completely alone in Human space. No Darius to share her thoughts and feelings with. No other Veelu to talk with across the vast distances of space. She didn't even have other crew members, be they Kin or Human, to talk with.

Lulu watched Darius and his mechanical ship, *Orion*, flying toward the human space station Euthalia. The ship grew smaller and smaller until it was barely visible.

The space station had insisted that Lulu stay outside the range of most of the mechanical sensors Humans employed on their ships. The station had also routed all space traffic away from her.

No one except a couple of people on the station knew she was there.

Darius had insisted that was a good thing.

Lulu's sensors were better than the mechanical versions that Humans built. Even from this distance, she could identify the "petal" jutting out from the circular top of the space station where *Orion* landed.

It was just her imagination that she also felt when Darius disappeared inside the station, placing more metal and mechanics between them.

Lulu had told Darius that she would wait for him, like one of those ridiculous romantic heroines from the dramas that the Kin liked to watch and perform. However, there was no *forever* involved. Lulu had put a time limit on it. Darius had exactly one month to return to her, thirty days as both the Kin and the Humans counted these things.

Then Lulu would leave.

She couldn't make it through jump space on her own and

return to Veelu space. Not that she would have been welcome there, having been labeled a *wild one* and deemed unfit for civilized society. If Darius didn't return, she'd be stuck here in Human-occupied space, forever alone.

There was a very slim chance that she would be able to find another Human to share the *pikali* with. But that meant allowing humans into her space.

Chances were, she'd just fly into a sun when the time was up.

Lulu occupied herself while waiting for Darius by improving the cabins she kept for him. She'd originally grown the space for him behind the section that had been occupied by her Kin crew.

Darius was almost six and a half feet, in part because he hadn't grown up with strong gravity. The ceilings in his section were higher than those she'd originally built for the Kin, as those had been barely five feet tall. Plus, the mix of oxygen was different for Humans than for the Kin.

However, the ship breeders had deliberately placed brakes on Lulu's internal systems. While Lulu could grow rooms and make changes to her internal structure as required, for example, adding more cabins for crew or reconfiguring her storage compartments, she and Darius had discovered that it was practically impossible for Lulu to initiate the changes by herself.

Someone had to be there with her. It was as if she couldn't exactly pinpoint the location inside of body cavity on her own.

While Lulu felt as though she knew every inch of her external body, and could identify each individual scale across the vastness of her skin, her internal systems remained a mystery. She'd only been able to rebuild the kitchen galley with Darius standing there, enabling her to "find" the space.

Had this been a deliberate attempt by the Kin in order to keep the space flying Veelu under their control? To "enslave" them?

If there was ever a chance to go back to the Kin-occupied systems, Lulu had some sharp questions for the ship breeders, as well as things to tell the other Veelu.

So although Darius was gone (one day, three hours), Lulu had a cheat she could use. Darius had helped Lulu grow a Jason of the Argonauts medal on one of her walls. He frequently kissed two fingers of his hand and then touched the icon for luck. He wore a similar icon around his neck.

Lulu had directed extra nerve endings to be clustered in that medal so she could feel it intimately every time Darius touched it.

Now, she used those extra nerves to spread through her walls. She knew where the door was to Darius's cabin. She grew the complex net of nerves in that direction, spreading across the wall like vines growing in the hot sun.

Would Darius be able to see the change in the wall when he returned? Human eyesight was much better at close up, detail work, than the Kin, who were flying hunters originally.

Out the door and to the left ran a hallway to the galley where Darius cooked his food. (Lulu had to admit that before he'd shared the taste of cooked meat, she'd been as grossed out about it as the Kin. Searing meat ruined all the delicate flavors. However, he'd shared meals with her through the *pikali*, showing her that his way of preparing it was quite tasty as well.)

Lulu grew the nerve network out the door, then tried to push that wall further out. Darius's quarters were at the rear of Lulu's body, close to her tail. She willed the wall to extend outward, using her head as a reference point.

The nerves bunched up across the wall, but she couldn't feel any movement.

Damn it! Was she too far away from her starting point?

She upped the number of nerve endings throughout the network. She tried to replicate the feeling that Darius had when he blew across his arm, how sensitive his skin felt.

Then she pushed again. She got a little further, feeling the wall give slightly, but it was taking too much effort. She didn't want to have to leave the station and draw closer to the sun to refuel herself.

She quadrupled the number of nerve endings that ran across the surface of her walls, until just the slightest touch of Darius's fingers would have caused her to shiver. A hard push of his hand would have been painful.

There. That was the key. She needed to have that many nerves in an area internally to be able to "find" it without external help, someone standing in the area for her to focus on.

Again, was this a deliberate attempt on the part of the ship breeders to better control Lulu and the rest of the space flying Veelu? Most of the other space fliers that she knew wouldn't go to this much effort.

Plus, the Kin were too careful and organized for Lulu to believe it was accidental.

Happily humming along, Lulu pushed at the walls, extending them forward, enlarging Darius's quarters. Now, they didn't end at the hallway to the galley. Instead, they grew up along Lulu's torso, extending another four feet.

Lulu paused for a moment, pleased with her progress. She reinforced the external skin of the area, keeping a solid barrier between her precious passenger and the deadly vacuum of space.

When she was satisfied with her expansion, she absorbed

part of the nerve network back into herself. It wouldn't do for her to deplete herself.

Now, came the hard part.

Lulu wasn't sure exactly how to create windows. She'd grown them before for the crew. But the ship breeders had always been there, directing her. They'd also helped in the process, by applying chemicals to her skin that she could absorb and then use to change her tough hide into a new substance that was transparent.

She had no ship breeders. No extra help. She would have to figure this out on her own.

A wave of sadness washed over Lulu. She was truly all alone here.

When Darius had been with her, she hadn't felt lonely, or even sad that she'd left her home. There had been too much to look forward to.

She would admit now that she'd been infected by Darius' excitement to return to Human-occupied space.

There wasn't anything she could do about that now, though. She'd rejected her Kin captain and crew. Entered into the *pikali* with a Human. Left Kin-occupied space.

She could never go home.

The weight of it caused her to draw her great wings back toward her body. Darius had told her that she resembled a great manta ray, an ocean creature from the Human's home world that they'd brought into space with them.

Lulu had more reach with her wings than a manta ray did with its flappers. With effort, she drew them in closer. She couldn't quite touch her chest with her wings. She still enveloped herself with them.

Humans called it hugging.

Lulu hugged herself as best she could.

She stayed frozen like that for over an hour, processing all that she was feeling.

When she released herself and flowed back into her normal stretched out position, she felt as though something inside her had shifted. The new room still needed work. And she still had to figure out how to grow windows.

However, Lulu felt as though she'd gained purpose.

She would absolutely give Darius the thirty days she'd promised him.

Then she'd give herself thirty more to explore Human-occupied space, the area around the *New Athens* system.

She might still end up throwing herself into a sun, but she was determined to give herself a chance to find a new home, first.

"Spaceship *Lulu*? This is the space station Euthalia. Come in please."

An unfamiliar voice was hailing her.

Lulu drew her attention back from her latest window failure. She just couldn't find the right combination of chemicals to make the windows work right. The best she'd managed so far was a cloudy view.

"This is Lulu," she said, acknowledging.

Unlike a Human, her heart couldn't suddenly start beating faster when she grew excited. What she felt instead was a tingling along her outer scales. They lay flat against her skin, but she felt them almost rise up, like the hair on a human would.

Was Darius coming back? Why wasn't he talking to her directly?

"Prepare to receive transmission," the voice said.

"Ready," Lulu said. What did the station want to send her?

A stream of…something…came toward her. Lulu

captured it, but she wasn't sure what she needed to do with it. It seemed like a bunch of data.

Lulu had no computer capacity. Both the Kin and the Veelu had an aversion to anything mechanical. Communication between ships primarily occurred through talking.

The ship breeders had given her a crude ability to record vocal messages. However, her playback of them left out a lot of the nuance that the Kin used in their speech.

"What is this?" Lulu asked. What was she supposed to do with it?

"Video clip," said the station.

"I have no ability to view it," Lulu said. While her Kin crew members had watched their entertainment videos, they'd done so on their own personal devices. (Nothing *mechanical*, mostly organically grown in one of the Kin factories.)

"Please hold," the station replied.

Lulu found herself growing anxious. Chills ran down her long spine, making her swish her tail. What was it the clip contained? Was it a video recording of Darius? Why wasn't he speaking to her himself?

It had been three days, six hours, since he'd left.

It took another two hours before someone from the station hailed her again. Lulu couldn't concentrate on anything, not the windows, not her internal systems, not even trying to follow her own slow steady heartbeat.

"Space flier *Lulu*?"

This was a familiar voice. Norm, the Allied Worlds representative who'd Darius had gone to meet.

"This is Lulu," she confirmed. "What happened to Darius? Is he all right?"

A heavy sigh came across the channel. "Dude. I'm so sorry to have to tell you this. Darius is dead."

Lulu felt as though another Veelu had suddenly appeared and thwacked her across the broad expanse of her wings.

"What happened?" Lulu asked. She had no mechanism for breathing. But she'd shared Darius's inhale and exhale for long enough that she felt as though she couldn't catch her breath.

"Darius had a contract with the Pineapple Express Transport people," Norm said.

Lulu knew that. It had been part of what had drawn the pair of them together. While Lulu hadn't actually been a slave, not like Darius, she still felt his pain. Their situations had been similar. Particularly given how Kin had been treating her at the time.

"Captain Alana came and got him. Then she sent us the video of her spacing him," Norm said.

An electric shock ran through Lulu's systems. She shuddered as if she'd been hit with one of the lasers from the war.

"When?" she asked.

"Earlier today," Norm said. "The video clip has a timestamp on it. Look, I'm sorry. I really am."

Lulu hadn't been around enough Humans to judge the validity of Norm's words. She couldn't tell if he was angry or relieved or actually sad and sorry.

Darius had always believed the man.

"Why would Captain Alana send you such a video?" Lulu asked. She didn't think that the executing of people was normally shared.

Then again, she didn't understand at least half of the recordings that the Kin made. What was so cute about watching fluffy, domesticated baby birds teetering on the edge of their nest, then falling back in among their siblings? Or seeing baby birds dressed up like famous Kin from history? Though the baby birds had no capacity for speech, they seemed to have developed their own language, completely illogical and ungrammatical.

"Captain Alana told me that she'd 'take care' of Darius," Norm said. "No way would I have thought she meant spacing him. That's just…rude."

"I see," Lulu said.

She'd felt alone before. Now, it felt as though the cold tendrils of space pressed against her wings, seeing a way into her heart.

"You okay?" Norm asked. "Is there anything I can do? Want me to send some crew over to keep you company?"

"No," Lulu said. She knew she sounded harsh. "That won't be necessary."

Darius was gone.

"Look, I'm sorry," Norm said. "I really am. Darius seemed like a nice kid, you know?"

Lulu felt herself pause at that. Darius had believed that Norm was the same age as he was.

Calling Darius a kid meant that Norm was older. Much older.

Suddenly, Lulu couldn't shake the feeling that Norm was lying to her. About Darius? Captain Alana? Both? Neither?

After a long pause, Norm asked, "You let me know if there's anyone I can send over. Or if there's anything I can help with."

"Thanks," Lulu said. "I will."

She cut communication with the station. If they tried to contact her again, she wouldn't hear it. Not for a while. She felt herself compress down into a crackling ball of rage and pain.

How dare they take Darius from her? Their *pikali* was still fresh and new. It wasn't fair. They hadn't had time to develop their relationship, to learn everything there was to know about the other.

Lulu had no weapons, like the lasers the Kin had used during the civil war. Even if she could somehow figure out how to buy weapons, it would take a lot of time (and money that she didn't have) to graft them to her system so that she could fire them at her will.

Besides, those were *mechanical* things.

That didn't mean that Lulu couldn't figure out how to take her revenge on Captain Alana and the ship *Xu Shing*.

Devil's tails, as both the Kin and Darius had referred to them, were actually derived from the Veelu ability to delve down into jump space.

Lulu had experienced jump space more than once. However, she couldn't achieve it on her own. As Darius had explained to her, she needed more weight to flow down into it. Which made sense: it took the combined mass of two to three Veelu to reach jump space.

However, it wasn't just weight. Other factors also came into play.

While the Humans had their physics and their machines to find jump space, the Veelu just had their instincts and will.

All Veelu had tails. She knew that the ship breeders had tried, very early in their attempts to create space fliers, to breed out what they considered an unnecessary appendage. The Veelu had rebelled, and the ship breeders had stopped the program.

While Lulu could swish her tail from side to side, particularly if she was agitated, it wasn't prehensile. She couldn't pick something up with it. And it didn't really aid her when she flew, not as it did her smaller cousins who were planet bound, who needed them for gliding.

What the Kin didn't learn about until much, much later was that the tails of the Veelu actually helped them when they dove into jump space.

The things that Darius referred to as devil's tails were actually shifters. They phased a ship in and out of regular space. Not quite to jump space, but not fully in normal space anymore either.

During the war, the ship breeders had grafted shifters onto the bellies of the fighting Veelu to give them more natural defenses beyond their tough skin and scales.

While the Veelu could shift on their own, it took a lot of energy and training, time and effort that the Kin hadn't wanted to spend.

Every space flier was taught the basics. Lulu used her tail instinctively when it came to achieving jump space.

Now, she had to figure out how to use it as a shifter.

She left Darius's quarters semi-blind, the white windows looking opaquely out at the stars, and turned her attention to her tail.

It was as much feel as anything else. But Lulu had been practicing that the last few days by focusing on growing Darius a new space.

(And every time she thought of him, she remembered how hollow her heart felt.)

The space station had wanted Lulu isolated, alone, so no other ships could see her, no one else at the station could interact with her.

Lulu didn't know what would happen if she suddenly disobeyed their orders and flew closer to the station. She was pretty sure they'd shoot at her. Lasers and other weapons that may or may not damage her scales.

Humans were good at warfare. Much better than the Kin and the Veelu, who tended to try to get along for the most part. They didn't have a huge long history of one battle after another, but instead, had centuries of peace interspaced with occasional conflict.

Since at least some of the humans knew about the Veelu and the Kin, Lulu had to assume that the Humans had already started developing weapons that would destroy the aliens specifically.

So Lulu wasn't going to ram into the station, as tempting as that might be.

Instead, she was just going to disappear.

It took another three hours for Lulu to get the pattern just right. There was a specific angle that she needed to dangle her tail at, while at the same time, concentrate on trying to make that leap into jump space that wasn't really there, that she couldn't really get to.

Darius had once told her a joke about how Humans had learned to fly—by throwing themselves at the ground and missing.

That described how Lulu felt. She was diving into jump space and missing, landing in an alternate state instead.

Something pinged Lulu's consciousness, bringing her focus back to the rest of her body. Was someone from the station trying to communicate with her again?

No, that wasn't it.

When she looked around, she realized that four smaller flitters had been slowly approaching her, inching forward.

What, did they think she couldn't see them if they approached slowly? That she wouldn't notice them?

Then again, she had been focused on other things. They'd come very close, had more than halved the distance between Lulu and the station.

"Approaching ships," she called out, hailing them on the

normal Human frequencies. "This is the space flier Lulu. What is your purpose? Why are you approaching me?" She'd thought that the station would continue to ban any ships from approaching her.

Static greeted her.

All the ships noticeably speeded up.

Were they coming to shoot her? Ram her? Maybe do something really stupid and try to use a net on her?

Lulu didn't know, and didn't plan on sticking around to find out.

She dropped down out of their plane quickly. While Darius had jiggered *Orion* to be able to do some tricks, most ships couldn't follow her aerobatics.

Plus, when she and Darius had approached the station, she'd purposefully taken a long time to come to a halt.

Darius had wanted the humans to underestimate her capabilities.

Seemed he was right. Again. As always.

Lulu laughed at the other ships trying to dive down after her. Though these pilots may be good, they would never be as good as her.

She spun around them, moving much more quickly now, herding them together, as the ship herders had once guided the pod of space fliers she'd grown up with.

One of the smaller fliers shot at her with a beam weapon.

The beam bounced off her back, a warmth spreading there.

For a moment, Lulu was worried that she was damaged. She flexed the scales in the area where she'd been hit.

Fools didn't realize that the Kin lasers had been specially tuned.

The wrong frequency just fed Veelu. Like sunlight. Made her stronger.

Could she get them to shoot her again?

She stood up on her wings, gliding away from the cluster of smaller ships, exposing her back to them.

Pout. None of them wanted to play.

So she turned, spinning on her long axis, before she abruptly leveled herself out again, bashing one of the smaller ships with her great wings, sending it skidding into its neighbor.

The others finally saw the stupidity of being grouped together and tried to spread out.

Lulu flew around them again, harassing them, keeping them bunched up.

As one, the ships suddenly fired at her again. It was a much stronger beam striking her.

Lulu veered away. *Ouch.* That stung. Could she still absorb the energy from the weapons? Not as well. And they could damage her if they kept it up.

Should she let them separate? So they couldn't coordinate their attacks? Or keep them bunched together so they were easier for her to attack?

They fired again, this beam hitting her at the base of her neck, where her wings started their spread from her torso.

Lulu howled in anger. She dropped into the blast range of her vocal abilities. She'd been able to seriously shake up an attacking Veelu by shouting in this tone.

The ships couldn't shake their heads like a Veelu. They did seem to lose power abruptly, as if the shout had somehow drained them.

Huh. Interesting. Lulu was going to have to remember that, see if it was effective against Captain Alana and the *Xu Sheng.*

Because Lulu was still determined to get her revenge.

Time to get going, before the human pilots came back to their senses.

Lulu made a swooping run at the small cluster of ships, as if she was going to bash all of them at the same time.

They opened fire on her head, one of the most reinforced parts of her body. She could survive a headshot better than a neck shot.

Just before she reached them, Lulu *shifted.*

The ships rocked, as if hit by a great sound wave. Or psychic wave. Or something.

Lulu laughed as she flew away. She couldn't hear the chatter between the ships, but she imagined they were all confused as hell about how such a large ship as herself could suddenly disappear off their screens.

Now, she only had to find Captain Alana.

See how her ship faired against a vengeful Veelu space flier.

Lulu lurked closer to the space station Euthalia, while staying in shifted mode. It was more difficult to pick up the stations communication transmissions this way. But Lulu quickly learned how.

She listened for some clue as to where *Xi Sheng* might be found. She knew that Captain Alana had been to the station previously. Darius had explained all the various ships that *Xi Sheng* had carried with her, cargo ships like *Orion* as well as smaller flitters for carrying personnel, some that were capable of jumping in and out of a planet's gravity.

Lulu went through the list of ship names that Darius had reeled off at one point. She'd been curious about how the ships had been named. While *Orion* came from a myth that was part of Darius's Greek culture, others had named their ships a variety of things.

Lulu kept half of her attention on the station's

communications, while the other half maintained her shifted condition. She was glad she didn't carry any passengers at that point—they might have complained about the conditions. Or gotten sick.

Darius had told her that all of his surroundings had a red tint to them when he'd shifted. Plus, he'd said it always smelled like something was burning, plastics or rubber wires.

Lulu burned through her reserves of energy staying hidden, but finally, she had a target: the spaceship *Triumph* was asking for a departure window.

Hopefully this *Triumph* was the same ship that Darius had mentioned.

Lulu followed the small flier, staying behind and on top of it. It took two long days, but eventually the flier led Lulu directly to a ship that she readily identified as *Xi Sheng*.

And it was close to a sun.

Lulu flew out of sensor range of the Human ship, closer to the sun, basking in its warm rays, refueling herself. She caught a little of the communications traffic from the ship to its smaller ones. A cargo ship arrived, and three more departed.

They had no idea of the monster lurking just off their bow.

Lulu refreshed herself, growing stronger, until finally, it was time for her to attack.

DARIUS

"Really?" Darius asked Shelly, after being handed the new identification discs that Captain Alana had ordered for him. "Jason?"

Shelly smirked at him. The older man was as tall as Darius, though possibly weighed twice as much. His round face beamed with mirth. He kept his head shaved, though a short rift of white stubble still crowned the back of his neck.

"It could be worse. She'd originally wanted to name you Hercules," Shelly said. He spread his hands wide across the desk that took up most of the space in his tiny office. Huge monitors and fine electronics covered every available surface. After just a few minutes, Darius was already feeling claustrophobic. "Lucky for you, I was able to talk her out of it."

Darius rolled his eyes. "Thanks," he said, though he really wasn't sure that Jason was much better. He stuffed the ID disc into his pants pockets. He wore a spacer's jumpsuit with many tight pockets in the front. It was blue with gray stripes, and luckily fit him across the shoulders. The legs were a little short, and were pulled snuggly around the tops of his ankles. It would be easy to slip on an EVA suit over it.

"You're still from *New Athens*," Shelly continued, telling Darius about his new identity. The captain had supposedly killed him, as a sop to the Allied Worlds. But also to protect him. Darius Linus was officially dead. He needed to become someone else.

"With that nose and coloring of yours, nothing else would really be believable," Shelly said.

Darius nodded. A complete new body was out of the question. While the technology existed to permanently change hair and skin color, as well as reprogram your DNA to grow you different fingerprints, it was excessively expensive. Only really rich criminals could afford to do that.

And Darius was kind of already indentured to Captain Alana and the Pineapple Express Transport company.

However, with a new identity would come new contracts.

And Darius had something to bargain with, this time.

After gathering up his new identity, Darius left Shelly's tiny office, located on one of the upper levels of *Xi Sheng*, and headed for his next meeting. The hallways up here were better than the general crew quarters. A soft, navy blue material covered the floor, making it more comfortable to walk on. Sunlight yellow paint covered the walls, so the hallways seemed wider. Recessed doors leading to mysterious rooms branched off the corridor, nothing numbered or named.

At almost every place where the hallway branched, Darius had to present his new crew badge, coded blue, instead of the plain white one he'd had before. Captain Alana ran a tight ship. Even if he'd been able to sneak up here to this level, he wouldn't have gotten very far.

He'd been aware that Captain Alana kept a lot of guards.

Now he understood why, given that she'd joined forces with the rebellion against the Allied Worlds.

The door to the conference room was already open by the time Darius arrived. Kwasi, Captain Alana's second in command, scowled at Darius as he walked in.

Darius had met Kwasi twice before. He was a towering black man who was constantly smiling, as if each day was a gift. Like Captain Alana, there were rumors of his past, that he'd been trapped on a mining world, a true slave.

Why was he so angry now?

"Sorry, am I late?" Darius asked as he sat down at the conference table. It was made out of a plastic formed and colored to look like highly polished beach wood. There was enough room for four of them around the table. The air in here smelled stale, as if the room was rarely used.

Actual papers lay in front of Kwasi. He transferred his glare from Darius to them. "No," Kwasi said. His tone was gentle and deep, like Darius had just woken a sleeping giant. "But I have more important things to do than to babysit you."

"Understood," Darius said, nodding. Was there some emergency that needed Kwasi's attention? Nothing that dire had to be happening, or Captain Alana would have canceled the meeting.

Kwasi flipped the papers around and pushed them across the table, in front of Darius. "Your new contract. You'll sign here, here, and here," he said, stabbing the various lines with his fat finger.

Darius swallowed against a dry throat. "I need to read it first."

Kwasi narrowed his eyes at Darius. "Really?"

"Yes," Darius said, his voice more firm. Was Kwasi really angry? Or was he playing the role of an asshole as part of the contract negotiations?

After a few more moments of staring at Darius, Kwasi finally nodded. "If you insist."

Darius's stubborn Greek nature rose up.

He slowly reached for the first page of the contract and started reading it. Then he grabbed the pen on the table and struck several paragraphs from the first page, and the second, then rewrote most of page three.

Kwasi reviewed the pages as Darius finished them. He didn't seem to know whether to be shocked or amused. Maybe a bit of each.

"Is that all?" Kwasi rumbled when Darius was done.

"I cannot speak for the space flier Lulu," Darius said firmly. "I cannot legally sign a contract for her. She needs to be here to represent herself."

Kwasi blinked as if this had never occurred to him. "And you think this is going to stand with the captain?"

Darius shrugged and leaned back. "Yes," he said simply.

"Why would you think that?" Kwasi asked. Seemed as though he was going for outraged. "What makes you so important? You're just another peon."

Darius nodded to himself. Kwasi was merely playing the role of a hard ass. He bet a lot of people first coming onto the ship would be cowed by Kwasi.

Darius knew better.

"I am different because I have something Captain Alana wants," Darius said. "A Veelu space flier. Lulu will represent herself."

Kwasi glared at Darius. "And the rest of it?"

Darius shook his head. "I won't sign it." He wasn't about to put himself back into indentured slavery.

"You aren't that special," Kwasi sneered.

Darius merely shrugged. Sure, Captain Alana could actually space him at any time. Darius was betting, though, that she wouldn't. Not at this time.

"This will never fly," Kwasi eventually said. "Stay here."

Darius nodded as if he didn't have a care in the world. "Take your time," he said airily as Kwasi left the room.

Once the towering man had left, Darius let go of a deep breath. His hands shook as he spread them out across the tabletop.

He knew that this was all part of the captain's game. Kwasi and his anger, then letting Darius stew and wait. Particularly since she knew that every minute they waited here was another minute that Lulu would falsely believe Darius was dead.

He didn't like to think about how much pain that was causing her.

If the situation was reversed, Darius knew he'd be going through Hell.

Already was, actually, as there was a good chance that Lulu would fly into a nearby sun before he returned.

Still, Darius tried to wait patiently. He slouched down in his chair, tipped his head back, and closed his eyes.

Part of his training as a pilot had been gaining the ability to sleep pretty much at the drop of a hat.

Despite his worry and his position, Darius didn't wake up until he heard the door opening behind him.

"What the hell are you after, mister?" Captain Alana came steaming in.

Darius held up his hand. "Give me a minute," he said. He stood up, then reached down to touch his toes, stretching out his back.

Yeah, sleeping in a chair probably wasn't the smartest move. Maybe he should have moved to the floor instead.

"Are you finished?" Captain Alana snapped at him.

"Yes, ma'am," Darius said. His tone didn't hold much insolence. Much. He dropped back into his chair.

If they could play this game, so could he.

Captain Alana took the seat the Kwasi had vacated. She wore a spacer's jump suit, like Darius's, though hers fit much better and was made out of a soft orange material that went well with her dark coloring. The scar that covered most of her left cheek blazed white, the tissue never seeming to fully heal. Her black hair was shorn short, easier for putting on helmets and such.

She probably was only five feet four, but her presence filled the room.

"What is this all about?" Captain Alana said as she angrily thrust the contract back at Darius.

"As I explained to Kwasi, I cannot sign for Lulu," Darius explained. "She is a sentient being. I have no legal standing with her. I cannot legally represent her. So most of that contract isn't legal."

Captain Alana narrowed her eyes at him.

"Look, I'm just trying to save you some time at court," Darius said, his hands spread wide, as if he was just being helpful.

"Right," Captain Alana said. "And the rest of it?"

"If you try to make me a slave again, you'll never get Lulu to cooperate," Darius said. "Did I mention that she has a will of her own? Kind of stubborn, actually? You try to indenture me again and neither of us will ever be able to get her to cooperate."

"I'm not sure that her cooperation is all that important," Captain Alana said.

"You're lying," Darius guessed.

Captain Alana grew very still.

Darius realized he'd overstepped his bounds.

"Do tell," Captain Alana purred.

Darius took a deep breath. Captain Alana was always most dangerous when she grew quiet.

"You told me about your operation. I've spent the last

two days delving deep into the delivery side of things. And remember, I'm really good at learning things."

That ability had saved him more than once. He paused, putting his words together.

"You're fighting a losing battle. There isn't a pattern of attacks on the gathering side, when you go out and get supplies. On the delivery side?" Darius shrugged. "You're getting your ass handed to you by Allied World ships."

"Tell me something I don't know," Captain Alana growled.

"I don't think you have a spy on the ship," Darius continued. "The attacks are mostly random, and seem to occur as much by chance and opportunity, rather than planned."

Captain Alana blinked. He knew that she'd been assuming she had to have spies.

And possibly she did, but they were further down the line, not on *Xi Sheng* itself.

"It's really a question of supply and demand," Darius said. "You have a lot more worlds to draw from for supplies. But there are a limited number of worlds that you want deliver to. So the Allied Worlds are focusing on those."

Captain Alana narrowed her eyes at him. "Go on," she said. The dangerous quiet tone was gone, replace with more curiosity.

Darius still didn't think he was telling Captain Alana anything new. She'd seen this pattern, or one of her crew had already told her about it.

"What you need to do, in order to make more successful deliveries, is to carry more per trip, as well as randomize more," Darius continued.

"And so you think that Lulu will just fix all my problems?" Captain Alana asked, the sneer evident.

"Not all of them," Darius said honestly. "But some of

them, yes. She's larger than most of the cargo ships. Huge, actually. She can grow specialized compartments, so in a single run, we can deliver both chemicals as well as supplies. There is a *possibility* that with some additional work she'll be able to achieve jump space on her own."

Darius and Lulu had talked about whether adding some heavy equipment to her cargo holds would be enough for her to achieve jump space.

"And when she get attacked?" Captain Alana said.

"I don't know if she'd agree to being modified so she could carry her own weapons," Darius admitted. "But her scales are a natural defense. And she can fly much, much better and faster than any ship you've ever seen of that size."

Captain Alana appeared to be considering his proposal. "How long before the Allied Worlds figures out what she is and starts preparing for her?"

"Don't know," Darius said. "But once they do, we switch to pickups again. It's expensive for the Allied Worlds to keep ships out there, patrolling 'just in case' a pirate shows up."

"You realize all this is moot until you go and get her," Captain Alana said.

Darius nodded. "So let's go."

"I will need your word that you'll return to *Xi Shing* once you've accomplished your rescue mission," Captain Alana said seriously.

Darius bit his lips together. Unlike most people, when Darius gave his word, he'd keep it. It was a point of honor with him.

He understood what the captain was asking. Once he was away from the ship and back on Lulu, there wouldn't really be any reason for him to return. He had a new identity. They could just disappear into the vastness of space.

He didn't want to promise Captain Alana that he'd come back.

"Without your promise, your word, I won't move forward. I'll keep you here under your old contract. You'll only have scut work on this ship," Captain Alana said firmly. "You'll never fly again."

Darius swallowed hard. He knew that she meant every word.

While she really wanted to get her hands on Velluthian space flier, and was willing to negotiate on that, what Lulu could do for Captain Alana's operation was strictly theoretical. Captain Alana was willing to bet that she'd find a different way to replicate what Lulu could do, if Darius wouldn't give his word.

"Fine," Darius finally said, nodding. "I give you my word that I will return to *Xi Sheng* after I go and fetch Lulu."

Captain Alana gave him an evil grin. "I will hold you to that, hero. Then we'll restart the negotiations. But Lulu had better live up to her end of the bargain."

Darius merely nodded.

"Report to space dock. You'll be a passenger on the ship *Lucky Eight*. Your cover is visiting the space station Euthalia to pick up a package for me. You will need to stay on board the ship the entire time," Captain Alana said as she stood up. "You are not to step one foot on the space station. Your ID is good, but you may be recognized."

"Thank you," Darius said. He meant it. He knew that without her help, he might already be dead.

"Don't thank me until you get back here," Captain Alana growled before she swept from the room.

Darius took a deep breath, feeling his chest expand. She always made him collapse in on himself, as if protecting his vital organs from the hit he feared was coming.

Maybe some year he'd be able to face the captain without such an extreme reaction.

Then again, maybe space monkeys would come flying out of his butt.

Darius took another moment to stretch before he left the conference room and headed down to the space dock, humming with excitement.

Finally, he was going to go get his girl.

"What do you mean, there's nothing there?" Darius asked, panic setting in. He tried to keep breathing, though the air in *Lucky Eight* had tasted sour the entire trip. The pilot's cabin was cramped, like the rest of the ship. It was more modern than *Orion*, but to Darius, felt more plastic, more like what he figured an office would feel like, not a home.

Darius hadn't been allowed to fly any of the trip, but had been stuck as a passenger, without much to do, while Enrico and his partner, Samantha, handled everything.

The pair of them were opposite in every aspect: Enrico was short, round, dark-skinned and older. Samantha was at least a foot taller, thin and willowy, pale as an underground slug that never saw the light of day, her hair a pale blonde-red, her eyes a faded gray. They worked together well, completing each other's sentences and communicating with just grunts sometimes.

As they'd drawn close to the station, Samantha had given up her seat so that Darius could see out the front windows.

They'd approached the station from the direction that Darius and Lulu had first come in. He'd hoped that she'd still be there.

But she wasn't.

The sensors didn't really need to tell him that, actually.

He couldn't feel her.

Or had she broken the *pikali*? Was he no longer connected to her?

No, she had to be there.

Before Darius could demand that Enrico do another pass, a ship hailed them.

"Unidentified ship, this is Euthalia system guard. What is your purpose?"

Now the *Lucky Eight* spotted the tiny flitter that appeared to be patrolling the area.

"Euthalia guard, this is *Lucky Eight*. We're here for a package pick up," Enrico replied in a bored tone. Both hands flew over the sensor boards, his fat fingers rapidly adjusting balances, belying his casual tone.

Darius realized it wasn't just one flitter, but three.

Not flitters. Fighters.

Armed to the teeth.

Darius shuddered. Had they been sent by the station to attack Lulu?

If she'd been damaged, there would be remains spread through this area.

"This is a restricted area," the guard replied. "You need to leave this arc of the Euthalia station space immediately and use a different approach."

"Why?" Enrico asked, sounding belligerent. "That's just a waste of fuel. Besides, there weren't any markers warning us away."

"Unscheduled asteroid collision," a different guard replied. "Markers are just being deployed now."

At the far end of *Lucky Eight's* sensors, they now picked up the automated drone that would place markers all around the forbidden zone. The drone was very similar to the one that dropped markers for a claim in an arc of an asteroid belt.

Was there something else there, lost in that vastness expanse of space that the station was rapidly closing off?

Something beyond the sensors of *Lucky Eight*? Parts of Lulu that had been exploded off of her? Why else would they say it was a biological hazard?

"Fine," Enrico said. The exasperation was evident in his voice. "You guys need to get better organized." Then he cut communications.

"I'm sorry," Enrico told Darius softly. "But I can't get into that area."

"I know," Darius said. "Can you skim the side of it?"

"Like I'm an ass of a pilot tired of this shit and willing to cut corners? Absolutely," Enrico said.

They had to be warned away twice more before Enrico finally corrected his course well away from the area.

However, the ship's sensors didn't pick up anything out of the ordinary as they flew by.

Darius would bet that Lulu was no longer there.

Where had she gone? Had she already flown into a sun? How was he going to find her?

While Enrico and Samantha were on the space station Euthalia picking up their package, Darius stayed hidden in his cabin. It was as cramped as the rest of the ship. The room's single bed took up most of the space, though it wasn't long enough for Darius to lay down fully. Almost all the cabinets that took up the walls were locked.

At least Darius could stand up fully without banging his head.

Enrico had piped the ship's comms back to Darius's room, so he could listen to the station chatter.

Like all the ships in Captain Alana's fleet, *Lucky Eight* had special programming and equipment that allowed it to access many of the secured channels of the station. Not the highly encrypted channels, but that generally wasn't necessary.

Or maybe Captain Alana didn't want her common pilots to have such access.

Darius kept himself awake the entire time by switching from one channel to the next. However, no one was talking about a great alien ship hanging out close to the station. There were some rumors about a chemical cargo that had spilled, but no one knew for certain. The primary chatter was from pilots bitching about what a hassle it was going around it.

Where was Lulu? Where would she go? Had she already killed herself? Though Darius couldn't feel her, there was a part of him that believed she was still alive.

It was a stupid hope. But hey, his father used to say that as a Greek, foolish hope came as natural to him as breathing.

With a heavy heart, Darius agreed to turn back to *Xi Sheng*. Enrico and Samantha seemed to have come to some sort of agreement about leaving Darius alone for the return trip, not trying to engage him in conversation.

Darius spent most of the time in his tiny quarters, trying to figure out his next move.

If he had no Lulu, what could he use to leverage his position with Captain Alana? She might have at one point been impressed with his pilot skills. He hoped that his time with Lulu had sharpened them.

She had better analysts than him, however. People with more smarts, who figured out her operation without her having to point it out to them.

He was going to end up being indentured for life if he couldn't figure out something. He'd lost *Orion*, this time for good. And a Veeluthian ship.

"Darius, you need to see this," Enrico's words came unwelcome over the system.

Darius's first response was to ask, "Why?"

But he didn't allow himself to ask that, particularly not in the nasty, grouchy tone he heard in his head.

"On my way," Darius said. The lifeless tone worried him just as much.

However, there really wasn't anything left for him to see. Just a question of how much time he'd have with Captain Alana before she either drove him to kill her or himself. Or both.

Darius flung himself up to the front pilot's cabin, crowded in there with both Enrico and Samantha.

His mouth dropped open and the sour air of the cabin filled his lungs as he gasped.

It took him a moment to interpret exactly what he was seeing.

Lulu.

Flying directly at *Xi Sheng*.

She looked like a great gray bat attacking a much darker cousin, built out of metal instead of flesh.

Crap.

One of Lulu's wings just impacted the ship, shoving it to one side, knocking it off its course.

"Lulu!" Darius screamed.

Captain Alana opened fire.

LULU

Lulu focused on attacking that nasty ship, *Xi Sheng*.

Captain Alana had killed Darius.

Lulu would die killing her and her ship.

She screamed again, that sonic blast, watching as lights on the ship blinked off and on.

Then she batted the ship with one of her wings, shoving it to the side like a bad child being punished, the metal dented and crushed under her blow.

Xi Sheng opened fire on Lulu's exposed chest.

She laughed at the feeling. The heat tickled her, lightened her heart.

It couldn't penetrate her armor.

Lulu turned on her wings, hitting the ship with her tail, now. While she'd been soaking up energy from the nearby sun, she'd been practicing her tail strikes.

What exactly would happen to a ship if it was struck by a tail that was just starting to phase shift?

Lulu could only imagine the creaking of the metal as the entire ship shuddered under her blow.

It made her giggle like a girl. Joy bubbled up through her.

Wait.

This attack should be done in anger. Not joy.

Darius's touch further breached her consciousness.

Lulu froze. Shivers ran up and down her spine, to the tip of her tail and along the edges of her wings.

With a snap, the *pikali* came back to life.

Lulu turned her back on *Xi Sheng* and flew unerringly toward the tiny flitter approaching her.

Was Darius on that ship? She couldn't see him in the pilot's seat. But she felt him.

The *Xi Sheng* fired more lasers on her back. She ignored them. They weren't tuned correctly to give her damage. Yet.

Belatedly, Lulu remembered to turn on her communications channels.

Darius's voice came flooding through her system. "—she won't hurt you, she just doesn't know I'm alive, stop shooting her! Let me talk with her first!"

"Darius?" Lulu said, breaking into the conversation.

"Lulu," Darius breathed out. She wasn't close enough to feel his heartbeat, but she knew it well enough to guess that it had just spiked hard. "I'm here. I'm alive. I'm so sorry. I didn't know they would send you that recording, tell you that I was dead."

"What happened?" Lulu asked.

"Can you two lovebirds take this offline? While I attend to the damage on my damned ship?" Captain Alana came on the line, bitching as usual.

Lulu felt her entire being light up with emotion.

She hated that bitch. Not only had she first enslaved Darius, she'd been the one who claimed he was dead.

There wasn't any point in continuing her attack, however. Darius was here. They could leave. Together.

Because if they didn't…Lulu would still have her revenge.

Lulu had already prepared an entrance for Darius. She wasn't about to wait three days while she grew something for a ship to dock to. Instead, Darius donned an EVA suit and traveled the short distance between *Lucky Eight* and Lulu.

The other Humans on the ship didn't want to come over. Or maybe the bitch captain had ordered them back to *Xi Sheng*.

It didn't matter. Lulu wasn't keen on opening herself up to a troop of Humans wandering inside her.

The "door" of the entrance was made up of a special membrane that Lulu had grown specifically for the purpose of Darius entering and exiting her internal systems. She didn't have a locking system like the Humans built. There was no reason. She wouldn't suddenly lose power, all her systems malfunctioning.

Or rather, if the entrance blew, that would entail a catastrophic system failure and her entire crew would already be dead.

Lulu still had the chemical pattern she'd extracted from Darius the first time he'd passed through a membrane, coming from *Orion*.

Then she keyed the new entrance to Darius's DNA. No other Human would be able to come through that entrance without him. If they tried, again, Lulu would have to already be dead before she'd allow anyone else to board her.

It took Darius a few minutes to push through the foot-thick membrane. Lulu caressed his body as he passed through, the nerve endings thrilling as his beloved form returned to her.

As soon as Darius was in the hall, he stripped off his helmet and gloves. "Lulu!" he called.

She detached a communication filament from the wall directly next to the entrance.

Darius grabbed it, like a drowning man reaching for a rope.

Lulu let Darius's presence wash over her. The smells and taste of him. The pattern of his thoughts. The depth of his feelings. The love and grief and joy and sorrow.

They reveled in each other, exchanging feelings more rapidly than any words could have conveyed.

After a timeless time, Darius finally came up to breathe. "Okay," he said shakily. "Can I take off the rest of my spacesuit now?"

Lulu laughed. The joy that she'd believed had fled the universe was back.

It didn't matter so much that she was the only Veelu on this side of Human space.

Darius had returned.

DARIUS

Through words and sharing, Darius told Lulu all that had happened to him since he'd left, how he'd been betrayed by Norm/Norman, how Captain Alana had actually saved his life, how her operation supported those planets the Allied Worlds had conquered, absorbed, tried to force into the melting pot of humanity.

He didn't lie to her about Captain Alana's first contract, how they'd tried to get him to sign Lulu's life away. He sensed a reserve in her whenever he mentioned the captain, but he couldn't blame her, not really.

Lulu had attacked *Xi Sheng*. Done it some damage, actually. And they'd fired back. It would take a while before Lulu had warm and fuzzy feeling toward the captain, if ever.

Darius marveled at her ability to defend herself without specialized weapons. He was shocked to learn about the devil's tails, how they helped her. He knew he would have a lot of questions about that. She would have to show him later.

He understood why she'd never mentioned them before

—it wasn't something that the Veelu shared with many of the Kin.

Darius spent the time flat on his back in his quarters, communication filaments wrapped firmly around both his wrists and his ankles.

It was how she expressed holding onto him.

Honestly, he felt the same way, as if he never wanted to let go.

The air here smelled sweet, so much better than *Lucky Eight* or even *Xi Sheng*. It had personality. It reminded him of her.

The temperature was instantly responsive to him, along with the humidity. He barely had to think of a change and she responded.

Then again, he did the same for her. The hint of a request and he complied, leaning against a wall or laying down again, ready to be embraced.

Finally, after twenty four hours, Lulu announced, "*Xi Sheng* is hailing us."

Darius grimaced. "You understand that Captain Alana is going to be pissed off because you damaged her ship."

"She deserved it," Lulu said.

Again, that stiffness in Lulu's attitude. If she was an upright bipedal, she would pull herself up taller when she made those statements.

"I know," Darius said. "But she saved my life by acting as she did."

Lulu didn't reply. Instead, she opened the communication channel.

His faked death was a wound that wouldn't heal overnight.

"So have you two lovebirds made up?" Captain Alana asked. The sarcasm set Darius's back up.

"We are ready to entertain proposals at this time," Darius responded.

"Oh, really? Do I need to remind you of your promise, young hero?" Captain Alana said.

"Promise?" Lulu interrupted.

"I promised to return here after I found you, that we wouldn't just fly away together," Darius explained.

"You specifically promised to return to *Xi Sheng*," Captain Alana said. "Or do I need to replay the conversation to you?"

"I'm not leaving Lulu. Not yet," Darius said firmly. He couldn't just leave her again. That would be like rubbing alcohol across newly healing skin. The constant pain would drive him crazy. He wouldn't be able to think.

"You promised," Captain Alana said flatly.

"Look, we didn't fly away or depart the system as soon as we could," Darius explained. "We haven't gone anywhere. Just—I can't leave Lulu right now. It wouldn't be good for either of us."

"Right," Captain Alana said, her disbelief evident.

"I have *not* broken my word," Darius said stubbornly. "I'm still here. I'm living up to the spirit of the agreement."

An idea came to him. It seemed to just pop into his head, almost as if someone had placed it there.

"Look, why don't you come over here?" he proposed.

"Just step into your den?" Captain Alana asked.

"Bring all the guards you want," Darius said. He held up his hand so Lulu wouldn't start protesting immediately. "You'll be safe here."

Silence came through the other end of the line. Who was Captain Alana consulting with? Kwasi? The head of her guards? Darius wasn't sure.

"I will come over with a team of four," Captain Alana

said. "If anything happens to me, well, I wouldn't worry about being departed from one another, as I'm going to escort you *both* into death. You hear me?"

"Loud and clear," Darius said.

"Give us an hour to prepare," Lulu suddenly added. "The membrane used for entrance isn't currently capable of accommodating other Humans."

Understanding came flowing through the communication filament. "It's keyed to my DNA only," Darius said. "Lulu needs to adjust the chemical composition to allow humans, in general, through."

Darius grinned. He could practically hear the wheels churning in Captain Alana's twisted brain.

"Fine. We will fly a general transport into proximity in one hour, but won't attempt to cross over until you give the go ahead," Captain Alana said.

The communications channel was cut.

"Is everything all right?" Darius asked Lulu. She seemed, well, cold, for the want of a better explanation. It was as if the *pikali* hadn't fully re-established yet.

"Everything's fine, love," Lulu responded. "Why don't you sleep for a while? I'm going to have to concentrate deeply to make this change." She shared some of the chemical processes that she was going to have to go through in order to transform the membrane into something more accepting.

Darius hadn't felt tired up until she'd mentioned it, but yeah, he could sleep. "Get me up in time to actually wake up," he requested as he fell back on his sleeping platform, asleep before any more questions came up.

Darius and Lulu shared a nervousness as they waited for Captain Alana and her guards to make the crossing from the little flitter to Lulu's side.

The guards landed first. Darius could feel them as they attached to Lulu's side. She'd thoughtfully grown a handle outside for them, so they had something to grab onto.

Darius stood on the far side of the membrane. Lulu assured him that it was safe, but he still felt a shiver of fear as the guard first pushed a hand holding a gun through the foot-thick membrane, followed slowly by the rest of him.

He stood in the hallway looking around, not taking off his helmet. Darius assumed that he was reporting in, telling those behind him what he was seeing.

Darius tried to look at Lulu's hallway anew: fleshy, pink walls enclosed the space. Nothing came to hard corners like in a human-manufactured system, instead, it was all rounded and natural, one section growing into the next. If the guard looked really closely, he would be able to see the faint lines of Lulu's veins pumping through the system, and after a while, even watch her slow heartbeat.

Eventually, the guard put his gun away and took his helmet off.

"Hi!" Darius said. "Welcome aboard. I'm Darius."

The guard merely nodded. "All clear," he said, obviously talking to the others on the comm.

A second guard pushed through. Then a third. The hallway was now quite crowded, as only two people could really stand abreast in it.

Captain Alana came next. Or at least Darius assumed it was her, based on her much smaller stature. Plus, she wore the best suit of the others, and though she carried a gun and had other weapons attached to her belt, she wasn't as heavily armed.

Then the fourth and final guard came through.

Captain Alana finally took off her helmet. She sniffed in disapproval. "You're sure the air is safe?" she asked. "Kind of stinks in here."

"The air is set to Human standard," Lulu said, addressing Captain Alana directly.

The guards jumped. Captain Alana just grew still.

"Is this the ship Lulu that I'm address?" Captain Alana asked.

"It is," Lulu said. She followed that with a short phrase in Veeluthian, basically saying, "Welcome aboard."

Darius smiled. That was his clever girl.

"You can leave your suits here. Or be uncomfortable and wear them," Darius said. He'd changed back into loose pants and a T-shirt. Lulu had kept the clothing he'd brought aboard from *Orion*.

Captain Alana nodded and started to shuck off her suit. The guards remained standing at attention, their eyes darting everywhere, as if afraid of some alien would pop out of the walls and attack.

Darius rolled his eyes at them. It was safe here. Just him and Lulu.

Once Captain Alana had stripped off her EVA suit into her light gray spacer jumpsuit, she seemed to strip off some of her attitude as well.

"Thank you for welcoming me aboard," Captain Alana said as she studied the walls around her. "All living flesh?"

"Yes," Darius replied. "Lulu's organic. Nothing mechanical."

"Huh," was all that Captain Alana said in reply.

"This way," Darius said, directing them back down the corridor toward his quarters. They passed the galley, then entered his rooms through the side wall.

"What are those?" Captain Alana asked immediately, drawn to Lulu's failed windows.

"An unfinished project," Darius said smoothly.

The windows weren't transparent, but instead, covered with a sticky white film. Darius had promised to bring a piece of the material used for windows on the human ships so that Lulu had a template, and could maybe figure out what chemicals she needed to create her own.

Captain Alana walked over to the windows to inspect them more closely. She reached out to touch one before Darius could warn her.

White goo covered Captain Alana's palm as she drew her hand back. "What the…"

Her eyes grew cloudy.

"Captain?" Darius asked. He stepped closer to her.

A *thump* at the side drew his attention.

The guards had all slumped over and fallen onto the floor.

Captain Alana turned to Darius. "You promised," she said weakly as she fell against the wall, held tightly by tendrils that sprang up out of the smooth surface.

"Lulu?" Darius asked, turning to the empty room.

"You get to sleep too," Lulu murmured.

Darkness rose and Darius fell to his love's betrayal.

***

When Darius awoke, he found he was sitting against the wall, fully restrained by straps growing out of Lulu.

"Lulu!" he called. "What the hell are you doing?" he asked. "I promised Captain Alana that she'd be safe!"

Just across from him, cocoons of living flesh held the guards and Captain Alana.

"*You* promised," Lulu pointed out. "I did not. You never asked me."

Darius suddenly realized his mistake. It wasn't that the *pikali* hadn't been fully established.

Lulu had been holding back.

As had he.

The initial *pikali* had been overwhelming in so many ways. Darius remembered his guilt at his relief at being alone when he'd first left.

That sense of solitude had stayed with him. He had never really fully committed back to Lulu and the *pikali*. He could see that now.

"I'm sorry," Darius said sincerely. He flooded their connection with all the emotions running through him; the sorrow that he'd not treated her better, more like a partner than just a ship; how ashamed he felt that he'd not consulted her and her opinions, or even letting her make the call about who came over and who didn't; the guilt he felt about needing to be alone; as well as the determination he had for making their relationship work, regardless.

"Please, forgive me," Darius added out loud.

Lulu appeared to be ruminating. "Sometimes, one of the Kin who bonds with a Veelu also needs that time alone," she said. "We always pity the poor Veelu when that happens."

"I'm sorry," Darius said again. "But you need to believe me that I want to be with you the rest of the time."

"Hmmm," was all the reply he got.

It seemed as though the straps holding him tightly against her wall had loosened.

"What are you doing with Captain Alana and her guards?" Darius asked.

"Reabsorbing them," Lulu said cheerfully.

Darius gasped when he realized what exactly that meant.

Lulu was in the process of devouring the five humans. It wasn't easy. It involved determining the exact chemical composition of their skin then finding right solution to strip off one layer at a time. After that, she'd start on their internal systems.

"No! You can't!" Darius said. Horror washed over him.

"But she was going to enslave you again," Lulu pointed out. "That isn't a problem if she's no longer around."

"We need them," Darius said, his thoughts frantic. "She's helping the war effort."

"The war's over," Lulu said dismissively.

"But the wrong people won," Darius said. "Norman and the others who want to *absorb* the differences of each and every culture, to make everything all one flavor, all one religion, all one point of view." He paused, then added, "And they're going to attack the Veelu and the Kin as soon as they have the opportunity. Kill all aliens."

He could tell that made Lulu at least stop and think for a moment.

"Captain Alana is still a complete and total bitch," Darius agreed. "But she's doing more good than harm." He was firmly convinced of that after carefully examining her operation for a few days.

"But your revenge!" Lulu reminded him. "And mine!"

"We can't," Darius said. "I won't just kill people. Not like this."

Sure, Captain Alana teased him by calling him *hero*. But a hero didn't kill defenseless people. Not after promising their safety.

He pushed all his feelings and resolutions about that toward the ship. He knew he wouldn't be able to live with himself if they died. Something inside him would also die. It would doom their relationship.

"I'm not sure I can reverse the process," Lulu said after a moment.

Lulu showed him where she was in terms of her progress. She'd absorbed almost all the skin off the captain. She hadn't gotten as far with the guards, as they still had their EVA suits on, and she'd had to go through those first.

"Can you grow back her skin?" Darius asked.

"Maybe?"

"Use samples of mine," Darius said firmly. "I don't care if you have to remove strips from my hide to do it. Just grow skin back on her."

"You're sure?" Lulu asked, her voice still a little distant.

Darius sighed. "I know I'm asking a lot from you. I will owe you a lot. A lot of favors." He nodded to himself. "I don't know how we're supposed to work together. I've never done something like this before. You have to promise me you'll tell me when I overstep like I just did."

"I'm sorry," Lulu said after a moment, absorbing all that Darius was feeling. "I think I overstepped as well, just enacting my revenge without telling you. We both need to be better at communicating."

Darius snorted. "You mean we're both going to have to grow up?" he teased.

"Probably. At least some of the time," Lulu replied. He could hear the smile in her voice. "Okay, now I need to concentrate on fixing the captain. She's going to be so pissed when she recovers."

"I know," Darius said. "And I'm willing to take the blame."

"No, we both will. But I won't be enslaved," Lulu warned.

"We'll have to burn that bridge when we come to it," Darius said.

He knew the captain would be pissed. He didn't see what good could come of this.

Darius found that the sense of time that he'd first noticed when he'd initially left Lulu had stayed with him. Without consulting any clock, he knew that it took Lulu approximately forty-three minutes to grow back the captain's skin.

While Lulu had focused on the captain, Darius had been in touch with *Xi Sheng*, assuring them that Captain Alana was alive and would be speaking with them momentarily.

Oh, and please don't shoot at them.

Lulu released the captain just as the last of her skin healed, waking her up in the process, so that Captain Alana hadn't really been aware that she'd been strapped to the wall.

Mind you, she could probably figure out what had happened when she looked over and saw the guards in their cocoons, still wrapped in layers against the wall.

Darius had clothing ready for Captain Alana as she stumbled naked into the room.

She blinked and stretched her jaw out, as if finding all the muscles in her face again. Her skin was a lighter color than it had been, as Lulu had had to base the new skin on Darius's, and he was several shades lighter than the captain. Her head was bald, all the dark hair absorbed. She was muscular and lithe, like a dancer.

"What the hell just happened?" Captain Alana said, turning on Darius and stomping over to him.

Darius handed her the clothing in his hand silently.

Captain Alana ignored them. "What. Happened."

"I made a mistake," Darius said. He gestured with the

clothes again. "You only had my promise that you'd be safe. I didn't check with Lulu. I didn't ask her for permission for you to come over. I just assumed that it would be all right. I apologize for my mistake. I won't make such a mistake again."

He kept his eyes on the captain's face, not allowing them to wander over the rest of her naked body. He hadn't ever seen a naked or completely hairless woman in the flesh before.

He found it disturbing.

Captain Alana looked different, now. It wasn't just the lighter colored skin.

It took him a moment to register the primary difference: Lulu had healed Captain Alana's scar.

"What, so because you didn't talk with your partner here, you put me at risk?" Captain Alana asked. She finally reached for the clothing. "And I suppose the same thing that happened to me happened to the guards as well.

"Yes, ma'am," Darius said as he promptly turned around to give her a touch of privacy while she dressed.

"Oh for gods' sake turn back around," Captain Alana groused. "You're not embarrassing me by looking. I was raised in a commune. We spent a lot of time naked. There's no shame in it."

"Really?" Darius said. He turned around, but he stared stubbornly at the floor. Huh. He never would have guessed that.

"It's why I make new recruits strip," Captain Alana said. "They can't handle it and it doesn't bother me in the least."

That made a kind of perverted sense.

"So explain exactly what happened, both to me, and the guards. And why I shouldn't order *Xi Sheng* to blow you out of the sky," Captain Alana asked as she finished pulling on the last of Darius's clothing.

The shirt hung on her like a dress. She'd rolled the pants

legs up so she wouldn't trip. She looked younger in the outfit. However, that didn't decrease the sense of fierceness that Darius got from her.

"Speaking of *Xi Sheng*..." Darius said.

Lulu opened up a communication channel. Captain Alana spoke some code with Kwasi, something about pawn taking bishop and the red hatter wanting tea, before announcing to them that she was fine and would be back in contact in fifteen minutes.

And that if she missed that deadline they should open fire.

Darius knew that Lulu would keep track of the time, as would he, making sure they didn't miss the deadline by even a single second.

"Again, what happened?" Captain Alana asked.

Darius explained as well as he could the process that Lulu had used to absorb her skin, then regrow it. He apologized for the attack three or four times until Captain Alana finally told him to knock it off. He also explained that the guards were still held in stasis for now, that it was much more important to bring her back to consciousness first.

"And, ah, one other thing, captain," Darius concluded. "The scar on your face has been healed."

That seemed to shake Captain Alana, more than being captured by an alien ship who had been intent on devouring her. She reached up with one hand to feel where the wound had once been.

"My scar..." she whispered. "It's gone. No matter what treatment I took. It would never heal."

Darius rocked back on his heels. He'd always thought she'd be prettier without that scar, and had assumed she'd kept it so as to retain her image as a badass pirate.

"What about my back?" Captain Alana demanded. She

turned and lifted up the back of her shirt. "What do you see?" she said after a moment.

"Nothing?" Darius guessed. "Smooth skin?"

"There had been an organism implanted into your dermis," Lulu said quietly. "I didn't reintroduce it when I regrew your outer covering. It seemed to be a parasite."

Captain Alana turned back around slowly, nodding. "That's why my scars could never heal. You completely regrew my skin," she said. She ran her fingers down her bare arm, as if she was finally realizing all the consequences of that. "I'm lighter colored than I was."

"That's probably my fault," Darius said. "I told Lulu to use samples of my skin as a base."

Captain Alana merely nodded. "What about fingerprints? Can you grow new fingerprints for a body?"

Before Lulu could ask, Darius reached out and touched Lulu's wall, explaining the concept, letting her feel the ridges and whorls on his own fingertips.

"Probably," Lulu said after a moment.

"What about eye shape?" Captain Alana asked. "Or the retina?"

"Probably not," Lulu said. "Eyes are very complicated."

"So, *Jason*," Captain Alana said, turning to Darius.

It took him a moment to realize that she was using his new identity.

"You need to become somebody new if you ever want to leave this ship," she continued. "Lulu? How much can you change him? Make him someone new, someone that no one will recognize? It will protect him, and you, in the long run."

"I can change a lot," Lulu said. "There's essential DNA that I can't process. But there are a lot of things that I can change."

"Do it," Captain Alana said.

"Now?" Darius asked, incredulous.

"Now," Captain Alana said firmly. "Prove to me that I can trust you and your ship when you're not here."

"What about the guards?" Darius asked.

"They're fine where they are," Captain Alana said, waving a hand in their general direction. "Let's see what Lulu can do to you, first."

"Lulu, are you okay with this?" Darius asked, reaching out and touching Lulu's wall again. He wanted to make sure that he wasn't making decisions for them on his own again.

"What she's asking makes sense," Lulu said.

Where Darius touched grew warm, and a strong sense of well-being flowed through their connection.

"You've explained your new identity and how it will protect you. I want to keep you shielded as well," Lulu continued.

"Ah, do you want to go back to *Xi Sheng* while Lulu works?" Darius asked the captain.

"Nope," Captain Alana said with a wicked grin. "This will give us girls the chance to talk."

Darius gulped. He wasn't worried about Captain Alana being able to influence Lulu. The Veelu was plenty stubborn.

What schemes would they hatch together?

This time, Darius asked without words if Lulu was comfortable with this, with having Captain Alana alone.

Lulu replied with gentle amusement and great curiosity. Darius had been the first human she'd ever met. It was time to meet others. Plus, Lulu replied to Darius's unspoken question—she wasn't going to harm Captain Alana at this time.

Darius understood that while Lulu would keep her word for now. However, if Captain Alana ever did something egregious, Lulu would restart the reabsorption process.

After another moment of silent reassurances on both sides, Darius asked, "Where do you want me?"

"Press your back against the wall next to Captain Alana's cocoon," Lulu directed.

Darius did as he was instructed. A great sense of love and tenderness washed away his general nervousness.

He trusted Lulu. He didn't trust Captain Alana. But he knew that he had to allow the pair of them to work things out.

Or else they'd probably end up killing each other.

———

Darius felt himself falling. He stumbled from his bed, no, wait, he'd been standing. He was still on his feet. All his skin felt overly sensitive. He shivered, and the goose bumps that raised across his flesh were almost painful. The sensation faded quickly.

Captain Alana stood in front of him, looking him over critically.

Darius forced himself to stand there and take her stare, though he really wanted to use his hands to cover himself.

Huh. He looked at his arm. The skin was definitely darker than it had been, and hairless. That would grow in over the next few weeks. His skull was bare as well.

"Here," Captain Alana said, thrusting a small, hand-held mirror at him.

Where had she gotten that? It wasn't from Lulu. How long had he been out?

One hour, thirty two minutes, it appeared.

Wow.

Darius's new face was similar to his old. He still had the same proud Greek nose, wide set eyes, and full lips. But he didn't look like himself. Or how he remembered himself. He looked more like an older brother to the Darius he'd once known.

His fingers had no calluses and his hands were completely smooth as well. He'd have new fingerprints now, to go along with his new ID.

He tilted the mirror to look at his neck.

Then he gulped.

There, in the middle of his chest, grew a tiny Jason of the Argonauts medal. He reached up to touch it. The tiny spot was covered with nerve endings. The skin there felt very sensitive.

Darius knew that Lulu had embedded some of her own unique DNA into the medal. When he touched it, he'd be touching her.

"Thank you," he told Lulu softly.

"My pleasure," she said truthfully.

"Now what?" Darius asked as he started putting on the T-shirt and jeans waiting for him near his feet.

"Seems as though Lulu is much more useful than as a mere carrier," Captain Alana said. She sounded as though she blamed him for not telling her before. "She can give new identities to people who need them."

"How many people need them?" Darius asked.

"More than you can imagine," Captain Alana said. "All the leaders for the rebellion. All the people in the spy networks." Her eyes unfocused as she thought for a moment. "And all of them are going to pay a premium."

Darius's breath caught. Working as a carrier, he and Lulu would have been able to buy out his initial debt to Captain Alana.

Working as a type of illegal hospital? He might get out of debt within a year.

"Wow," Darius said after a moment.

"Lulu and I have worked out some of the details," Captain Alana said. She glared at the dark spot on the wall, the place where Lulu generally spoke out of. "She wouldn't finalize anything until after she'd talked with you."

Darius just nodded. Then he paused. "You realize that I'm going to insist that we give identities to the people who really need them, to those who can't afford them."

Captain Alana snorted. "Of course. *My hero.*" She sighed. "Lulu had insisted on that as well."

Darius smiled and reached up to touch the Jason medal embedded in his chest. That was his girl.

"Can you change the guards now?" Captain Alana asked. "Using the specifications we agreed to before."

"Yes," Lulu said. "I'll do Fan Di first."

"Good," Captain Alana said. She nodded at Darius and said, "I need to get back to *Xi Sheng.* I'll be sending the guard captain over shortly so that she can explain what happened to the guards as they finish their processing." She paused. "I'll give you two lovebirds the chance to catch up."

"All right," Darius said, already reaching for the communication filament that Lulu was dangling over his shoulder.

"Yeah, that's still creepy," Captain Alana announced before she marched out of Darius's quarters.

Darius shrugged. He knew what it looked like to an outsider, the living skin wrapped firmly around his wrist. How his own face sagged a bit and his eyes grew vacant as he concentrated on the living being who sang in his blood.

Eventually, they wouldn't need the filaments to communicate. The process would be much quicker now that Lulu had implanted a little bit of herself inside him. Their *pikali* would be stronger than ever.

They would still be separate sometimes. Darius would need to be alone, or he'd need to go to get supplies or meet with other people.

That was all right. Darius would also need to return to her, just as much as she needed for him to return.

It was in his blood, now.

The past few months had taken a lot of work and coordination between Lulu, Darius, Captain Alana, and the others. They now flew over *Síocháin,* one of the planets hardest hit by the war. They wouldn't be here long.

A ship carrying half a dozen people was slowly making its way to where Lulu held herself. She had grown a new space just for them, with cocoons already prepared. It had taken a bit of experimentation, but they'd determined that half a dozen was the most patients Lulu could work with at one time.

Darius waited on the far side of the new docking system that Lulu had grown just for this purpose. It was one of the many changes she'd made for him, for them, for their future.

Given the prices that Captain Alana was charging (which, she assured him, was much less than a regular hospital would charge) they would pay off all of Darius's initial debt in a year's time. They'd also be safer, as they weren't smuggling supplies. Plus, Captain Alana had assigned a half dozen fighters as Lulu's escort, to protect her.

What would they do then?

They'd talked about it, dreaming about the time when the Allied Worlds would be defeated and Lulu would be free to roam all of Human space, whether to go back to the Kin-occupied space, or to have adventures and go exploring all on their own.

Darius knew in his heart of hearts what they were really doing, though.

They would pay off their debt (as Lulu had insisted that it was now partially hers, since they were joined.) They would help out the rebellion effort as much as they were able, both as a hospital and occasionally as a transport system.

And they would wait for the war with the Allied Worlds to start again.

READ MORE!

Are you a traveler? Do you enjoy exploring strange new worlds, new cultures, new people?

Journey into the various lands envisioned by Leah R Cutter.

Sign up for my newsletter and I'll start you on your travels with a free copy of my book, *The Island Sampler*.

I will never spam you or use your email for nefarious purposes. You can also unsubscribe at any time.

http://www.LeahCutter.com/newsletter/

ABOUT THE AUTHOR

Leah R Cutter writes page-turning fiction in exotic locations, such as a magical New Orleans, the ancient Orient, Hungary, the Oregon coast, rural Kentucky, Seattle, Minneapolis, and many others.

She writes literary, fantasy, mystery, science fiction, and horror fiction. Her short fiction has been published in magazines like *Alfred Hitchcock's Mystery Magazine* and *Pulphouse*, anthologies like Fiction River, and on the web. Her long fiction has been published both by New York publishers as well as small presses.

Find Leah's books on Knotted Road Press at (www.KnottedRoadPress.com)

Follow her blog at www.LeahCutter.com.

Read her essays on her Patreon, get free stories, and more! www.Patreon.com/leahcutter

Reviews

It's true. Reviews help me sell more books. If you've enjoyed this story, please consider leaving a review of it on your favorite site.

Come someplace new…

Are you a traveler? Do you enjoy exploring strange new worlds, new cultures, new people?

Journey into the various lands envisioned by Leah R Cutter.

Sign up for my newsletter and I'll start you on your travels with a free copy of my book, *The Island Sampler*.

I will never spam you or use your email for nefarious purposes. You can also unsubscribe at any time.

http://www.LeahCutter.com/newsletter/

ABOUT KNOTTED ROAD PRESS

Knotted Road Press fiction specializes in dynamic writing set in mysterious, exotic locations.

Knotted Road Press non-fiction publishes autobiographies, business books, cookbooks, and how-to books with unique voices.

Knotted Road Press creates DRM-free ebooks as well as high-quality print books for readers around the world.

With authors in a variety of genres including literary, poetry, mystery, fantasy, and science fiction, Knotted Road Press has something for everyone.

Knotted Road Press
www.KnottedRoadPress.com

www.ingramcontent.com/pod-product-compliance
Lightning Source LLC
Chambersburg PA
CBHW070517100726
47907CB00004B/872